DEVIL AMONG US

Jack Winnick

To comment on this book or to leave a message for the author, please e-mail: DevilAmongUs@live.com

Dedication

Every day, in this country, and indeed the rest of the world, there are groups of armed men and women whose sole aim is to spread terror among civilian populations. In many cases they are, unfortunately, successful. In many others, they are thwarted by the tens of thousands of brave individuals who risk their lives to protect our way of life.

These people, whether they are part of our CIA, FBI, Joint Terrorism Task Force, or military agencies, go about their dangerous job without expectation of fame or monetary reward. The same is true for Israel's security forces, whether it be Mossad, Shin Bet, AMAN, or other anonymous organization. Their job is even more critical, if that could be possible. The future of their very nation is at stake.

It is to these unnamed individuals to whom we owe so much, that this book is dedicated.

ACKNOWLEDGEMENTS

Devil Among Us is a work of fiction. As such it is based on many hypothetical situations and imagined events. But it is also based on facts. There is a vast storehouse of information in the open literature. More can be gleaned from news items, interviews and private sources not able to be verified. I am grateful for the help of the office of the Director of Mossad, Mr. Tamir Pardo.

An author of fiction must rely on several sources in order to put together a readable and reasonably conceivable stream of events. But we must be constantly held in check by an editor who has the feel for what the writer is trying to say and allows him rather wide boundaries within which to say it. Ms. Joan West, has, as she did with the first novel in this series, *East Wind*, offered guidelines and suggestions throughout the creation of this work.

My constant source of energy and ideas continues to be my sweetheart, Gisel, who never fails to keep me on the right track. Without her encouragement and help throughout the project, this work would never have begun.

Jack Winnick, Los Angeles
November 2013

Chapter 1

Yehudi Bar-lev dressed slowly for the afternoon Yom Kippur services. This was to be a special Yom Kippur for the Bar-lev family, no doubt about that. He had just celebrated his bar mitzvah earlier that year but that wasn't the only reason he was so excited. Soon his family would be a part of history.

Even though Yom Kippur always appeared on the same date every year on the Hebrew calendar, it was late this year on the English calendar; so it was unusually cold outside the Bar-lev's Brooklyn apartment. Over all his necessary religious clothing, he added a heavy black woolen topcoat, and of course the black fedora over his sequined yarmulke.

Yehudi's parents tried to hide their own excitement. Yehudi was their only son, and in fact their only child. So Saul and Esther Bar-lev carefully dressed in the Orthodox Jewish tradition, and also added topcoats against the cold weather.

After checking each other's appearances, they strode out of their third-floor Williamsburg apartment into the face of a cold and buffeting wind, whipping their long coats against their legs, stinging their faces with its icy fingers. Hundreds of their neighbors, as far as the eye could see in either direction, pushed through the streets on their way to services, heads down against the frigid, biting wind. Of the many synagogues in the area, the Bar-levs belonged to one of the largest of the Orthodox congregations.

The Bar-levs had lived in this neighborhood only four years, having emigrated from Israel, but as is customary, they knew most of the community. In fact, Yehudi's bar mitzvah had been attended by hundreds of their neighbors. Several had commented on the fact that Yehudi's *peous*, or side-locks, were growing and so thick and curly black.

A large crowd of congregants milled in front of the open doors. Most of the high holiday services were open only to members of the congregation, due to the large percentage of members who came to services on those days, filling the synagogue. The afternoon or Yizkor, service, on the other hand, was open to all who wished to attend. This was the service where the prayers were said for departed relatives, so it was a mitzvah, a good deed, to allow nonmembers to say these prayers.

A contingent of police stood at the entrance, along with ushers, to check on worshipers who were not recognized. This precaution had been installed after the terrorist attacks of 9/11. The Bar-lev family, along with all the other well-established congregants entered with a nod, shaking hands with the other families, wishing them a happy and glorious new year.

As in all Orthodox synagogues, the main floor was divided into two parts, one side for the men, one for the women. The children were seated on the lower floor, where the service was broadcast through amplifiers. The Bar-lev family split up as they always did and sat in their accustomed seats, nodding to all of their friends. Yehudi, as usual, sat next to his best friend and competitor for top student honors, Benjamin Cantor. Benjamin noticed that Yehudi seemed flushed and somewhat nervous. He attributed this to the fact that this was Yehudi's first Yom Kippur after his bar mitzvah, and the first time for him to observe the fast, which would come to a close at sunset.

The Yizkor service proceeded for about an hour and a half until it was time for the prayers for the dead. Upstairs, Yehudi's father nervously looked at his watch. As the final Hebrew word was uttered by the Rabbi, the elder Bar-lev mumbled something unintelligible, took a deep breath, and pressed a button under his coat.

The sound of the blast tore through the synagogue and the streets of the borough of Brooklyn. The door of the synagogue blew outward, into the street, smashing into a passing FedEx truck. Stained-glass windows exploded outward, raining shards of glass mingled with bits of clothing, flesh and blood.

Later, in the stillness that followed within what used to be one of the oldest Orthodox synagogues in the borough, only quiet moans could be heard. Outside on the street, after a brief moment of disbelief, the shrieks and screams of terror of the passersby blotted out the everyday noises of a Brooklyn street.

Chapter 2

The Grand Mufti of Jerusalem, Muhammed Amin al-Husseini sat comfortably on cushions in his apartment in Ramallah. At the moment, his giant flatscreen television was tuned to CNN international; he switched back and forth between this channel and Al Jazeera. Outside, hordes of young men danced in the streets, waving the flags of Hamas, the Palestinian Authority, and Hezbollah. They shouted as they danced, feeling the same intense glee as the Mufti. He hadn't been this ecstatic since that wonderful evening of September 11, 2001.

He watched as CNN over and over showed the carnage that destroyed the Orthodox synagogue in Brooklyn. While not nearly as many Americans had died as on that glorious day a few years ago, this time all of the dead were Jews. Praise be to Allah!

His predecessors, Kamil al-Husayni, who spied for the Germans in World War I, and especially Mohammed Amin al-Husayni, who spied for the Nazis in World War II, would have been proud to see so much Jewish blood spilled. The latter had actually been a personal friend of the great Adolf Hitler. They had been so close to eliminating the Jews not only from Palestine but from the entire world.

Oh well, yesterday was but the first step in the true final solution to the freeing of the Holy Land. He sighed blissfully, and selected another sweet pastry from among those Hakim had laid out for him. He took another sip of the strong, syrupy Turkish coffee. *Not quite sweet enough,* he thought, and daintily added another sugar cube, stirring it with a tiny silver spoon. *What could make this day even more wonderful?*

The answer came quickly enough: the lovely Seera, his latest wife. Only 14 years old, she had yet to learn the intricacies of giving him pleasure, but teaching her was part of the entertainment. Slim and graceful, her appearance was not much different from that of a young boy; perhaps that explained part of her allure. He clapped his hands to get the attention of Hakim, who would bring her to him. Hakim, he knew, was jealous of the attention that used to be lavished on him, but he would learn to accept it.

Chapter 3

Sgt. Brian Davis of the NYPD took another look around the grim scene of the slaughter, as the coroner's squad continued their awful task. *How could this possibly have happened?* he asked himself again. The police had meticulously searched both levels of the synagogue before the afternoon service, every stranger entering had been searched, wanded and swept for chemical residue. Yet, three simultaneous blasts had sent shrapnel of all sorts through the innocent crowd. Over 150 men, women, and children lay dead, and others severely wounded filled the neighboring hospitals. Terrorists had managed to do the unthinkable, killing over 100 worshipers on their holiest day.

One of the Jewish religious societies sent a team in for the ghastly task of trying to put together the remains. According to Orthodox Jewish law, they told him, each person needed be buried whole, that is, with all their parts, bones and flesh. This almost impossible task had to be carried out without delay because the law required the victims be buried within 24 hours whenever possible. The team proceeded with their grim task, their religious garb hidden beneath protective clothing.

The bomb squad first cleared the area of any possibly undetonated explosives. There were none: only the three simultaneous blasts clearly outlined in the concrete where the three seats had once been bolted down. One seat near the center of the children's section on the ground floor; the two others on the main floor, the adult section --- one on the men's side, one on the women's side.

Who could have carried out this act? Davis wondered for the 20th time. *And how could they have gotten through the tight security?* Three different Palestinian terrorist groups already had claimed credit for the massacre; but all their accounts lacked the proper detail and so had been dismissed.

And why? What reason could anyone possibly have to kill all these innocent people? Davis had only a passing interest in the affairs of the Middle East; but all of these victims, as far as he knew, were Americans. He had a vague knowledge of the atrocities committed in World War II by the Nazis, when literally millions of German citizens, most of them Jews, had been murdered. *But in the United States?* It certainly looked like a hate crime, and was being treated as such, but who and where were the criminals?

Still numb from the scene, grief wasn't the right word, this went beyond that by far. He felt grief when he saw a child killed in an automobile accident or a murder committed during a holdup. Now he felt utter shock and disbelief; none of his experiences on the force had prepared him for the human devastation that lay before him.

The joint terrorism task force (JTTF) would arrive any minute and a six block area surrounding the Temple had been cordoned off. The mayor of New York, a non-Jew, intending to make a televised thirty minute speech, found himself so overcome with emotion, he floundered and had to cut it short before he hit the twenty-minute mark. He did manage to say decisively that the person or persons who had committed this horrendous act would be hunted down if it took every resource of the city and the federal government. The leaders of various Jewish groups also appeared on television offering $10 million in rewards for the culprits. They seemed to have no doubt that the guilt lay with one or more of the Palestinian terrorist organizations.

The prime minister of Israel, as shocked and grief-stricken as his American counterparts, made a plea for information.

The Cable News Networks interrupted their heavily-edited coverage of the grisly event with video of Palestinian youths dancing with wild enthusiasm, waving various flags, as gleeful as they had been on September 11, 2001. There seemed little doubt that when the truth came out the same sort of group would be found responsible.

Lara Edmond, Special Agent with the FBI, was at her desk at the JTTF regional office building in lower Manhattan when the news broke. The terrible scene covered the special closed-circuit networks available for the task force. She received orders almost immediately to head down to 26 Federal Plaza, the location of the FBI's national security branch headquarters in New York City.

Lara, a trim, attractive young woman with shoulder-length straight blonde hair, raced down the six flights of stairs to the garage with the rest of her team, Tim Farley, Roger Fairburn, and newcomer, Isaac Niebuhr. The four grabbed a slick-back sedan, and made for the Federal Plaza building, where they found a scene of near chaos; uniforms and suits racing through the headquarters lobby.

Lara's team quickly scanned their badges and headed up to the eighth floor. Hadley Parkinson, the acting chief, was in his glass-walled office, clearly in a state of total turmoil. Hadley, a 55 year old man, nearly completely bald, a little overweight, appeared close to having a heart attack. Uniforms were dashing in and out of his office with faxes hot off the machine. Five flatscreen television monitors blared out gruesome details of a scene in Brooklyn that could have come from a Tarantino movie.

Without so much as a preamble, Parkinson shouted at Lara to hustle her team down to the Brooklyn massacre in Crown Heights at flank speed. Parkinson, an old Navy man, still used a lot of the old lingo.

Other teams were headed out as well; camera crews, witness identification crews, and high-ranking officials. Jumping into another slick-back sedan from the Federal Plaza garage, it took them just 17 minutes, sirens screaming, lights flashing, to race across the bridge and reach the remains of the synagogue.

Local NYPD uniforms from the 77th precinct had set up barricades, keeping the frantic crowd back from the devastation. Lara saw the front door of the synagogue lying in the street; otherwise, the building maintained its structural integrity. Unfortunately, that structural integrity had intensified the effects of the blast inside the building, the shock waves reverberating back and forth causing even more death and injury.

They raced up the steps, identified themselves with their badges and photo IDs, and peered inside at the wreckage. The NYPD bomb squad, which had arrived almost immediately, had chalked out the three explosion centers: two on the main floor, and one on the lower floor.

The main floor, which had been about half a flight up from street level, was broken in two. Bodies, and pieces of bodies, lay everywhere; even though a triage center had been set up, and many of the wounded had been taken to local hospitals.

Lara approached Brian Davis and, reading his name tag, asked, "Have any of the wounded been questioned to any extent, Sergeant Davis?"

"I don't know, agent," he said, "We've been too busy separating the dead from the injured to do anything else."

"The Rabbi stands on the stage, about five feet above the main floor. Perhaps from that position he might have an insight into what occurred," she said, "That is, if he survived. Do you know his name or if he survived, sergeant?"

Davis pulled out a cell phone hit a few buttons and scrolled down a list. "Yes, he did make it, Agent ...," he paused, glancing at her name tag, "Edmond. His name is Josh Goldstein. The list indicates they put him into an ambulance headed for Presbyterian, three blocks north, one block west. He's not marked as 'critical'; maybe the lectern he stood behind absorbed most of the shrapnel that came his way," Davis speculated.

Lara's cell phone rang. Her boss wanted a first-hand report from Lara and Tim. He had seen most of the details on TV; now told her to get back to his office posthaste, leaving Roger and Isaac to interview any witnesses they could find.

Tim was not much past teenage, maybe into his mid-20s, with a lead foot developed from growing up in rural Tennessee. He still had the slender, blond semi-hick look about him that hid a tough, capable FBI agent.

With Tim driving, sirens blaring and lights flashing, it took them less than twenty minutes to get back to 26 Federal Plaza, then another five to stow the car and take the elevator up to the eighth floor where Parkinson strode around the room in a frenzy. He had been a homicide Lieutenant with the NYPD for 12 years after leaving the Navy, before he moved over to the FBI. He arrived there just after 9/11. Parkinson, a no-nonsense cop, had seen all the bloody misery that New York had to offer. He was a family man, whose only son had been the victim of a senseless drive-by shooting six years earlier when he happened to be in the wrong place at the wrong time. The shooter or shooters had never been found, a bleeding sore that he carried with him day and night.

Barely stopping his aimless wandering, Parkinson ushered Lara and Tim into his office, and waved them into chairs.

"Whatta we got I haven't seen on TV?" he asked without preamble. "Survivors, witnesses?"

"The few survivors are all in pretty bad shape in the hospitals," Lara replied. "Our best shot may be the Rabbi. He was up behind the *bimah*, the lectern, and from what the cop on duty tells me, it may have saved him from getting hit too bad."

"What are the chances we get an interview?" Parkinson asked.

"Don't know," Tim replied, "he may be in shock."

"Damn right he's in shock," Parkinson shot back, "but he may be our only witness. He would have been facing out toward the auditorium, so maybe he saw something, anything." Parkinson finally sat down and spun his swivel chair around. "While you were gone, I got a list of their enrolled congregation. The secretary, who wasn't at the services, also sent me a map of the synagogue. She faxed me this seating arrangement of both floors. You know, people tend to gravitate to the same seats, in schools, in theaters and in churches; every time they go. It's a familiarity thing."

"So you mean the Rabbi might be able to tell us who was sitting in those seats?" Tim interrupted.

"Exactly. Now here's the thing: there were three explosions, three seats, three people. Three suicide bombers the way I see it. What are the chances they were unrelated? Zero. I figure a family, or three people who at least knew each other. And if we show this map of the synagogue to the Rabbi, he may just be able to tell us who that family is. But we gotta get to him while the thing is still fresh in his mind, shock or no shock. Let this thing go a day or two, I'm afraid we're out of business. Traumatic events have a way of disappearing from memory,"

"I know, it's one of the mind's ways of dealing with severe tragedy, but that's kinda tough on the guy just hours after he's seen his whole congregation wiped out," Lara said.

"It'll be a lot tougher on him a week from now when he can't remember, and he realizes he's let our best chance slip by. Tim, you stay here and go over this list of congregants and see if you can pick out any families of three."

Chapter 4

It took Lara less than fifteen minutes to get to Presbyterian. She presented her shield and ID to the administrator, but it still took some explaining before he allowed her to enter the Rabbi's room. Eventually she made him understand the necessity of speaking to him immediately. He phoned the nurse on the floor and told her it was urgent that the FBI agent speak to the Rabbi as soon as possible.

Lara entered the room to find the Rabbi bandaged, with an IV bag hanging from a pole, but apparently not badly injured. He had received several shrapnel wounds in his arms and legs, and lost some blood, but was not in a life-threatening situation. He was a small man, or at least seemed that way in the hospital bed. He was younger than she expected, perhaps in his late 30's, long black beard and earlocks just tinged with gray. He didn't seem to notice her as she walked quietly to his bedside. His eyes, rimmed with red and caked with salt, were fixed on a book; his upper body moved gently to and fro as he mouthed inaudible words. It was clear to her that he was saying prayers for the dead, and possibly asking forgiveness for himself. There was no question he, of all people, would be suffering what is known as survivor's guilt.

Before she spoke to him she motioned the nurse aside and asked quietly, "Did he ... that is, does he have a family, and do you know if they were there at the services?"

The nurse glanced over at the Rabbi to make sure he wasn't listening. Then she said in a hushed tone to Lara, "He has a wife and son, but fortunately they weren't at the afternoon service. From what I understand, the boy is only about seven years old and was a little tired from the morning service, so his mother kept him home, thank heavens."

That was the most encouraging thing Lara had heard all day; she couldn't imagine the grief of losing one's own family along with the whole congregation. Knowing that, she felt a little more able to approach the Rabbi.

"Rabbi Goldstein," she said softly, "my name is Lara Edmond, I'm with the FBI." The Rabbi did not seem to notice that she had spoken; he simply continued with his prayers. Tears welled in his eyes, ran down his cheeks, and soaked his bedclothes.

Lara waited half a minute, then spoke again. "Rabbi, there's no way I can express how sorry I am for this unspeakable act of terrorism. I can only imagine the terrible grief you must be feeling."

Still no response came from the Rabbi; he continued his praying and silent weeping.

"Rabbi," she began again, "this terrible tragedy affects not just you and your congregation, but the whole nation. We are all stricken and in a state of shock by this terrible act."

Slowly, Rabbi Goldstein looked up. "Why? Why would anyone do this to our peaceful congregation? Who could possibly have in their hearts such unspeakable evil?" His eyes still swollen with tears, he searched her face for an answer, beating his fists angrily against the bed.

"That's what we're going to find out," she replied, "if it takes every person in the Bureau." She sat down in the chair next to his bed, leant forward reassuringly, and told him quietly, "Rabbi, this is in no way your fault. Every reasonable precaution had been taken before the service, we know that."

"Then how could this possibly have happened," he shrieked, "if we had done our job -- if I had done my job -- all those people, all those children ..." He broke down again, wailing, continuing to beat his fists against the bed, trying desperately to tear his bedclothes.

Lara had been trained in grief counseling as part of her work with the FBI, but never had she encountered an event of this magnitude. She wondered if he knew how many of his congregation had been killed or maimed. She thought it best not to bring the subject up.

"Rabbi," she said gently, "I know this is a terrible time for you, and I hate to bring these things up. But, if we're to find out who's responsible for this outrage, it's urgent that we gather as much information as possible while the events, as awful as they are, are still vivid ..."

The Rabbi looked up at her, seemingly recognizing reality for the first time. Obviously, with great effort, he pulled himself together. "Yes, I can see that," he said quietly. "What can I do?"

Lara breathed a sigh of relief. She might be able to get something from this stricken person after all.

"It was the afternoon service, the Memorial service, is that right?"

Rabbi Goldstein nodded, "Yes, the Yizkor service. I remember we had just finished saying the prayers for the dead." At that he broke down again, weeping, his body rocking back and forth.

"Rabbi, this is important, really important. Anything you can remember about the congregation during that Memorial service, anything unusual, will be of immense value to us."

He looked at her with a new realization on his face. "The afternoon service ... We allow others in, I mean, nonmembers, so they can at least say prayers for their departed. The other Yom Kippur services are so crowded with our members we have little room for others. These strangers, these are the ones who must be responsible!"

"These 'others'," she asked, "do they sit amongst the members?"

"No, typically they take seats at the rear."

"You know Rabbi," she added, "all of the nonmembers were searched very carefully before they were allowed in." Lara thought deeply for a moment before she made the next especially disquieting disclosure. "Rabbi Goldstein, the information I'm going to give you now must remain confidential, for the sake of the investigation. But I have to tell you that there were three separate explosions, all originating from seats well within the area occupied by the membership."

Goldstein looked at her in disbelief. "That's not possible! I know every one of our congregants. I know ... knew everyone ... personally. There is no way any of them could have been responsible for such a monstrous act."

13

"Was there any animosity within the congregation?"

"No, not the slightest. They all know each other, they all live in the same neighborhood. You see, we Jews, whatever differences we may have in business or in our recreational activities, that all gets put away when we come to the synagogue. Here, we are all the same, all equal in God's eyes, all brothers and sisters, descendants from the same line of ancient Hebrews. All of us, Ashkenazim, Sephardim, even our black brothers from North Africa. We all have the same seed of Abraham in our blood and there is never even a harsh word, and especially not during the High Holy days. This has to be the act of an outsider, someone filled with evil ... someone ..." He paused and shook his head, gazing down at the book in front of him.

Lara paused for a moment, carefully considering her next words. "Rabbi," she said quietly, "is it even remotely possible that some in the congregation have been disguising themselves, even for some period of time?"

"What do you mean?"

She knew she had to be careful here. "We have very good evidence, that the explosions took place at three specific locations, that is, three specific seats in the auditorium. We have the exact rows and seat numbers where the blasts occurred."

"That's impossible!" The Rabbi exclaimed; the entire auditorium was searched by the police bomb squad, I was there myself!"

Lara paused again. "Yes, Rabbi, we know," she said, looking out the window, afraid to face him as the implication was driven home.

After a long pause, the Rabbi turned to her. "You're not suggesting that someone; no, three people intentionally ... three of our congregation ... No, that's out of the question!"

"I know this is difficult, Rabbi, but it's essential that we get started on our investigation as soon as possible. We have to use the evidence we have. Incredible as it may seem, it does appear that three people in the congregation intentionally ... that there were three suicide bombers ..."

The Rabbi turned to her enraged, his face florid. But before he could say a word, Lara explained, "It's possible that three of your congregation were not Jews at all; rather they were terrorists pretending to be Jews, possibly for years, waiting for the right moment to ..."

"No," he interjected, "I interviewed all of them; they all spoke Hebrew, knew their Talmud, Torah, the holidays, the prayers ... it's not possible."

"I know it's a cliché to say someone looks Jewish, I mean it's idiotic. But were there some in the congregation who were obviously non-ethnic Jews, converts perhaps...?"

"Yes," the Rabbi said, smiling ever so slightly. "I know what you're saying. But you see these days, Jews come in all shapes and sizes. Maybe you know that we now have many black Jews, from North Africa, taken in darkness from dictator-held countries, to live in Israel in freedom and equality with Caucasian Jews. And there are black Jews born in the U.S. who have chosen to convert. We welcome everyone; but do not proselytize. That is, we don't go out looking for conversions. Anyone who wants of their own accord to become a Jew can come to us, study, and after a long period of time, if they still so desire, can join our flock and become as much of a Jew as one who was born a Jew."

At that point, the nurse silently entered the room and handed Lara a fax. "Your Lieutenant, or whoever he is, told me this was extremely important and I should get it to you as soon as possible." Lara glanced at it and saw that Tim had indeed searched through the list of congregants, and circled those families with at least one child. Those that had only one child he had circled in red. This information couldn't have come to her at a better time.

Glancing quickly at the list in her hand, she saw ten circles of red; families with one child. She turned back to the Rabbi. Armed with this new information Lara had to get the conversation back on track.

"What I was getting at," she said, "is that perhaps there were some of your members who just didn't seem to fit in, maybe not by appearance, but by manner, speech, anything ..."

The Rabbi shook his head. "No, as I said, our congregation covered the whole spectrum, old, young, single, married, those with children, those without ..."

This was the opening Lara had been waiting for. "Families with children, Rabbi, did you know all of them?"

"Yes of course, these were my favorites, why do you ask?"

Now came the hard part. "Rabbi, there were three distinct explosions in three specific seats that we have pinpointed. They happened simultaneously. This could not have been a coincidence. One seat was in the men's section, one in the women's, and one in the children's."

"What are you suggesting?" The Rabbi looked at her incredulously.

"I'm suggesting, horrible as it may seem, that this massacre was carried out by Islamic terrorists masquerading as a Jewish family."

There was a long pause as the Rabbi shook his head and stroked his beard. "I want to say impossible, but I can't."

Lara took the opportunity to show him the map of the synagogue seating. She also showed him the list of families of three circled on the list they had received from the secretary. "Looking at this map, Rabbi, and the seats that are marked, can you think of any individuals who commonly sat there?"

He looked at the map for several minutes, and shook his head and shrugged. "No, no specific individuals come to mind; men, women, or children."

"All right, now take a look at this list of families that each have one child. There are ten of them. Do you recognize them all?"

"Yes of course," he said, as he perused the list. Then he burst into tears again as he recalled each of them. "Oh my God," he wailed, "the Solomons, the Ginsburgs, the Bratmans ..." He had to turn his eyes away.

Lara had one more card, and tough as it may be on the Rabbi, she had to play it now. "The individuals who did this, they had to have clothing that could hide the explosive vests they were wearing. Does that thought trigger anything? Were any of the people at the services dressed differently from the others, possibly with heavier clothing? Think especially of these families of three that you just looked at."

The Rabbi looked up at her, seemingly more aware. "Many of the Sephardic Jews, those whose ancestors emigrated from Spain and Portugal during the Inquisition, and settled in North Africa and the Middle East, have traditional head coverings that are quite a bit bulkier than those of the Ashkenazi Jews." In response to Lara's quizzical look, the Rabbi added, "The Ashkenazis were those Jews who immigrated to Europe from Russia; they have slightly different customs."

His eyes lit up suddenly. "I see what you're getting at: yes we do have a small percentage, I guess I should say had ... a small percentage of Sephardim who covered themselves with relatively bulky clothing along with heavy black overcoats. But to think that any of them would ..."

"Now Rabbi," she interrupted, "think as carefully as you can. Were any of those families of three of Sephardic descent?"

The Rabbi looked carefully again at the list of names. "Yes, three of them: a family from Persia, one from Morocco, and one from northern Israel. They all have young sons ..."

"Persia," Lara exclaimed, "you mean Iran!"

"I see what you mean," the Rabbi said, smiling for the first time. "No, the Rahlevis were friends of the Shah; they lost everything in the revolution. Immigrated here in 1979, despised everything about the Islamists. You can scratch them off your list."

"And the Moroccan family?"

"Oh yes, the Kadouchs: Talya and Matan. They have a ... had a boy, Nissim ... it means 'miracle,' ... they had tried for so long, and then he was ... you know ... somewhat ..." The Rabbi's tears flowed again as he recalled the anguish of the parents when they realized their son would never be the gift of God they had hoped for and for so long a time.

"And the family from northern Israel?" she asked.

"Oh yes," he replied, "the Bar-levs. They were from a place called Beit She'an in the upper Galilee, a highly Orthodox community. The son, Yehudi, one of the best Talmudic scholars we have seen, he had his bar mitzvah recently, and I remember he was just glowing this morning ..."

"One last thing Rabbi, and believe me I know this is very difficult for you, but have these families been in your congregation long?"

"Well, let's see: the Rahlevis, they've been with us since they escaped from Iran in 1979. Nothing remarkable about them that I can recall; they contributed, money I mean, every year, but rather a minimum amount. Their son Gilad was not one of our most religious students, but still a nice young man, about 18 years old.

"The Kadouchs, on the other hand, came here from Morocco about fifteen years ago, I'm not really sure of the date. But as I said, their only child, Nissim ... He was, as you say, 'the apple of their eye'."

Lara realized at this point that she had pushed the Rabbi as far as humanly possible. "... And the Bar-levs ...?"

"A wonderful family," the Rabbi said, memories flowing through his grief-stained mind. As I recall, they came here about four years ago when Yehudi was only nine. But he already had the mind of a Talmudic scholar, one can tell. And of course, coming from Israel, his Hebrew was excellent, but with that certain kind of accent that you hear from people of the Galilee region. He has ... had ... the makings of a Rabbi, scholar ..."
And then the Rabbi broke down completely; this session was over.

She did have a couple of leads. She couldn't discount everyone else, but she did have a couple of leads ...

Chapter 5

"Well, boss," Lara said to Chief Parkinson, after she returned to the Federal Building and apprised him of what she had learned, "what do you think?"

"I think you call your buddy in Israel, that's what I think. If there's anybody who can help with this impersonator idea, it's going to be him. You worked with him before and it worked out pretty well, as I recall."

Lara read through the veiled implication and knew he meant Uri Levin, the Mossad agent who teamed up with Lara and the Bureau a few years ago in the destruction of a Hezbollah gang operating in the U.S. They threatened to annihilate the country using nuclear weapons if the government did not comply with their demands for the isolation of Israel. Parkinson's unspoken reference was to the romantic attachment that developed between the two during that successful operation.

Parkinson knew, no doubt, that they had lived separate lives in the years since. The idea tore at her; on the one hand, in the years that had passed, she had desperately thought of ways to communicate with him without appearing, well, desperate. On the other, she knew he had a wife, or ex-wife, in Israel, and Lara was totally uncertain of his situation.

Lara had relationships with men since him, of course; a beautiful young woman surrounded by eager men. But she and Uri had been such a fiery exploration both of body and soul that he had been hard to replace. Those few days when it seemed the whole world depended on their actions, and perhaps it did, had made an everlasting impact on her psyche. She found herself immediately, overwhelmingly, captivated by the opportunity of seeing him again.

She had enough sense and self-dignity, however, to suggest that Hadley himself contact Uri and make the suggestion. Meanwhile, she felt terrified by the idea that he might not accept.

"In the meantime," she said, "I think we should isolate the apartments of the three most likely suspect families, even though at least two seem unlikely to have been the bombers."

"Right," he agreed, "the sooner the crime scene tapes go up, the less likely any confederate might enter the scene and remove important information."

The order went out, and uniforms in squad cars shot out to the addresses given to them by the secretary at the synagogue. It had been less than two hours since the explosions and they hoped the neighbors would be suspicious of any strangers entering the apartments of those killed earlier that afternoon.

Luckily, the three suspect families lived within just a few blocks of each other; a common occurrence among congregants in this Orthodox part of Brooklyn. The uniforms got to work blocking off the buildings and wrapping crime scene tape around all the entrances and exits. Formidable spiked bars protected the windows of the buildings; anti-Semitic acts by gangs from other neighborhoods were uncommon but not unheard of.

Once the tapes were in place, and the other residents of the buildings interviewed, plainclothesmen sitting in unmarked parked cars watched for any unusual activity. The other families in the buildings were informed that the families of the bereaved had asked that the belongings of their departed be guarded from possible vandalism. These went beyond the ordinary precautions. If the residents saw any unusual activity they were asked to call the precinct immediately.

Of course, the desk at the 77th precinct had been ordered to inform the task force at 26 Federal Plaza if any leads developed.

Lara and Tim, dressed in plainclothes, went that evening to each of the three suspects' apartments. Bringing the usual booties and latex gloves, they spent an hour in each apartment, accompanied by the uniform placed at the location.

The Rahlevis, clearly not an affluent couple, had lived in a small, one bedroom apartment on the third floor of a brownstone. The furniture appeared basic, probably obtained in a secondhand store. Persian jewelry and mementos lay everywhere, as if they were trying to remember life before the Islamic revolution. On the floor of the small living room sat an ornate Persian rug they must have somehow managed to get out of the country when they fled. Tim took pictures of each of the rooms, getting as much detail as possible.

They next went to the apartment belonging to the Bar-levs. A slightly larger place than that of the Rahlevis, it had two bedrooms and a large walk-in closet. Old-fashioned furniture filled the rooms, typical of the neighborhood; pictures of the family, a menorah, and trinkets they had brought with them from Israel completed the scene. A picture of the Orthodox community in northern Israel by the Sea of Galilee from where they had come, hung in prominence on the main living room wall.

Lara and Tim followed the same routine as before, taking detailed pictures in every room. As with the Rahlevis, nothing eliciting any excitement struck them. One thing Tim noticed, however, was the typical low priced wall-to-wall carpeting in the living room; beige in color, it matched the rest of the décor.

Lara, about to give up, headed for the door, when she heard the slightest squeak as the uniform, a burly guy named Flanagan, moved across the living room floor.

"Hold it!" she said, "Walk back the way you just came from."

Flanagan moved back, crossed the living room floor toward one of the corners of the room. As he neared the corner, they heard the same slight squeak.

"Now come back this way again."

This time when they heard the squeak they could pinpoint it at about two feet from a corner of the living room that would normally not receive much foot traffic. He moved back and forth across the spot, each time producing the same small sound.

"What the heck," Tim said, "just a squeak in the old floorboards."

"Maybe, maybe not," Lara moved closer to the spot where they heard the sound. "Let's take a look under the carpet."

"It's wall-to-wall carpet," Tim argued. "It's been nailed down ever since it was installed."

"Take a look down there in the corner anyway."

Tim, accustomed to following orders, dutifully got down on his hands and knees in the corner, moving a floor lamp a few feet to one side. "Yep, nailed down solid right into the bottom of the wall, just like I ... wait a minute, this part here right by the corner isn't nailed, it's Velcro'd! What the hell!"

Lara, excited now, got down on her hands and knees with Tim, and helped him pull the rug up, starting at the corner and going out about 4 feet in both directions. The exposed wood floor, rather than just being plywood, proved to be hardwood planks each about 6 inches wide.

"Nothin' unusual about that," Flanagan observed from above. "Some folks just don't like walking on the hardwood floor."

"Yes," Lara said, "but then why Velcro just one corner and leave the rest of the carpet nailed down?"

Flanagan reached up with one hand, removed his cap, scratched his nearly bald head with his gloved hand, thought for a second, then said, "Good point."

He got down with them on the bare floor, and the three of them ran their hands over the smooth wood, taking special notice of the places where the planks were joined.

"Whoa, Nelly!" Flanagan said suddenly, "Feel this right here."

Tim ran his hand over the spot Flanagan indicated. "There's an indentation here, all right. Got your Swiss Army knife?"

Flanagan gave Tim a look, took out his NYPD-issue knife, and gently lifted the plank, which moved easily from its neighbors.

Tim looked down into the recess and let out a low whistle. Lara and Flanagan stared with him at what they saw crammed into the small space. Flanagan reached for a multicolored rug rolled up in the center.

"Don't touch a thing!" Lara shrieked. "Let's get some pictures first!"

With his cell phone, Tim took close-up pictures of the contents of the recess. Some silk garments were crammed in on one side of the rug and on the other side two small, leather covered, well-worn books. Next to them were three small blue

22

booklets, which Lara recognized immediately as Israeli passports. Some writing in Hebrew, decorated the cover, along with the words "State of Israel" in English. A picture of a menorah blazed in the center. A seven digit number, punched into the paper, appeared at the top of each cover.

"Look at that," Flanagan declared as he grabbed one "They open backwards."

"Hebrew is written from right to left," Lara informed him, as she gently took the passport back and replaced it in the box. "And be careful not to damage anything."

Only after getting complete pictures of the setting did they carefully remove the items. They took the rug first. "It's an ornate Jordanian prayer rug," Lara said definitively, after examining the plush, mostly gray, wool item measuring a little over two feet by three feet. The ornate image in the middle could have represented any of a number of famous mosques.

Lara took the passports and looked closely at the photos. She compared them with a professionally-taken family photo on one of the living room walls. The father, a dour-looking man of about forty, sat in a chair in the center; the mother, a frightened looking woman of nearly the same age, stood on one side; and a chubby little boy stood on the other. The father, bearded with curly sidelocks, wore a black hat. The mother, also dressed primly in black, stood next to him, her hand on his shoulder. The only smile in the picture belonged to the boy. A few other pictures graced the walls; one of a happily grinning boy during his bar mitzvah, surrounded by proud congregants at the synagogue, clearly the same boy as in the family picture, just a few years older. The parents, also in the bar mitzvah picture, appeared to be those pictured on the passports. All were of dark complexion, and could have come from anywhere in the Middle East.

As Tim took photos of the pictures on the wall, being careful not to use his flash, Lara noted a clearly amateur photo of an arid-appearing landscape with a few goats grazing in the background. She had Tim get a shot of this, too.

They went back to examining the items contained in the box. "What about these leather-covered books?" Tim asked, looking at Lara. They opened from left to right as had the passports.

"They appear to be a copy of the Qu'ran and some of the books of hadith. They're all written in formal Arabic."

"I know the Qu'ran is sort of like the Arab Bible," Tim said, "but what's the other stuff?"

"From what little I know," Lara replied, "the hadith are sets of rules of behavior. They've been set down by Moslem, well, they call themselves Muslims now, scholars ever since the time of Mohammed, and they're different for the Sunni and Shi'a sects. Let's get some pictures of the covers and a few of the pages and we'll get some experts downtown to tell us a little more. Too bad we can't take this stuff with us."

"Now wait just a minute," Flanagan interjected, getting more and more interested in the project, "I'm just a regular old Catholic, but I sure wouldn't expect Arab stuff in a Jewish apartment, right? Especially hidden away under the floorboards." The others just looked at him, then at each other.

"What about these silk scarves?" Tim asked.

"They're called hijabs, or headscarves," Lara replied, "One hadith says a woman's prayer will not be accepted by Allah unless she is wearing a certain type of head covering. That's what these are."

Flanagan shook his head. "You mean, there are different prayin' rules for men and for women?"

"Women get killed every day in the Arab countries for things men don't even have to think about. Just read the news," Lara pointed out. "Main thing is, we've found our fake Jews. They were Arabs who were willing to learn enough about Judaism so they could kill a couple hundred of their 'friends.'

"All so they would be greeted by the open arms of Allah," she continued. "and receive his grateful blessings for their courageous act. The more innocents they kill, the more benefits they receive when they reach paradise --- don't get me started." Lara looked as though she were ready to throw up.

"I thought I'd seen it all in my twenty-five years at the 77th," Flanagan said, "but this sure takes it. So it's the same guys who took down the towers, right?"

"And the ones who nuked Los Angeles a few years ago," added Tim, speaking to Lara.

"Maybe not the same exact groups, but certainly with the same purpose: to bring us and the rest of the Western world to our knees."

Tim took pictures of the prayer rug, and silk scarves. All three took one last look at the items, now carefully replaced in their hiding place in the floor, put the floorboard back, then replaced the carpet. They pushed the edges of the carpet back against the wall, then moved the floor lamp back to its original position.

Before they left, Lara asked Tim to take a few more pictures of the living room as a record of how they had left it. They removed their gloves and booties, quietly opened the door to the hallway, checked to make sure it was empty, locked the door, and re-sealed it with the yellow crime scene tape.

Lara and Tim reported back to 26 Federal, where Hadley took down their report and got copies of the pictures Tim had taken. He shook his head sadly and lifted the phone to contact one of their few Arab speakers, Saad Azad.

Saad had been born in this country, a second-generation Jordanian. Even though he'd been vetted repeatedly during his 10 year tenure with the FBI, he was still looked on somewhat suspiciously by many at the JTTF. He had long ago converted to Christianity, and loathed especially the vicious practices of the jihadists. Several of his friends, and even one of his cousins, had been killed on 9/11. They had worked at a Jewish-owned brokerage firm.

He looked carefully at the pictures Hadley showed him. "The prayer rug seems standard enough, I don't see anything unusual about it. Also, the silk scarves are used as head coverings during prayer, and sometimes in public, by the women, in this case the mother. It's too bad you couldn't bring the actual books you found. The copy of the Qu'ran is a standard one, could be found anywhere. But there is some writing in Arabic on the inside cover that I want to look over more carefully. This copy of the hadith you found is most interesting. As you know, the hadith contains writings that are claimed to be the thoughts of the prophet Mohammed.

"This first chapter, 'Revelation,' listed in the table of contents, is one where Mohammed supposedly authorizes the killing of infidels. It also authorizes the beating, stoning, and mutilation of disobedient women. Some Muslims believe much of the hadith to be a total misinterpretation of the sayings of Mohammed. The jihadists, on the other hand, take 'Revelation' quite literally as justification for their obscene acts. By the way, there are other places in the hadith that are just as extreme in the treatment of nonbelievers."

The three sat thoughtfully for a moment, then all agreed they needed to await the forensic findings before taking any further action. They also needed information gleaned from the Arabic texts, and word from the Israeli Consulate where they faxed the photos of the passports and the landscape.

The Consulate was close-by, at 800 2nd avenue. Lara had become familiar with the consul general, David Peretz, who had taken over a few months after the nuclear attack in Los Angeles. He had called her at her office immediately after the synagogue bombing and offered any assistance the government of Israel could provide.

They didn't have to wait long. Within an hour, Peretz himself called Lara and told her that while the passports appeared to be genuine Israeli issue, they were forgeries. Even though the photos looked genuine, the seven digit identification numbers did not exist. The visa stamps showed entry through JFK four years ago, but at that time, the customs officials hadn't had any reason to verify the numbers. The photos could be of any Sephardic Jewish family; or Arabs, posing as Jews.

The task force left the tape around the Bar-lev building as well as the other two in question, so as not to focus public and media attention on any one in particular. A uniform had been stationed in each of the buildings, as were plainclothes officers outside on the streets in various types of non-cop vehicles: cable vans, plumber trucks, Con-Edison vehicles, and so on. They rotated every few hours. To keep up the image, they even had suited up "workers" going in and out.

And then they waited …

Chapter 6

Two days passed without anything suspicious being reported. The expected gawkers and newsmen buzzed around, but nothing more. The uniforms inside the buildings kept watch on the suspect apartments from positions hidden from public view.

The break happened on the third day. A man wearing a dark suit and black Fedora strolled by the Bar-lev's building a couple of times during the afternoon, duly noted by the suits sitting outside in a plumber's truck. On his third trip past the building, he stopped, looked around as if expecting someone and casually slipped under the crime scene tape at the front door. A few neighbors in the foyer spoke to him briefly; he smiled and tipped his hat, then used a key to enter the inner door. One of the suits outside immediately contacted the task force at 26 Federal, and radioed the uniform inside to watch where the guy went, but to do nothing to stop him.

Lara and Tim raced to the scene in an unmarked slickback. By the time they got there, the suit outside told them the stranger had spent about fifteen minutes in the building, and that the uniform had watched him from behind a water heater as he used a passkey to enter the Bar-lev's apartment, slipping under the crime-scene tape. The stranger carried a typical, large lawyer-type briefcase. He left at a leisurely pace, still carrying the briefcase, and headed down the street in the general direction of an IRT subway station. One of the cops in the plumber's van quickly threw off the overalls that up until then had been his "cover," revealing the street clothes he wore underneath. He jumped out of the van and followed the suspect at a discreet distance.

Constantly in contact, 26 Federal alerted a set of agents already in the Brooklyn area. They had his description and would be ready at any of the stops along the line. The officer from the car, now in plainclothes, was ready to follow the stranger onto the subway or to keep up with him on the street. The stranger in the Fedora entered the IRT station and headed down the stairs. The cop radioed the information downtown, and agents set up at every stop in both directions; meanwhile he continued to follow the guy down the stairs and watched him drop a token into the turnstile and head for the westbound platform toward Manhattan.

The uniform in the apartment building had noted the people the stranger had talked to in the lobby, and directed Tim to their apartment. Tim showed his badge and ID, and after some initial reluctance, they told him the stranger, who was after all dressed in the usual garb of the Orthodox neighborhood, had identified himself as the attorney for the Bar-lev family. Since he had a key and seemed intimately familiar with the Bar-levs, they had reluctantly let him pass.

Lara and the uniform cut the tape and entered the apartment. Tim joined them in a few minutes. They all put on booties and latex gloves and first took a cursory glance around. Nothing, it seemed, had been disturbed or obviously changed since the first look they had on that terrible day of the explosion. They had with them photographs taken immediately after they had spoken to the Rabbi in the hospital, when they had first examined the apartment.

A slight film of dust coated everything, which was to be expected if nothing had been disturbed. After a few minutes of careful searching - kitchen, the two bedrooms, the closet and the bathroom - nothing seemed disturbed. Yet the stranger had come for something. They had a pretty good idea what, but before checking, Lara had Tim take pictures from every possible angle with his cell phone, which they could later compare more carefully with the pictures taken earlier.

The floor lamp in the corner had been moved ever so slightly. They had all they needed; they pushed it aside and lifted the carpet and the loose board. The box was gone.

The "plumber," Sergeant Michael O'Connell of the NYPD, followed the stranger with the briefcase as closely as possible, A burly man now dressed in street clothes, carried his 9mm Glock hidden in his shoulder holster.

O'Connell saw the man leisurely board the next westbound train and stand near the door. O'Connell waited as long as possible, then boarded a few cars back. The train started to pull out, when suddenly O'Connell felt it lurch to a stop, temporarily throwing him off balance. A few cars forward, the suspect leaped from the train with unexpected grace and raced for the exit stairs. O'Connell forced open the doors of his car, and followed the man's lead. By the time he reached the next landing, his prey had vanished. On the floor lay a black tie, overcoat and Fedora and, a few feet away, a lifelike black theatrical-quality beard next to a briefcase, empty except for an ornate prayer rug.

O'Connell radioed headquarters to alert all agents stationed at the westbound IRT stops; however, none had managed to arrive yet at the departure station. It took the squad car only five minutes or so to squeal to a stop at the subway exit, but the officers had no real way to identify the suspect. He had made his escape leaving behind the prayer rug and carrying with him the smaller contents of the box: the prayer books, the passports and the headscarves, all were easily hidden in a man's pockets.

Ali Azad, known on his passport as Yehuda ben-Zion, walked away from the subway station at a pace matching the other commuters, headed towards an MTA station he knew would take him into western Queens. By following the route map, he got close enough to the Al Masjid Oman mosque to walk leisurely by the building, pause at a convenience store, and purchase a copy of Al-Ahram. He paused again outside and pretended to read it. Seeing no apparent observers, he entered the mosque and sought out the imam.

He only had to wait a few minutes before one of the imam's assistants saw him with the Arab language newspaper in his left hand, and nodded to him almost imperceptibly. Azad followed the assistant to imam Hussan's study where the man told him to wait.

The assistant disappeared for just a few minutes returning with the imam who ushered him into the study.

"A*s-salaam 'alaykum*," the imam greeted him.

"W*a'alaykum salaam*," he replied.

"Much has occurred in the last two days, my friend," the imam said in Arabic.

"And all of it good, thanks be to Allah," correctly replied Ali. They kissed each other warmly on each cheek, and sat at the imam's desk.

"So the material had not been discovered?" inquired the imam.

"I brought it all with me," said Ali, taking the passports, scarves, and prayer books from his pockets.

"Allah truly is with us," said the imam, kissing the Qu'ran and hadith. "You left the photographs on the walls?"

"Indeed, the pictures of the pious Orthodox Jewish family remain for all to mourn."

"To mourn or to blame: what could be more perfect?" the imam said. "The Prophet himself could not have devised a better plan. Already the New York newspapers have been asking the question: why would some members of a synagogue kill others?"

"Does this mean the police have already discounted the idea of jihadists exacting their revenge on the Zionists?"

"Not completely, but from what I read, the police are insistent that they thoroughly examined everyone entering that accursed place. That is, everyone not known intimately by the other Jews."

"But what if they suppose the bombs were planted before the service?" asked Ali.

"The police also searched the infidels' *zamhareer* with their wands and chemical detectors and so on, *before* the service. So they are convinced the detonations were performed by the Jews themselves.

"Imagine the agony those wretched transgressors are suffering right now. Perhaps now these Zionist devils have some idea of what our people have had to deal with since they stole our land and put our people in prison."

The imam rose, kissed Ali on both cheeks, and bade him, in the Arabic tradition, "God is great," *Allah hu Akbar.* Then added, "May he bless you forever, *jaza kablah.*" Simultaneous with this blessing, the imam gave the slightest nod of his head to his assistant, while showing Ali to the door. As they reached the door, the assistant pulled his *janbiya* from his belt, grabbed Ali by the hair, and neatly slit his throat, slicing both carotid arteries and jugular veins. A mix of bright red and purple blood flooded onto the floor. As he fell, Ali's eyes opened wide in astonishment and incredulity.

The imam told the assistant to wrap the body in the cheap, imitation Persian rug that lay on the floor, and remove it to the basement for disposal in the dumpster in the alley. He made sure that he included the passport, wallet and all other documents. It was indeed wonderful how efficient these Americans were at waste disposal.

Aamal djaid, well done, the imam said quietly to himself as the job was finished. Alone now, he went to his wall safe and retrieved his secure satellite phone. He smiled as he made the call he knew would set things in motion.

Chapter 7

Uri sat reading, alone as usual, in his small apartment outside Tel Aviv. Most of the time, including when he was alone, he wore a black eye patch to cover the hole where he had lost an eye during the battle with the Hezbollah operatives in Chicago. He considered it something of a badge of honor for the dismantling of their nuclear threat. He also appreciated the way it made him resemble his hero, Moshe Dayan. Even the same eye, the left, had been lost.

The downsides were formidable. First, his loss of vision had forcibly removed him from the field, which was his first love: he had been a Kidon, a supreme assassin of the Metsada, the army of force of the Mossad. Now he had to settle for a desk job, still with Metsada, but no longer able, or at least allowed to, remove the terrorists from existence.

Second, he felt nothing less than a curiosity, wearing that eye patch, even though it garnered appreciative glances from the many Israelis who recognized him. For reasons of security rather than vanity, he agreed to be fitted with a prosthetic eye for times when recognition could be a liability. The eye, produced by the finest craftsmen Israel had to offer, was an amazing match to the real one. On trips abroad Uri inevitably wore the prosthesis, and was always amazed at the lack of attention it received.

His secure cell phone rang at about 1700; it was a number known only to a few people at the Mossad. He recognized Shimon's voice immediately and knew something important was up.

"The synagogue bombing in New York: they want you there."

Of course, Uri had followed the case from the moment it had been reported. Part of him, the part that he kept hidden even from himself, wondered if Lara would be involved in the investigation. Memories of her brought back those strong feelings he struggled so hard to keep buried so he kept the thought veiled. Their operation in America a few years ago had been the highlight of his career. But it also established a romantic relationship that could never go any further. Lost possibilities agonized him daily. Now it seemed inevitable that if he were to go to New York to work on this case their paths were sure to cross.

The other part of him, the Metsada part, was overjoyed at the possibility of solving what seemed to be an impossible situation. The idea that a few Orthodox Jews, as was now currently believed, according to the press, had deliberately blown up a synagogue, he found incredible. He knew from reports that the FBI had narrowed the list of suspects, but even the Mossad was not privy to any more details. The fact that they were asking for him specifically indicated to Uri that there must be a connection to either Hezbollah or Israel itself.

"When do they want me there?"

"You're on the El-Al red-eye tonight, or I should say tomorrow morning. You'll leave Ben-Gurion at 0100 hours and arrive JFK at 0700, 7 am their time. You'll have time to get a hotel room and clean up before you report to 26 Federal Plaza at 0900. Hadley Parkinson, eighth floor, is head of the task force. Leave your weapon; they'll fix you up there." Just before he hung up, Shimon added, "By the way, she's working the case." It seemed everyone, at least at the Mossad, knew where his thoughts were.

It'd been a while since Uri had to prepare for a trip across the ocean at the last minute, but old habits die hard. He was packed and ready to go long before he needed to be. He looked glumly at the Desert Eagle pistol he had become attached to since his return to Israel. The .357 Magnum Mark XIX was a smaller version of the famous .50 caliber weapon, admired and feared throughout the world. With only one working eye he had become proficient with it on the range, and felt a little more secure knowing its deadly impact. He hated to leave it behind, but recognized the impossibility of bringing it along. Reluctantly, he placed it in his hidden wall safe.

He headed to Ben-Gurion airport, known locally as "Natbag," three hours early for the rigorous ordeal he would have to deal with. Even members of the Mossad were given scrupulous inspections; with his prosthetic eye in place he looked like an ordinary traveler. The retinal exam they subjected him to when he presented his credentials ended up speeding the process, and gave him a chance to get a prime aisle seat.

The long hours on the plane gave him more time than he really wanted to reflect on the all too short time he had spent with Lara those few years ago. He tried to wrestle his mind away from those thoughts and more towards the horrible synagogue bombing. Few details were available about the investigation; he knew little more than what he read in the media. Secure as their transmission lines were, the FBI still felt it best to wait until they could talk to him face-to-face in New York.

At any rate, his efforts to remove Lara from his thoughts were for the most part in vain. As he drifted off into thoughtful episodes of light sleep, he remembered precisely what she had looked like, sounded like ... everything. It was crazy, he told himself, to fantasize about the future. What they had was not likely to be resurrected.

After checking into a moderately-priced midtown Manhattan hotel Uri arrived at 26 Federal Plaza 20 minutes early, typical for him. After showing his credentials to the guards downstairs, they gave him a badge that permitted him access to the eighth floor only with an escort. His escort appeared five minutes later, dressed in a trim, dark blue business suit, looking every bit the way he remembered her. Her hair was trimmed to shoulder length, still blonde. She smiled at him, and when he saw those brilliant blue eyes; a lot of his Metsada training disappeared. She offered her hand, and as he took it, he wondered if she could feel the way his pulse was racing. There was of course no hug; these were two professionals meeting for the first time in a while, colleagues joined together on a case after a few years apart. At least that's the way it was supposed to look to the others in the lobby.

He made the requisite pass through the metal/explosive detector; then they rode up the elevator together with only small-talk. Cameras and monitors recorded movements everywhere. No discussion, even of the case would take place until they had entered the strict confines of the chief's office. Though she had never seen his prosthetic eye, she only gave it a quick glance, not wanting to embarrass him.

At precisely 0900 the desk sergeant showed them into Hadley Parkinson's office. The men didn't know each other personally, but each knew of the other's career. Uri could tell, as they shook hands, that Hadley was giving his left eye close scrutiny. "Good prosthesis isn't it?" Uri said to loosen the tension, "They do good work in Tel Aviv."

The three of them laughed as Hadley offered them chairs, then sat himself. Lara took the chance to sneak a glance at Uri, and realized at once that her feelings for him hadn't changed a bit in the few short years since they had worked together foiling a Hezbollah plot in the United States.

She snapped back into the moment as Hadley got right down to business. "The reason we asked for you," he said to Uri, "is that we have every reason to think that the synagogue bombers weren't Jews at all. We're pretty sure they were deep-cover Islamists. We even have a pretty good idea which family strapped on suicide vests and blew up the place. What we don't know, is what their motive could be, aside of course from the obvious one, of killing a couple hundred real Jews.

"We haven't let any of this into the media, not even to the NYPD. Whatever these folks are up to, we'd like to stay one step ahead. The reason we asked for you, specifically, will be obvious once Lara shows you what we've come up with so far. But basically, we think the Bar-levs immigrated here illegally, from a Hezbollah base in southern Lebanon. Like I say, we don't know what they're up to, and we're afraid there may be lots more of them."

"How do you know all that already?" Uri asked.

Hadley replied quickly, "Lara will fill you in on the details. The main thing is, we found three Israeli passports hidden in one of the suspect families' apartment. Your consul general in Manhattan checked the numbers, found they were fraudulent. Muslim holy books were hidden there too. The family, who called themselves Bar-lev, emigrated here four years ago, supposedly from a place called Beit She'an. Been members of the synagogue ever since—that is, up until ..."

"What makes you think they were Hezbollah?"

"Our resident expert looked at the copy of the Qu'ran and hadith Lara found along with the passports. The handwriting inside the covers looks to him like Lebanese-Arab. He says a photograph on the wall, a landscape, could very well be a region near the Golan Heights. You can take a look, see what you think."

Beit She'an, Uri knew well, was a religious community in the northern Galilee just a couple of miles from the Lebanese border. It had been the site over 40 years ago, of a massacre carried out by Hezbollah, or their admirers, the Palestine Liberation Organization from Lebanon. The raiders deliberately targeted unarmed civilians, mainly children.

"You still have all the stuff?" Uri asked hopefully.

"No, we got some pictures but we left everything in place, hidden under a floorboard. We were hoping to catch somebody coming in the apartment later to pick it up," Lara said quietly.

"So what happened?"

"I'll give you all the gory details later, but the main thing is, some guy did come and pick the stuff up, but we lost him ... and the stuff."

Lara and Hadley looked at each other in embarrassment, the implication being this would never have happened with the Mossad.

Uri, remembering some recent failures by the Mossad, failures splashed over the international press, quickly relieved them of any guilt. "Nothing *we* haven't done, and a lot worse. The whole world knows about our screwed-up assassinations lately."

Hadley, rubbing salt in the wound, remarked, "Yeah, that business in Dubai was embarrassing."

Not wanting to show irritation, Uri said, "Believe me, we were not too pleased by it. Shook up the whole department, as you probably know."

Lara recognized Uri's demeanor, never wanting to develop friction on a working team, no matter how unprofessional a colleague, in this case Hadley, behaved.

Feeling he had made his point, and shown who was boss, Hadley relaxed a bit, leaned back in his chair, and smiled smugly. "Well," he said, "I think the first thing you ought to do is to contact the Israeli consul and see how much he can tell you. Then come on back and we'll work out a plan."

Lara saw that, as usual, Hadley automatically addressed the male part of the team, even though Uri was a foreigner. Not even a member of the FBI or JTTF. With anyone other than Uri, Lara would've been offended by this behavior. But she knew that Uri recognized the effrontery and their partnership wouldn't be affected. He even gave her a glance as Hadley looked away for a second, and what Lara saw as a little grin. Her feelings for him, hidden away for a few years, surged back. Compared to all the men she had met in the FBI, Uri was as sensitive as he was competent. As dreadful as this case was, a large part of her looked forward to working with him on it.

Hadley sat forward in his chair, indicating that this meeting was finished. Lara and Uri both stood and shook hands with him. They were getting started.

They rode back down in the elevator together and went into Lara's small office, which she shared with Tim. One small window that looked out onto the busy street was the only relief from the pale green walls.

Tim was out so Uri took his chair. "You want to call him or you think I should?" she asked.

"You've already made contact with him, why don't you call and make an appointment?"

Lara spun around, hit a couple of buttons on her telephone, and left it on speaker. She gave her name to the receptionist and asked to be put through to the consul. He picked up right away. "Hello David,' she said warmly, "I've got your colleague Uri here. He just got in."

Uri and David exchanged a few words in Hebrew, and then they got down to business. "Listen, Uri," David began. "Can you and Lara come over here this morning? There's something I need to show you. It's important."

"You bet, of course," they each replied almost simultaneously. This had to be something important. "We'll be there in twenty minutes," Lara said. They practically ran to the elevator with their briefcases, and instead of grabbing an agency car, hailed a taxi to take them the short distance to the Israeli consulate. Both dying to speculate on what the consul had discovered, they were disciplined enough not to talk about it in the cab.

The trip took only ten minutes. In the lobby, they walked briskly to the receptionist, not wanting to cause panic. After all, Israeli consulates all over the world were on high alert for terrorist attacks. They showed their IDs to the woman. She alerted David of their arrival, and, after they passed through the detectors, showed them into his office.

The office was spare, simple and pleasant. A couple of windows looked down onto the busy street, a simple blue carpet, an average sized wooden desk, totally clear of papers or folders, and four chairs for visitors completed the furnishings. A United States flag stood on one side of the windows, an Israeli flag of the same size on the other. A few photographs adorned the walls: the current U.S. president and Israeli prime minister most prominent. Other photographs were of the Israeli president and U.S. secretary of state. Further around the room, they noticed old photos of notable Israelis such as David Ben-Gurion, and noted U.S. presidents such as Harry Truman. Truman, of course, had been instrumental in establishing the State of Israel back in 1947.

David Peretz, a slightly built man about 45 years of age, and less than average height, walked around his desk to greet them. Dressed neatly in a blue suit and tie, with a U.S. flag pin in one lapel and a Star of David in the other, he shook hands with Lara first, warmly but professionally. Then he reached out and hugged Uri, muttering something in Hebrew. Uri returned the embrace and also said something Lara could not understand. David showed them to their chairs and walked back around his desk.

David could not help but notice the electricity between the young, blonde Ohio farm girl and the ruggedly handsome

Mossad agent. Uri had that combination of fine, sculpted features and trim, athletic body that seemed to attract women. His demeanor of quiet confidence added to his charm. Lara, on the other hand, concealed the knowledge and expertise of the finest FBI agent, behind her seemingly innocent appearance.

"What have you found out?" Uri asked before Lara could even open her mouth. "We're dying of curiosity here."

"Let me show you," David said, nodding toward Lara. "Remember those photographs you took of the material you found hidden in the apartment?"

"Yes, of course," she replied, "you told us you discovered the passports were forgeries."

"Well," David added, "we had one of our experts examine the writing, the Arabic writing, found inside the holy books. He's almost positive it's Lebanese."

"How could he tell that?" Uri asked; this confirmed the FBI analysis.

"Let me show you." David opened a folder he had taken from a drawer in his desk. "Look at this writing inside the Qu'ran you found. You see these Latin letters mixed in with the Arabic? That's typical of modern young Lebanese, who use a lot of Latin letters, especially in their electronic transmissions. Other Arabs typically don't do that, at least not yet."

"Hezbollah?" Uri offered.

"When you add it in with everything else we know, there's not much doubt. The passports were probably forged in southern Lebanon. I wouldn't be surprised if our friends the Bar-levs were trained in their Jewish-ness somewhere near the Israeli border."

"There are some ultra-Orthodox settlements in the Galilee," Uri said. "You don't think ..."

"I can't speculate on anything yet, but the matter sure needs quick investigation."

Lara had to get in on this conversation. "Are you trying to say that there may be some real Orthodox Jews in Israel connected with this somehow?"

"Not intentionally, I don't think, but like I said, we need to investigate. That is, you folks need to," David added.

"But listen," he said. "There's even more disturbing news. Right after the embassy found out about these three fake passports, they ran a computer check on all Israeli-issued passports that had come into the United States over the last five years. Fortunately, they record the passport numbers at U.S. immigration and make them available to the country of origin. Turns out there's a bunch of passport numbers registered that were never issued by the State of Israel. Looks like about thirty."

"Why hasn't this been noticed before?" demanded Uri.

"You know the U.S. government, if it's not a problem don't worry about it. There's never been a problem with Israeli citizens entering the country before."

"Well, do we have any idea who these people are and where they went?"

"Here's the thing: we do have the names on those passports and their purported destinations when entering the country. The names are probably fake, but every one of these people had a student visa. They were all headed for universities."

Exasperated Lara said, "I don't suppose we have any idea which particular universities."

"Believe it or not," David said, "we do have records of their primary destinations. Doesn't mean they stayed there, just that they went there first. With Israeli student visas, these people could go to virtually any of the best universities in the United States."

"Was there any commonality in the visas or the destinations?" Uri asked.

"Virtually all were headed to second or third tier technical schools; that is, for science or engineering degrees. Probably couldn't, or didn't want to, get into the first tier schools. Here's something you'll like: four of them showed West Texas Polytechnic University as their destination. Going there to study math or science or something. In order to get the visa they had to have gotten approval from the dean there."

"Any other common destinations among them?" Lara asked.

"A couple went to 'Florida AIMN and T'. Don't ask me what all the letters mean. It's in some little town in the Panhandle."

"Panhandle?" Uri asked.

41

"The northwestern part of the state. I have no idea how they picked that particular school."

"Any others ...?" Lara asked. This was looking like a wild goose chase.

"No, the others all went to places like North Dakota School of Ceramics and Metallurgy. That would be NDSCM. And Southwestern Mississippi Science and Engineering, in a place called East Ferriday. That's just outside Natchez ..."

"Okay, I get the picture. You think we can have these names and destinations? Maybe we can get on the phone to the deans and track 'em down." Uri was ready to get started, unless David had some more information for them.

"Sure, I've already had a list made up for you. If you want, you can use a couple of phones in our visitors' area."

Uri and Lara stood up simultaneously. "Sounds like a plan," she said, taking the list from David.

They headed for a secure phone bank in the next room. They split up the list, each pulling out a tablet computer and pad of paper. They quickly found websites for all schools on the list David had given them. Each website had abundant information about the school: exact location, available curricula, phone numbers for the administration, even listings of undergraduate and graduate students.

Lara got lucky immediately. She had that part of the list with the four "students" who had shown their destination as "West Texas Poly," which was in Waco. There on the list of undergraduates was one of their suspects, or at least someone of the same name. "Bingo!" she cried out. She then looked around in embarrassment to make sure no one besides Uri had heard her.

They examined the websites for several of the other schools, but either the suspects' names were missing, or there was no listing of students at all. Next, they phoned the Dean of Students office at each of the schools. Uri got through first, to the small North Dakota school. "I was wondering if you have a student enrolled there named Yoram Cohen?" he asked the secretary politely. Lara heard him say, "Yes, I'm his cousin from Israel, and I was hoping to reach him." Uri waited patiently for a couple of minutes then said into the phone, "Oh, I see. Well did he by chance leave a forwarding location? ... Oh really, well that's great! Thanks very much. Goodbye."

"They had a student by that name a couple of years ago, but guess what? He transferred after one semester ... to West Texas Poly."

After a few more calls with the same result they were starting to get a pretty clear picture of what was going on. From what they could tell, essentially all these "students" had headed for Waco, and West Texas Poly.

They packed up all their material and hurried back into David's office to give him the news.

"I bet I know where your next stop is," he said.

"Yahoo, pardner!" Lara said with a big smile, as they headed for the door.

Chapter 8

Lara and Uri took a cab back to the federal building, and rushed up to report to Hadley. He exhibited unusual enthusiasm. "That's very good news," he said. "I expect you want to head to Waco immediately."

"Yes, that's what we thought. Can your secretary arrange a flight for us?" Lara asked.

Hadley spoke into his intercom. "Doris, can you arrange transportation for Lara and Uri to, ah... where exactly was it again?" He remembered after a second and said to Doris ... "to Waco, Texas." He turned to Lara and Uri and asked, "Right?"

"No," Lara answered. "Waco's not far from Dallas, so I figured we would fly to Dallas, rent a car, and drive the rest of the way." She had already checked out the flights, and had learned that the short hop from Dallas to Waco would be a bumpy ride on a small prop plane. They both preferred to drive.

After a few minutes, Doris rang back with the information that a flight leaving that afternoon would get them into Dallas around 1900 hours.

"Just get them economy seats, Federal fare, from JFK to Dallas, and arrange for hotel rooms there for the night." He turned to Lara. "Anyplace special you want to stay?"

"Well, since you asked, I've always wanted to stay at the Anatole. It's got all this great art and I'm sure we can get a good government rate."

Hadley paused only a second to show his mild disapproval before instructing Doris to get them two rooms at the Hilton Anatole. "At the lowest government rate available," he added. The ultimate skin-flint when it came to his employees' travel, he insisted on a detailed receipt instead of the usual government per diem. "Oh, Doris," he added, "be sure to tell them late arrival." Pleased with himself for remembering all these particulars, he wished them luck, and asked that they check in at least everyday.

Before they left the building, Lara took Uri down to the third floor, where they checked out a couple of 9 mm Glocks. They weren't expecting any need for real firepower, just personal protection. The permits that came with the guns would get them quickly through airport security.

Lara and Uri rushed off separately to get their things together for the 1600 hours flight from JFK International Airport. Getting there from Manhattan in midafternoon would not be difficult.

They had no problem at the airport. Once they showed their Federal IDs, they were able to take their side arms with them.

On the plane, they found they had side-by-side seats in economy with no one else in their row. This was really the first chance they had to talk, but naturally, not about the case; no telling who might overhear. So the four-hour flight would be an opportunity for them to catch up on each other's lives.

"You're not married?" Uri inquired bluntly, looking at her bare left hand. Might as well get this out of the way, he figured. He recognized he was still crazy about her.

"No, you?" She noticed the ring on his left hand. "Danielle…?"

"No, I guess I'm meant to be a bachelor," he said with a small grin. "Just sort of got used to the ring," he added, glancing at the band on his own left hand. "But after the uh, 'business' here, when I got back to Israel, things were pretty much over."

She knew of course, he was referring to teaming up with her to quell the nuclear terrorism threat from Hezbollah, when he lost his left eye. "I couldn't help but notice," she said, looking at his glass eye.

He smiled and said, "Yes, I know I said back then I was going to wear a patch all the time. But I became too recognizable. It was uncomfortable as well as dangerous. They did a pretty good job of it, don't you think?"

She laughed and touched his hand, "Well, I did like that Moshe Dayan look, but, yes, you look fine."

Other than their handshake, this was the first physical contact between them. He noticed that she said, "You look fine," rather than "It looks fine." A glimmer of hope raced through his veins; he was glad he had his briefcase on his lap. "I've been mostly stuck behind a desk since then. Some reluctance to put me back in the field ..." He cleared his throat, wanting to get off the subject. "That's enough about me; what have you been up to? I see they moved you from Washington to New York." Actually, he had known about the transfer. His Mossad buddies had kept tabs on her without his having to ask.

"Yeah, I figured I needed a change anyway. It was a good move. And, yes, I've dated around a little since I moved up there, but nobody special. I still have that thing about, you know, the guys at work."

He knew she meant the macho FBI agents she worked with. They were not her type. They had a tendency to talk mainly about pecs and abs. She was, he knew, more likely to want to go to the art museums in New York, rather than the gym.

The overpriced meals they had ordered arrived and they relaxed and watched the onboard movie in silence, laughing at the absurd Hollywood version of gunfights and hand-to-hand combat. The four-hour flight seemed relatively short, and with the time change, they arrived at DFW airport just after 1900 local time. They found the government carpool on-site; Hadley had conveniently arranged a small, anonymous American sedan for them.

Lara drove the short distance to the Anatole Hotel, just off the freeway. It was a spectacular sight, with its Asian art, reflecting pools, and statues. Uri was impressed that their government rate was a mere $113. They had rooms on the same floor, but not next to each other. In any case, Lara insisted that they go around and see some of the art before they turned in for the night. Uri was happy for the chance to be with her a little while longer.

They walked leisurely through the various art collections, Lara commenting on the quiet beauty of the Asian paintings and sculptures. By then it was close to 2200 and the busy day had worn both of them down.

"Want a drink, or should we call it a night?" Uri asked.

"I think I'm ready for bed," Lara answered, stifling a yawn. They headed up to their floor and stood in front of her door for a second. Uri took her hands in his and looked in her eyes. She smiled at the same time, indicating they were not picking up where they left off a few years ago; at least not yet. "Breakfast, 0630?" she offered.

"Right," Uri replied. "See you in the coffee shop. Sleep well."

In their government car and on the road just after 0700, with hardly any traffic headed south, Lara had no problem driving a steady 70 miles an hour. She had made arrangements to see the Dean of Students, a man named Keltner, at 0900.

Being alone in the car gave them their first real chance to talk about the case. Even though this was a government car, Uri had taken no chances, and swept it for bugs before leaving the airport. "Have you thought at all about what these folks came here to accomplish?" he began.

"Sure, but I can't say I've come up with much, if anything at all. That first family, the Bar-levs, who blew up the synagogue, were here over a year before any of the others showed up in the country."

"Right," he said. "And they came here together. These others all came here individually. So maybe they waited to see if the Bar-levs would be discovered before they tried anything."

"So you figure their agenda is something different?"

"Right. If they were going to pull the same trick, they would've come as families."

"And anyway, they would figure we would be on to that immediately. Just like always, the U.S. closes the barn door after the horse is gone," she added grimly.

"You mean like with the shoe bomber and the underwear bomber and the liquids in the carry-on bomber ..."

"Exactly. So these guys are smart enough not to try the same trick twice. Whatever they are up to, it's not going to be the synagogue thing again. Anyway, the Bureau has put everyone available at all the large synagogues in the country. And the other synagogues have been put under the watch of the local police. The bad guys are going to know that we're stretched pretty thin."

Uri thought about that for a minute. "You're right; that's why they figure our quiet inquiry won't stir up the nest. So let's think like Hezbollah for a minute: why would they risk sending individuals to the U.S.? They can plan almost anything they want to do in Lebanon. With access to the Internet, and Google maps, they can send suicide bombers anywhere they choose, without even a rehearsal."

"You're right," Lara replied. "And besides, why send them to college, and why pretend to be Orthodox Jews?"

"The biggest question in my mind is why West Texas Poly? They all seem to be enrolled in technical curricula, but nothing they couldn't get at other schools ... unless ..."

"It's got to be something they're planning as a group. But a group terrorist attack in Waco doesn't make any sense, even for these guys," she said.

"So we're down to three questions: why are they pretending to be Hasidim; why are they all in college; and why are they all in Waco?" They pondered these questions as they drove, but came up with no answers.

Just before 0900, they arrived in the city of Waco. It appeared to be a clean, university town, typical of all those American cities built around private colleges. They learned while reading the brochures on the plane, that West Texas Poly had been founded as a Baptist college but had grown into a major university with multiple disciplines of study.

Under their cover as journalists doing an article on up–and–coming universities that would be attractive to international students, they were heartily greeted by the Dean of Students, Dr. Amos M. Keltner, in his opulent office on the top floor of the administration building.

Dr. Keltner turned out to be a short, corpulent man, about 60 years old, with a rather obvious toupee. Still, he exuded that Southwestern charm so commonly seen among businessmen in this part of the country.

"Have a seat, have a seat!" he said warmly, gesturing to two rich, red leather chairs that sat facing the corners of his desk. He plopped himself in a huge captain's chair unobtrusively placed on a hidden platform, to give him a few inches of height advantage over his visitors, much like a talk-show host. "I understand you want to do an article on West Texas Poly," he said, grasping his hands over his ample belly. "Well, you've come to the right place. What am I thinkin'?! Let me get y'all somethin' to drink," he said, heading to the bar. "Tea, coffee, ginger ale," he offered with a smile. "I'm sure y'all know we're a Baptist institution. But that don't mean we don't accept everyone as long as they follow the rules."

Lara and Uri both smiled in return, each politely indicating they had no need for refreshments.

"Well then," Keltner said brightly, "what can we do for y'all? I know you've come a long way."

Lara began, "As you know, we're doing an article on an organization that tries to place international students in well-thought-of institutions of higher learning. And, well I know you have quite a few international students so we are here ..."

"Yes indeed," Keltner replied, "of our 15,000 students, nearly 1000 come from overseas. We like to keep kind of a 'worldly' atmosphere here. You know, in a lot of schools around here in West Texas, students don't give a chance to rub shoulders with people from around the globe."

Lara also knew that colleges and universities around the U.S. were desperately short of funds, and were delighted to receive tuition from whomever they could.

"The thing is, Dean Keltner, many of the students we represent don't ... well, quite have the educational background necessary for them to meet the standards of a lot of U.S. universities. That isn't to suggest," she quickly added, "that West Texas Poly doesn't provide the educational opportunities that other more widely known U.S. universities might give; in fact, we feel the wide variation in educational background of the students here might be a great advantage for the individuals we represent. For even though their educational backgrounds may not have all the earmarks of the fancy private schools, the students still have all the initiative and desire for learning that anyone could ask for." She paused, slightly embarrassed, recognizing the length of the monologue she had just delivered.

Keltner sat up, clearly interested, and not at all offended. "Well, you know, little lady," he replied, "that really is the main concern in whom we admit here."

He cleared his throat and turned to look at Uri. "Of course, there is a limit, financially speaking, of how many students we can take. The price a' education here just keeps goin' up every year. We try to maintain the highest level of academic excellence ... why, you know we have the highest number of PhD's of any of the colleges in this here part of the country ... That is of the smaller private colleges," he quickly added for clarity.

"Oh," Lara interjected, so as to avoid Uri's Israeli–accented English from coming into the picture at this point, "we understand that completely. In fact, the students we're talking about here are, financially speaking, extremely well prepared. We've looked at your tuition and other costs per student, and are well able to meet your standards. In fact, we are willing and able to make a substantial contribution to the University in order to provide our students with the kind of well–rounded education they would receive in an institution like yours."

A bluebird might have flown in the window and landed on Keltner's shoulder from the smile this information produced. "Well then, I think we can start talkin' business here," he said brightly, leaning forward to bring out a hefty package of manila folders from his desk.

"Now then," he added in a businesslike tone, "just where y'all say these folks of yours will be comin' from? Not that it matters y'understand," he added quickly. "It's just we like to keep records of that sort of thing."

Now Uri entered the conversation. "For the most part, the students we're talking about are from the Middle East, Northern Israel actually, from agricultural communities where they haven't had the benefit of an urban education."

"Why, that's just fine," Keltner said, obviously relaxing. "Why, as a matter of fact, we have a goodly number of your folks here already. Fine members of the academic community they are, maybe you'd like to take a look at the list of 'em. Probably know some of 'em."

"Why that'd be great," Uri replied, "help us to see who'd fit in."

Keltner rose from his chair and made his way slowly across the room. "Thing is, an' I say this with the most respect y'understand. Most of the students we have here from Israel are the religious type, you know with the long sideburns an' all, an' ... don't get me wrong here ... they're doin' real good with their grades an' everything. Majorin' in all kinds of subjects, mostly technical—math, engineering, science—we have one of the best computer science departments in the state! They're fittin' in real well too, get along with all the other, that is the Christian students. All in all, we're proud to have 'em here, look forward to seein' more of 'em!"

A long pause followed as Lara and Uri tried to assimilate what they had just heard.

"Oh, I know what you're thinkin', how do they take care of all their Kosher needs an' whatall. But they manage an' are real happy doin' it." Keltner went back and sat himself down in his chair. "Tell you what, you got some time today, why don't y'all take a walk around campus, see what it's like, maybe talk to some of these students of yours."

Uri looked at Lara, received a confirmative glance, and stood up. "You know Dean Keltner, I think you have a pretty good idea there. We're going to take you up on it."

Keltner led them to the door and handed them the manila folder with the list of Israeli students, and their photographs. "An' while you're at it, get a look around Waco. It's a real special place you know, used to be a cow town way back. To get the cattle up north, they had to cross the Brazos River. Around 1900, folks built 'em a bridge, an' that pretty much put Waco on the map. West Texas Poly's pretty much the mainstay of the town right now. It's a pretty little town, with the new bridge they put in a few years back, it's one of the most modern cities in the state. Oh yeah, an' we got the gol-darndest football team you ever did see!!"

As Lara and Uri were leaving, Keltner slapped himself in the head and said, "Now how could I forget, you for sure got to go across that new bridge an' take a look at Mt. Zion!" He saw the uncomprehending looks on their faces, smiled, and picked up a card from his desk. "This bein' a weekday, ol' Len'll be workin' in his office. You just give them a holler on that phone number I gave you, an' tell him I sent ya'. An' come back anytime y'hear!"

As they left, Uri looked at the card Keltner had given him. It was a simple business card, with the words "Mount Zion" written in a crescent across the top. In the center of the card was the name, "Leonard Depew, Founder and Director." Below that was an address. From their map of the campus, they saw that it was on the other side of the river. At the very bottom of the card written in italics, was the word, *"Revelation."*

Lara and Uri left Keltner's office with the list of students from Israel, the information on Mount Zion, and more questions than answers. Getting in the car, parked in the visitors' lot outside the administration building, Uri opened up his laptop. "Let's take a look at that list of names he gave us." He compared it to the list of fake Jews that had entered the country with forged Israeli passports. A quick initial check confirmed that at least most of them were the same.

"I have an idea," Lara said brightly, "why don't you check a few of those names on Facebook?"

Uri didn't quite see what she was getting at, but went ahead and opened Facebook. He checked the first name on the list: Benjamin Aaronson. "Okay, now what?"

"Just take a quick look at his 'friends' and see how many of the other suspects are on the list."

"Very clever! Let's take a look." Uri compared the small list of friends claimed by Aaronson to the thirty or so Israeli students on the list given to them by the Dean. "Wow!" He looked at her in amazement. "None. Apparently Benny isn't friends with any of the others." He checked the next one on the list, Avram Cohen. "Guess what: Avi doesn't know the others either. What a friendly bunch!"

As they were talking and scanning the photos, Uri suddenly stopped and stared at one in particular.

"You see something special?" Lara asked. "Maybe someone you recognize?"

"No ... At least I don't think so," Uri replied. "Just these eyes, something about these eyes ..."

Uri and Lara walked briskly across the campus, headed for the technical center, which housed the math, science, and engineering buildings. They figured they'd most likely run into some of the Israeli students in that area. Sure enough, it wasn't more than 15 minutes before they saw two dark-complexioned Hasidic-looking young men, book-packs up over their right shoulders, in keeping with the rest of the students, chatting happily in English.

"Shalom," Uri called out to the nearest one, smiling and offering his hand. The two Hasids stopped in their tracks, took in Uri and Lara, hesitated, then broke into broad grins. "Shalom Aleichem," they said, hugging Uri and bowing slightly as they each took Lara's hand.

"Please, though, speak English, we need the practice," the first, and taller of the two, said with a smile.

The smaller, and obviously younger one, nodded, agreeing with his compatriot.

"This is Shmuel, and I am Michael. Let me guess, you are visiting from Israel," Michael said laughing.

"How did I give it away?" Uri replied with a grin. "My name is Uri; my friend here is Lara, she's an American. I know you're probably hurrying to class, but we're only here for a short time, and were hoping to meet some of the exchange students from Israel. We're part of a delegation to try and place more students like yourselves at West Texas."

After a slight pause Michael and Shmuel glanced at each other, seemed to come to an agreement, then Michael said, "Of course, what we can tell you in just a few minutes; we do in fact have to get to class."

"Well," Uri began, "basically we'd like to know how you like it here so far. How long have you been here now?"

Michael and Shmuel glanced at each other again, as if this were a complex question, and once again it was Michael who answered, "Actually we just got here this semester, but it's going real well. Listen, if you guys have time come on over to the

Kosher club where we eat dinner. You'll see it on the campus map you got there, it's called Hill Hall. But we gotta run now, see you later!" They scurried on off to class.

"Well," Lara said, "that was certainly interesting. What do you make of it?"

"Couple things," Uri answered with a quizzical look. "They seemed willing enough to talk to us, but just a little reserved. Did you see the way they looked at each other each time I asked a question?"

"I did notice that, but I thought that was mainly because they were so surprised to see us."

"It may be my naturally suspicious nature, but I had the feeling they were considering their answers before speaking -- not a totally natural response to meeting a countryman."

"What was the other thing you noticed?"

"It was the way they were dressed; they wore the typical Hasidic garb of the Ashkenazi Jews. Yet their complexions and facial characteristics are much more common to the Sephardic."

"You're telling me they look more like North African Jews, yet they were dressing like European Jews, right?"

"Exactly. It might not mean anything, but we combine it with what we learned from Rabbi Goldstein ..." He paused, trying to combine the information and come up with an answer.

"Anyway," he said, "we've got another trip to make today and I really can't wait to see what we're going to find across the river."

Chapter 9

Staunton Richardson looked himself over in the hall mirror in the grand entryway of Dale Simmons' mansion. *It might get a little dicey*, he thought, *but nothing I can't handle.* He adjusted his perfectly knotted tie, smoothed his perfectly groomed hair, and checked the shine on his thousand dollar, hand-made Italian shoes. *Perfect as usual*, he thought, smiling, *"I am the very model of the modern major general."* The quote from the Gilbert and Sullivan operetta always worked to calm him down.

The meeting had been called at Simmons' request. Nothing unusual there; it was the sense of urgency that gave Richardson some unease.

Their relationship began a few years ago when Richardson attended a meeting of an organization called the Texas Leadership Conference, a political action committee more commonly known as the "TLC." The organization sponsored conservative candidates ... conservative, even by Texas standards. Their positions on such issues as immigration, help for the needy, and foreign aid intrigued him. The TLC opposed them all. While Richardson had recognized a number of wealthy, conservative businessmen and politicians, it was Dale Simmons who had approached *him*. "Staunton Richardson, I believe," Simmons had said with a big smile, extending his hand.

"Call me Stan," he'd replied, grasping the hand firmly. Though he hadn't recognized Simmons, he certainly knew the name. The Simmons family was legendary in West Texas. Porter Simmons grew wealthy in the first oil boom, buying up mineral rights in the 1930s for virtually pennies. He used all his profits to buy up even more mineral rights, all through West and Central Texas. By the time his son, Blanchard, came on the scene in the 1960s, the game had changed. The young Blanchard Simmons figured out that if he bought the land instead of just the mineral rights, he wouldn't have to deal out royalties. He wisely figured that the price of oil would soon skyrocket, as the Arabs figured out how to manipulate us, and the doomsayers convinced the public that the supply of fossil fuels was nearly depleted.

His strategy worked magnificently. He bought up tens of thousands of acres of oil-rich property, then leased the land back to the former owners, so they could raise livestock. Simmons Oil prospered beyond anyone's dreams. They now owned hundreds of thousands of acres, produced millions of barrels of oil, and still qualified as a "Small Business" for tax purposes. The family purposely kept a low profile. They didn't run for public office; they sponsored politicians. They didn't become lawyers; they hired the best firms for their legal business. They didn't publicly endorse anything or anybody; they used their immense financial means to get the right people elected, and the right bills passed. The Simmons family, and others like them, kept Texas the friendliest state in the country for industry and accumulation of wealth. The laws they helped pass provided the least regulation on corporate behavior in the country. Dale, Blanchard's only child, took over the entire enterprise when Blanchard fell gravely ill.

"I recognized you from church," Dale said. "Our family been members for a long time now, from before you came on board. You're doin' one heck of a job with membership, Leonard Depew, our spiritual leader tells me."

Stan beamed at the compliment; he had seen the Simmons name on the membership rolls, and been aware of their generous contributions, but had no idea the Simmons knew of him. "Well," he said, "I think the church has had a wonderful, positive effect on the Christian community around here."

"More than you realize." Dale, a large, physically impressive man, a quality held in high esteem in this part of the country, wore a tan, Western-style suit. His cowboy boots, and immaculate, cream-colored Stetson made his appearance even more striking.

He steered Richardson over to the refreshments table and said, "Lemme buy ya' a drink." When he saw Richardson hesitate, he said, "Now I know drinkin' ain't strictly accordin' to church rules, but this here's a special occasion." Impressed by the social level of his new-found acquaintance, Stan allowed himself to be poured a relatively mild whiskey and branch water by the dark-skinned black man in the starched white uniform, tending bar. "Thank you, Cassius," Simmons said to the man warmly, pressing a five dollar bill imperceptibly into his palm.

As they sipped their drinks, Dale guided Richardson over to an unoccupied corner of the room. "I guess you're wonderin' what I want to talk to ya' about."

"Well, I uh ...," Stan stammered, still mystified by the attention he was receiving.

"I was just wonderin' what ya' thought of the talks here today."

The "talks" Simmons referred to were given by a number of noted statewide politicians and local businessmen. They were guiding the faithful, pointing out the need for resisting Washington's goals of taxing the wealthy, controlling air and water emissions, restricting oil and gas production on federal lands, and allowing unbridled immigration.

"As a matter of fact," Stan replied, "y'all strike a chord with me on all accounts." He affected a mild Texas accent to accommodate his host.

"Y' know, I had a feeling you were on the right side of things," Dale said, warmly placing a hand firmly on Richardson's shoulder. "But I wasn't sure. You know, you not bein' from around here—originally." Stan realized they had checked into his background and knew he had been educated at Tennessee Baptist University. "But I guess you don't like them New York lawyers any better than we do," he said, smiling.

By "New York lawyers" Stan knew instinctively Dale meant Jews. He sensed this was a test to see how much he agreed with the TLC. Although he had never actually met a Jewish person, he knew they did not believe in Christ, and were, therefore, doomed to eternal damnation. He was quite aware, even from his first visit, that the TLC vehemently opposed the enormous quantity of financial aid the Jewish state of Israel received from the U.S. It certainly made no sense to him that a Christian nation supported a country which opposed its very founding principles. Furthermore, he had heard how the Jewish immigrants, who had become rich in the US, mainly from the banking, newspaper, and entertainment industries, gave even more money to their Jewish brethren in Israel; therefore, he returned Simmons' smile and said, "No, I figure we got enough good Christian lawyers right here in Texas. And they sure do seem to be on the right side of things."

An ambitious man, Stan saw immediately how his position in the church could be valuable to these powerful men. His success in membership in just a few years had made a strong impression on the spiritual leader, Leonard Depew. The finances of the church had improved dramatically, as reflected in the unparalleled growth of the membership. He sensed that the TLC would like to have their "conservative" doctrines directed to the faithful, even if subtly.

From the first, the meetings between Richardson and Simmons continued regularly throughout the next few months. Then, one day after church, Dale approached Stan and asked him to his "place" for lunch. His driver, he told Stan, would pick him up at noon Tuesday, if he were agreeable. Richardson leapt at the opportunity, not knowing exactly what to expect, but realizing that the invitation had to have positive implications.

At lunch that day, about two years ago, Simmons had taken Richardson into his opulent, leather-bound library and disclosed his plans. That was Richardson's first visit to the mansion and he was suitably impressed. The driver, another near-silent black man in a tailored chauffeur's costume, had arrived to pick him up, promptly at noon in a black Lincoln town car. Richardson, not knowing exactly how to dress, chose to wear a light blue shirt, conservative tie, and summer-weight trousers. Torn between donning loafers or saddle oxfords, he decided finally on the latter.

After a short, 20 minute drive, they arrived at an electronic gate which opened on command. He heard a quiet rumbling as they drove over the metal cattle guard. The near featureless land spread as far as the eye could see, cattle grazing calmly on the sparse brush. Another five minutes passed before the "house" came into view. The road, changing from dirt to white pea gravel, led to a huge circular driveway framing a southern style mansion. Magnolias, cypress, a five acre lawn, an artificial pond with majestic swans completed the picture. All no doubt fed from a deep well system. To one side of the driveway, he saw a horse stable, corral and paddock. As they drove slowly past, Richardson noted two young people outfitted in British riding togs, cantering around the track.

All in all, the scene reflected the influence of European royalty on the gracious use of American wealth. To Richardson, it was a way of life that he had always dreamed of, but never really expected to encounter. As the limousine crunched to a halt on the white limestone driveway, Dale Simmons strode out from the veranda of the magnificent mansion, a wide smile creased his tanned face The chauffeur jumped out and opened the door for Stan.

"Thank you, Marcus," Dale said, as Richardson emerged from the car. "Great you could make it, Stan!" he said, putting his arm around Richardson's shoulder.

As if I would possibly miss this chance, Stan thought.

Simmons, attired in white linen slacks, blue blazer, and boat shoes and, of course, topped off with his white Stetson, made a nearly imperceptible gesture to the chauffeur, who saluted crisply, got back in the town car, and drove off, presumably to an ample garage somewhere out of sight.

In the sunroom just off the entrance, the men engaged in small talk as they sipped on light drinks. Hearing another limousine crunch into the driveway, Stan waited to learn the identity of the new arrival. When the door opened, he saw a man who looked vaguely familiar. Standing six foot two in his cowboy boots, he wore blue jeans and a leather jacket, his outfit topped off with the inevitable Stetson, this one a light tan.

"Roy!" Dale exclaimed, reaching out to grasp the visitor with a gripping handshake, the other hand grasped the man's shoulder. "So glad you could make it. Here, like you to meet someone; frienda' mine." He led the newcomer over to Stan, and the two shook hands, looking each other straight in the eye. Stan 64was taken with the man's startling blue eyes and perfectly groomed grey-brown hair, evident when he removed his Stetson.

"Roy, I'd like you to know Mr. Staunton Richardson, one of the leaders of the church, and a good friend." The two men nodded. "Stan, I'd like you to know Mr. Roy Blankenship, our new secretary of energy, and good friend of the family."

It hit Stan then; that's where he'd seen this man ... on television news about a month ago ... the Senate confirmation hearings. As he recalled, from the TV commentators, it had been a tough fight. According to the pundits, the only reason Blankenship had been nominated, was in exchange for the president getting the man he wanted as secretary of defense, a Mr. Frank McHenry. As it was explained to him by his political junky wife, Sally, "That's the way things work in Washington. It's all a matter of give and take."

In McHenry, the president had a man who agreed with his foreign-policy issues, especially when it came to the use of foreign aid and the use of force, when required. Blankenship on the other hand, had quite different views, especially when it came to land management, energy conservation, environmental protection, and perhaps most of all, foreign aid. He was opposed to all of them. To seal the deal, McHenry was a Texan as well.

Stan felt quite intimidated by these two powerful men, Simmons and Blankenship.

After some brief chatting about the weather, they went in for lunch. The three men sat at the dining room table partaking of a modest, but delicious Western lunch of perfectly barbecued ribs, sweet corn and baked beans. They dispensed with alcohol, and drank sweet iced tea. Stan let the other men lead the conversation. He feared they would drift into the world of politics, which would expose him as a babe in arms.

But it turned out to be a totally innocuous luncheon. Dale told Roy about Stan's work at the church, and asked Roy how he liked Washington. They talked about the local drought, how it would impact the farmers. They spoke of the price of grain, the price of beef, the price of land. They didn't exactly leave Stan out of the conversation, but they didn't ask for his opinion, and he wasn't about to offer it.

Stan's instincts were pretty good when it came to people. They told him that Dale had already spoken to Blankenship about him, and this lunch had a lot to do with Roy's getting his impressions of the new church man.

"Well, gentlemen, much as I'd like to spend the afternoon chatting with you, I have some other appointments that I couldn't break." Roy stood and moved away from the table.

The other men stood also and Stan extended his hand to Blankenship. "It's been a pleasure to meet you, sir."

"The same to 'ya, Stan. Keep up the good work you're doin' at the church."

Dale walked to the door with his guest and on outside where he lingered for a few minutes, alone with Roy, before the car drove off.

Back inside, Dale put his arm around Stan's shoulder. "Come on into the library for a minute, some things I'd like to talk to you about." He led Stan across the sumptuous foyer, opened a massive wooden door all of ten-feet-tall through which they entered a gleaming dark-walnut-paneled room interspersed with rich, red leather chairs. Huge shelves of books behind glass panels towered from tabletop level to near the ceiling. A round, mahogany table stood at one side of the room and next to it, two of the plush red leather chairs. *Fit for heads of state,* Stan thought.

Simmons motioned him to one of the chairs then sat in the other himself. A ceiling-high window, coated to avoid sunlight or the curious eye from entering, allowed one to gaze out onto the seemingly unending ranch. The only artificial light in the room came from hidden fixtures high above. Simmons must have touched a hidden button, because one of the servants appeared silently.

"Antoine, a couple of brandies, please," Simmons said easily, not asking Stan, but merely nodding in his direction, as if to say, "You will of course join me?" Richardson didn't bother to reply to the implied question, completely overwhelmed by the entire afternoon.

They engaged in small talk ... the weather, college football ... until the servant appeared again, walking silently on the plush maroon carpet. He placed the brandies on the table, cushioning the glasses with handsome leather coasters.

Simmons sat easily, crossing his legs, clearly at home in this situation, and also clearly in charge. Richardson sipped tentatively at his brandy. Unaccustomed to alcohol, and certainly to drinking it this early in the day, he waited for Simmons to begin the real conversation.

"Stan, I've got to tell you, I'm really impressed with the church's operations. Leonard is certainly moving things in the right direction, if you know what I mean." Stan wasn't sure to what he was referring, so just nodded politely and waited.

"I'm impressed with the Revelation concept, and so are most of the folks I've talked to about it."

So that's where this is headed, Richardson thought. *The idea from the Book of Revelation, whereby the Holy Land would someday be the place where the Savior would once again appear. Then the believers would be transported into heaven, the disbelievers consumed in flames.*

"Stan, I don't know about you, but I think it's a beautiful concept even if it might not happen in our lifetime. It gives folks a reason to live a good, wholesome, God-fearing life."

He waited for Stan to say something. Stan knew this was a moment of life-making or breaking proportions. Staunton Richardson had never been a devout Christian; the opportunity to handle the business of membership of this church had come his way and he had taken it. His parents had been Southern Baptists and had raised him in the church as well. Socially, it suited him, got him into a good fraternity in college, and allowed him to meet women whom he considered to be of a proper sort to be his wife and mother of his children.

It worked out well for him; his wife, Sally, had never pressured him to be anything more than a good husband and father. The chance for this position at Waco had come from one of his fraternity brothers, a friend who had gone into the business of "headhunting." The interview had gone well and Sally liked the idea of living in West Texas. While he attended services regularly, he thought of it more as part of his job than part of a lifelong devotion. Although he liked his job, he found that his adeptness in dealing with people indicated that he might be headed for bigger things in life. Heading into his forties, he realized life might have other horizons to offer.

Leonard Depew had never asked him for his deepest thoughts on the matter of Revelation; his performance as head of membership had been enough. Now, however, he would have to find an answer for Simmons. *Was this a trap of some kind?* he wondered, *or was this just an honest inquiry?* He took a deep breath, and decided to be straightforward. "Well, Dale, I've always thought of the Bible as a guide to living life the way God meant us to. But, I never really took it as a step-by-step command."

"I had a feeling you were that sort of fellow, Stan," Simmons replied, smiling lightly and easing back in his chair. He took a sip of brandy, as Richardson breathed again, not knowing what was coming, but now sure whatever it was it wouldn't be bad.

"You see, Stan, I couldn't agree with you more. What I'm specifically getting at is our strategy in the Holy Land. Now don't get me wrong; I'm all for this Mount Zion project the church is working on over there. I think the idea of getting our folks to see the land where Christ was born is just wonderful. There's not a doubt in my mind that someday that land will see the second coming of our Savior, and 'The Rapture'."

Stan nodded in complete agreement.

"What worries me is the money and men we're sacrificin' for the Jews who live there now. What if we sort of eliminated the 'middle men'-- you know how those Jews like to be wholesalers -- and speeded up things a bit. Why, how long do you think they'd last without our help?" Dale paused here, clearly waiting for a reply.

Stan hesitated for a second; he knew the right answer was critical here. On the one hand, if he showed complete agreement with what Dale had said, he would be, in effect, contradicting the precise views of his boss, Leonard Depew. On the other hand, an association with Simmons and the TLC could be a career-changing event of monumental size. "I see what you're getting at, Dale; what would happen to the region if the U.S. suddenly changed course?" Stan believed he had come up with a clever answer, that by posing his reply as a question, he had forced Dale to reveal more of his plans.

"Good point!" Dale replied. "I was hoping you'd ask." Stan relaxed slightly as he waited for the other man to continue. "We at the TLC governing board have given this a lot of thought. If the Arabs were to somehow get their wish and make that tiny bit of real estate their own, do you see the implications?"

Stan shook his head. He knew Dale had a well thought out answer to this question and that he was only expected to wait for it.

"Think about it a second, Stan. Arabs can't ever agree on anything; they're worse than the Jews. And speaking of the Jews, don't worry about them, they'll make out just like they always do. Most of 'em will end up here, in New York and LA, I mean; the rest will find other countries to go to. They're a resilient, clever people. Always have been.

"But getting back to the Arabs, without the Jews to fight, they'll fight each other. Sunnis, Shiites, and all kinds of other half-ass tribes -- there won't be a minute's peace. When you add to that mix the nutty Iranians, you end up with a massacre the likes of which the world's never seen. The Iranians hate the Arabs worse than they hate the Jews! And vice-versa. Why, we'd be doing the world a favor lettin' those crazy bastards have at each other."

This was a lot for Richardson to get his mind around in one sitting; Dale could see that, and didn't want to push the matter. He could see that Stan could be a valuable asset, and he didn't want to scare him off. "My gosh," Simmons said, "look at the time! Why don't you think over what I've said, and we can get together again. Kinda' talk it through a little more. In the meantime, let's just keep this conversation between ourselves, okay?" He stood, smiled, and grabbed Stan's hand to seal the deal.

Stan was more than glad to keep the meeting and the conversation between themselves. This had been an enormous unveiling, one that he would have to think about carefully over the coming days. *I won't tell Sally about this. No use complicating the picture. He knew he'd be able to bring her around when need be.*

Chapter 10

It was no more than two weeks later that Richardson received another invitation to Simmons' ranch. He knew he would have to be ready with an answer.

"Great you could make it out here again, Stan. I hope you've had time to think about ... well, about what we discussed the other day."

"You bet I have, Dale," Stan said. He sat again in the plush, red leather chair that Simmons offered. Instead of having a servant bring brandy, a bottle of the amber fluid stood ready on the table, along with two snifters. Simmons poured each of them about an inch of the liquor; this wasn't going to be a drinking party.

"Well, I've been wondering about the implications to the world at large, if things go like you say. And don't get me wrong," he added quickly, "I can see how they very well would."

"Well," Simmons said easily, "the first thing you want to look at is the world's economy. With all of OPEC at each other's throats, the production of oil is going to suffer like never before. For over 70 years, the presence of Israel has been like a buffer, keepin' things stable by bein' a target for all the hatred in the region. Now, without them, like I said the other day, all those Moslem, or 'Muslim,' countries are goin' to be fightin' for control. With the fightin', comes a huge reduction in oil production. And you know what that does to the price."

The clouds parted, and the sun shone through like never before. Staunton Richardson now understood everything. Like always, money and power were the keys. With Middle East oil in extremely short supply, the rest of the world would be looking elsewhere. Africa, North and South America, Russia, Asia -- all of the other oil producing areas would be forced to take up the slack. And, as the world had found in the 1970s, the price of oil was relatively "inflexible." A certain demand had to be met; a demand that was nearly independent of price. People had to have their cars, their air-conditioning, their electricity, and so on. The populations of the wealthier countries could afford to pay higher prices. The poor nations, well, they would have to make do as always.

Richardson got the point. The United States, more than any other country, was used to having an unlimited supply of energy. Americans would pay double, triple ... who knew the limit, and Simmons' company, along with many others, would profit like never before. New sources of oil on the North American continent would be opened: Shale oil, tar sands, offshore drilling, reopening of depleted wells -- all would appear. New jobs, absolutely. Environmental impact, not nearly as severe as would be restrictions on the nation's energy supply. The oil barons would prosper. Staunton Richardson wanted to get on board the train.

He sipped his brandy and considered his future. The opportunities for cooperating with Simmons appeared formidable. But what of his obligation to the church and its project in Israel? He asked Simmons directly, "What would happen to the Revelation Project, Mount Zion ...?"

"Like the sayin' goes, you can't make an omelet without breakin' some eggs. Over the long-term, our church would prosper. For one thing, Simmons Oil will sponsor education projects in its name all over the world. We're talkin' hundreds of millions of dollars ..."

"And in the short term ...?"

"Stan, you probably know that Israel depends mightily on U.S. financial support. Without it, they couldn't afford any kind of defense budget. Now that money depends on the will of the American people. Right now, Congress has the support of the Jewish lobby as well as us Conservative Christians. Take away either and, well, Israel's on its own. There won't be any negotiatin' table. The Arabs'll just take over."

"So," Stan said, "we somehow stop the Mount Zion project. How's that going to change people's minds?"

"It's the way that it stops; that's what makes the difference," Dale replied. Then he seemed to change gears: "What if Israeli Jews were to sabotage the project?"

"Why would they do that?" Stan asked, startled. "I thought the Israelis liked the idea of having Christian enclaves. Lots of money coming in, spirit of cooperation, that sort of thing."

"You're right. The vast majority, in fact almost all of the Israelis are delighted to have us come to their country -- for just the reasons you mentioned." Dale took another sip of brandy and seemed to consider how to make the next point. "You ever hear of a group called *Neturei Karta?*"

Stan shook his head.

"No, not many people in this country have. But strange as it may seem to us, there's a bunch of ultra-religious Jews in Israel, and even here in the U.S., who are vehemently anti-Zionist."

"Anti-Zionist?" Stan said, incredulous. "How could Jews living in Israel be anti-Zionist? That doesn't make any sense."

"Crazy as it sounds, there's this group and some others, who don't think Jews have the right to Israel until their Messiah appears. Till then, they think the land belongs to the Arabs."

"Let me get this straight," Stan said. "Some Jews living in Israel don't think they have the right to live there. Is that what you're telling me?"

"That's right. And let me answer your next question before you even ask. The Israeli constitution permits all Jews to live there, regardless of their politics. Remember now, we're only talking about a really small number, but they still get financial support from their government and don't even have to serve in the military."

"So I guess these folks aren't too happy about Christians who happen to be Zionist, either," Stan said.

"... or about any kind of project called "Mount Zion" supported by Americans ..." continued Dale.

"... who want to see Israel prosper as the homeland for all Jews ..." Staunton Richardson got the picture now.

The two men looked at each other over their brandies. Richardson waited for Simmons to get to the point: what needed to be done, and by whom? Finally he asked, "Just how would we get these ... what did you call them?"

"Neturei Karta. It's a done deal, Stan. We've already made the contact and gotten things rolling."

"What 'things' are those, Dale?" Richardson asked cautiously.

Simmons sat forward in his chair, resting his arms on the table, his gaze directly at Stan. "These Jews are going to sabotage the Mount Zion project. And you just watch how the Christian Right reacts. They are not gonna take kindly to Jews destroying American Christian property, whether it's in Israel or not. They'll combine with the ultra-liberal left, who already hate Israel anyway, to cut off any aid or cooperation just like that," he said, snapping his fingers forcefully. It was like a bomb going off in the silent room.

Stan sat back, took a sip of brandy and rolled it around in his mouth, savoring its rich flavor while he considered what he had just heard. If all this were true, he was being asked to participate in a world-shaking event. True, it would mean subverting the church's project; but in the long run, he could see how the church would prosper. As would he.

"And how would I be a part of this?" he asked.

Simmons leaned back; "Here's what you would do. We bring these folks into the country under student visas. "We get them to enroll at West Texas. While they're here in Waco, you help them mix in with the other students. Then you get them to come over and help with the Mount Zion project. Len will be tickled to have some honest-to-God Jews on the team. Then, at the right time, they'll go over to Haifa to help with the construction and ..."

Richardson thought about this for a minute or two. Simmons seemed to have it all figured out, except ...

"What happens after the, uh, event, and they get captured. Won't they give the whole thing away?" he asked.

Simmons smiled. "These guys are just like real Arab suicide bombers, only they're ultra-religious Jews. Won't be anybody left to question."

"I've got to admit, you seem to have it all figured out," Stan said admiringly. "But when you say 'bombers', won't there be Americans ..."

"We thought of that too. The 'event' as you call it will occur just as construction is completed; before any of our American

Christians go over there. We don't want to hurt any innocent people ...

"And while you're thinking about this, as part of the team, you'll get compensation in accord with the importance of what you're doin'. I'm thinkin' $500,000 a year to start, plus expenses. You'll be needin' to do a little travelin'."

It was all Stan could do to keep his eyes from rolling back in his head. The figure he had just heard amounted to ten times what he was making now.

"Think about it for a few days then give me a call in my Waco office," Simmons said, shaking Richardson's hand. "You're gonna be a fine addition to our team!"

Staunton Richardson felt his life was about to take a dramatic change of course.

Chapter 11

Lara and Uri walked back to the parking lot by the administration building and hopped in their government car. Using the city map they picked up at the carpool, they made it to the on-ramp onto what they read was the longest single span bridge in the world, leading to the other side of the Brazos River. They quickly found "Revelation Road" and a huge iron archway at the apex of a semicircular driveway. A shack stood at the entrance with a sleepy-looking guard who calmly asked, "Kin ah hep ya?"

Lara translated: "He's asking what we want."

Uri leaned across the window and said, "We're here to see Mr. Depew; he may be expecting us."

The guard, whose uniform draped across his scrawny shoulders as if it were on a hanger, thought about that for a moment, then pushed a button on his console.

"Coupla' folks here to see Mr. Depeeuw," he drawled into the mouthpiece.

"He expecten' em?" came the lazy reply.

"Don't rightly know, I'll ask." He turned back to Uri, "Whodya say t'was what sent ya?" he asked, barely audible from the back of the booth.

Uri looked at Lara again for a translation. "Tell him Dean Keltner from the University said he might have time to see us."

The guard, hearing the name "Keltner" spoke again into the console: "Seems as like they're friends a' Dean Keltner."

The disembodied voice on the other end of the console paused for a few seconds, then said, "Tell 'em to park in one of the visitors' spots, then to come on up to the second floor."

They left their car in front of the huge marble edifice that served as the church's office building, reminiscent of ancient Rome. Walking up the gleaming steps leading to the huge oak doors, they were absolutely breathless in anticipation of what they were about to find. As they ascended the steps, the beautiful

70

wood doors opened automatically in front of them, exposing a rotunda that could have come out of "Gone With the Wind."

"Come on up here, y'all," came a deep baritone voice from the top of the stairs, which were cloaked in a deep burgundy carpet.

Looking up onto the balcony, they saw a large man with silvery hair and a broad gleaming smile, composed of unnaturally white teeth. Dressed in a copper colored suit and bright blue shirt, the color of his tie magically matching his teeth.

They couldn't help but notice the array of biblical paintings that lined the staircase. The entrance would indeed stagger even the most jaded of worldly personages.

"Leonard Depew," he announced in his deep baritone, extending his hand first to Uri and then to Lara. "Y'all come in and have a seat. Any friend 'a Amos is a friend 'a mine."

They entered a sumptuous room, layered with a lush, golden-hued Persian carpet. A large, curved, immaculate walnut desk lay within the confines of a similarly curved floor-to-ceiling bay window. They felt as if they had entered the pearly gates. Depew closed the door silently behind them.

He sat in a maroon leather chair, set upon a hidden platform, similar to Dean Keltner's. Lara and Uri, at his bidding, sat in smaller, but similarly outfitted armchairs in front of his desk.

"Kin ah git y'all somethin' to drink?" Depew asked charmingly.

Uri by now had learned to translate the local argot, at least to a degree. "Water would be just fine, Reverend Depew," he said, knowing his answer would make due for Lara as well.

She looked over at him and smiled, as if to say, *"Go ahead, speak for me too."*

Depew flipped a hidden switch, muttered something, and as if by magic, a black man, immaculately clad in a gleaming white uniform silently entered the room. He held a silver tray on which were two beautifully crafted crystal glasses filled to within an inch of the top with ice water. He placed the glasses on coasters which were inset into the arms of their chairs.

Depew waited until the servant had silently left the room. He then got right down to business. "Amos tells me y'all are interested in our little facility here," he said, indicating both the building and the acreage beyond. Lara and Uri both nodded. "Well, our mission here is to do our part in bringing about the mission of the Book of Revelation."

He looked them over quickly in order to assess their reaction. He had, no doubt, had this discussion many times in the past. He could tell from the response of his audience immediately, whether they were Christians, and whether they were familiar with this book of the New Testament. From their rather blank stares, he realized he would have to start at the beginning. This was nothing new to him; in fact he rather enjoyed it.

The two agents sat back comfortably in their chairs and sipped their water; they could see that a lecture was on its way.

"We here at the church of Mount Zion are, most importantly, Christians. We believe deeply in the Bible, the Old Testament (he nodded politely to Uri), as well as the New Testament, the teachings of Jesus Christ. In the last book of the New Testament, the book called 'Revelation,' sometimes erroneously called 'Revelations'..."

He stopped briefly to take a sip of water and nod again at Uri. "... a Jewish prophet foretold the coming of what is known as 'the end of days.' By that, he meant that at some time in the future, during a period of worldwide war and degradation, the true believers would be swept up to heaven in what is called 'The Rapture.'"

He paused again and said, "Stop me if you've heard all this. I don't want to bore you." Lara and Uri smiled as if to say, "No, please go on."

"After this," he continued, "the Antichrist will appear and trick the remaining people into believing he was the real Messiah. Only after he is destroyed, would the true Messiah return to earth and bring everlasting peace."

The Reverend took another sip of water, examined the two visitors to see if they were still paying attention, and then concluded. "But you see, before any of this can occur, the Jews have to return to Israel and make Jerusalem their capital. The 'Third Temple' will be built upon the remains of the first and second: the Temple Mount." He once again looked at Uri for approval; it was clear he recognized his nationality, or had been told so by the Dean. Uri just smiled, trying not to look condescending.

"So you see," Depew said, "we Zionist Christians are wholehearted supporters of the nation of Israel. Many of us feel the Antichrist will appear from one of the Arab nations, or quite possibly Iran." He looked at his visitors again to see their reaction. Lara sat there, listening appreciatively; Uri nodded slightly in approval.

"The people, and the government, of Israel have given us unwavering support. Even though our religious views may not exactly coincide, our political aims are in complete accord. I guess I should qualify that a little; there is a tiny minority of Israelis, Israeli Jews, who reject the whole idea of Zionism. To its credit, the government tolerates these rejectionists, even though they call for the end of the Zionist State." He placed his hands on the table, indicating the lecture was over.

"Well, Reverend, speaking as an Israeli myself, we certainly appreciate all the Zionist Christians have done for us. The visitors you've brought to our country have been wonderful. I'm sure they bring back a positive impression, at least I hope so," Uri said, smiling.

"Oh, indeed!" Depew replied. "And that leads me to the next thing I want to tell you. We are building a Center, a visitors' center for Zionist Christians, as well as other interested parties." He paused here for emphasis. "And we're building it in the Holy Land, in Israel. In fact, construction is already well underway, on some beautiful land just east of your port, Haifa. You may be aware of it."

As a matter of fact, Uri was aware of a Christian center outside Jerusalem, but he was not aware of this one. "No, actually I'm not," he said, embarrassed, "but I've got to tell you I couldn't be more pleased. The more visitors who come and see what we've done with our little patch of desert, the better." He carefully avoided any discussion of religion; but his remarks

73

were genuine. They did reflect the views of over 90 percent of the Israeli population. The more the outside world saw, the less they would believe of the financially powerful Arab-Iranian propaganda machine.

"Well, that's wonderful!" Depew declared as he rose from his chair magnificently. "Now there's a couple a' things I'd like to show you." He motioned for them to follow him. He led them to a door at the right side of the rotunda. Opening it, they walked about 100 feet along a carpeted path, windows and biblical paintings along the walls. At the end of the path, Depew opened another door, which led them into another office, this one smaller and less grand than the one they had just left. This intimate enclosure suggested a place of study, similar to a monk's.

A simple carpet set off dark walnut walls in the room furnished with a study-type desk and an office chair; a reading lamp stood behind it. Tall columns of books added to the library-quality of the room. Three other chairs sat neatly near small windows at one side of the room.

"This is my private study, as you may have guessed," said Depew, closing the door. The two agents glanced approvingly around the room, waiting patiently for the next surprise. It was not long in coming.

"And this," said Depew triumphantly, opening a door on the far side of the room, "is our church."

Stepping through the door, Lara and Uri each took in a large lungful of air. They found themselves standing on the right side of a huge, theatrical type platform. The ceiling above them was at least 80 feet high, perhaps more. Behind them hung velvety, maroon and blue curtains, pleated beautifully. Rows of lights behind the curtains illuminated the painted ceiling. Stunned by a huge painting of Christ, hands held out to the multitude of believers and bathed in rapturous light, they gazed in awe at a ceiling clearly intended to rival the Sistine Chapel.

At the left they saw an enclosure meant to hold a choir. Uri estimated that it would accommodate at least 100 singers. At the center of the stage stood a splendid, carved wooden pulpit, hiding a raised platform and step, giving the speaker about 6 inches of added height.

But the audience area was the most astonishing. By far the largest arena Uri had ever seen, he could not estimate the occupancy. The rows swelled outward from the front of the stage to the rear of the auditorium, which was almost out of sight. Above the rear half of the audience area, cantilevered precariously, hung a balcony, also containing an inestimable number of seats.

Uri realized, to his embarrassment, that he had yet to resume normal breathing. Lara stood next to him, equally astonished.

"Really somethin' ain't it," Depew said proudly, his hand sweeping across the astonishing vista. "Holds just over 10,000 folks. We fill it too, twice every Sunday, and sometimes Wednesday nights."

Depew led them to a set of stairs at the very right side of the stage. As they followed him through the audience area, they noticed a number of workers busily placing pamphlets in the backs of the seats. They were all young men, about college-age, dressed simply, oblivious to anything but the task before them. As they walked up one of the aisles toward the back of the auditorium. Uri suddenly stopped, overwhelmed. Lara walking just behind, crashed into him.

"What in the world?" she asked. Uri continued to gaze at two of the workers; Lara followed his gaze. There amongst about 30 other young men, were five dressed in Hasidic clothing. Two appeared to be from the group of Israeli students they had seen on campus earlier.

Depew immediately saw the objects of their interest and motioned them to follow him through the outer doors into the foyer. "You noticed some of your boys there, I see," he said, smiling proudly. This remark was clearly aimed at Uri.

"Yes, I did," Uri replied. "Are they some of the students at West Texas Poly? The ones from Israel?"

"Yes, indeedy!" Depew declared. "They're some of the best volunteers we have. Came over here on their own, soon as they heard about it."

Uri was still in a daze. "But they're still dressed in their Hasidic, I mean their religious Jewish clothing ...?" he said.

"Oh yes, they haven't become Christians, at least not yet," Depew said, poking Uri lightly in the side, pleased with his little joke. "No, they just heard about our mission, our *Zionist* Christian mission to help Israel, and asked if they could help." Uri continued to stare, speechless.

"I can see you're impressed," Depew said. "But if I can borrow a phrase from somebody or other, 'you ain't seen nothin' yet.'"

Lara and Uri waited for his next surprise. It was not long in coming.

"Follow me out here," Depew said, leading them across the large foyer to the left-hand side. There stood large double glass doors leading into an enclosed space, perhaps equal in size to an ordinary theater. In the center of the space was a mockup, about 50 to 1 in scale, of a modernistic structure similar to the auditorium they had just left. This one however, had the futuristic character of a spaceship, destined to carry the faithful into eternity. Above the seating area they saw a saucer-like roof held in place only by slender columns around the perimeter. Lit by hidden lights around the ceiling of the enclosure the mockup was truly breathtaking.

"Now that's *really* somethin', wouldn't you say?" Depew's words broke. "If you hadn't guessed by now, this is what we're building outside Haifa ... already about two-thirds done."

Uri was now more embarrassed than ever. In the introverted state into which he had placed himself since leaving active duty, he hadn't even known of this stupendous undertaking.

Depew wasn't done yet. "And if you haven't guessed, some your boys are helpin' with the construction! Bein' as they are all studyin' engineerin' and that sort of thing, they volunteered to help put it together. Well, of course, we're payin' 'em a decent wage. But I've got to say, they're among the most dedicated of all the workers we got over there. Most of 'em work overtime, into the night."

Lara took over from Uri, "You mean, these students we met over at the college, spend time helping with the building over in Israel?"

"Oh no, not all. This program's been going on for some time. Some of your guys over there have already graduated. Got their degrees ... structural engineering, electrical engineering, mechanical engineering ... areas like that. I've got to tell you, when the congregation found out religious-type Israelis were helpin' out with the buildin', it sure did beef up the contributions. We're way ahead of schedule."

Lara and Yuri thanked Depew for the tour and the lecture. They had some work to do.

Chapter 12

The Grand Mufti of Jerusalem, Muhammed Amin al-Husseini, smiled with blissful anticipation as he digested the news he'd just received on his secure satellite phone. He leaned back on the cushions in his Ramallah apartment and smiled at his guests.

Everything was now in place; the crime would be committed and the Jews would be blamed worldwide. Nothing could have set the scene more beautifully than the plan he had set in motion, and was now being carried out. The United States would be helpless; how could they aid their friends the Israelis, when it was Israeli Jews who have carried out the heinous attack on the Christian enclave?

The American evangelical Christians of course, would be outraged not only that Jews, but the most religious Israeli Jews, had attacked their "Zionist Christian Center." After all the evangelicals had done in support of Israel, both financially and in Congress, to be spat upon by the very people they had been attempting to help. The repercussions could only be enormous. Add to that the help the Arabs had been given by the American Jews of the ultra-left wing, with their demonizing of Israel's attempted self-rule; even the most hawkish president would be helpless in now attempting to come to Israel's aid.

Further, the recent removal of the Syrian president, or more accurately, ex-president, acted to the Muslim Brotherhood's advantage. The peace-at-any-cost Americans saw only that a dictator had been vanquished. The fact that the Muslim Brotherhood had taken over complete control, as it had in Egypt, driving any and all secularists away from the country in droves, made no difference.

The new leader, Aboud Al Agha, was even more antidemocratic, anti-feminist, and religiously intolerant than had been the former president.

So then, as the Mufti had expected, support from both Aboud Al Agha in Syria, and Rabiah Tariq Al Khalid, the new violently anti-Western leader in Egypt, would be both rapid and overwhelming.

Even without the help of Jordan's weak king, the oncoming onslaught should be over in a matter of weeks. As should have happened seventy-odd years ago, the land of Saladin would be returned.

Of course, his contact in Jordan, Khalib al-Shammari, would be kept apprised of the coming events. An attack from the East, even a meager one, would force the Israelis to relocate some other forces. Add to that the effect of the Palestinian Authority, should they choose to participate, could only help matters more.

Then there was the matter of Gaza. The Egyptians still controlled the 40 odd tunnels that kept Hamas supplied with their weapons of terror. All their crude, home-made rockets did little in a strategic sense; they still provided something of the feeling of helplessness amongst the southern Israelis. Add to that the promised, more effective, long-range missiles from Iran, and Israel's vaunted IDF would quickly succumb.

"Well, my friends," he said with supreme confidence, as he faced his Syrian confederate, Yaman Al Mahainu, and the Egyptian, Merira ibn El Sayed, "you heard the same thing I heard: the game, as they say, is on."

"What do we know from the Palestinian Authority?" Yaman Al Mahainu asked. "Are they in or out?"

"All we can do at this time is wait-and-see. When they see the advances we're making from the North and South they will have no choice but to participate."

"And the Iranian missiles?" queried Merira ibn El Sayed.

"Their Sejjil 2 rockets are tested and ready. As soon as we give the word, they are ready to aid our effort. As you know, these new missiles of theirs have a range of nearly 1200 miles, far enough to strike Israel from Western Iran."

"You're talking about a huge escalation of this war. If Iran even prepares to launch these rockets, the Americans will spot them from their satellites and have the excuse they need to destroy all the Iranian missiles plus their nuclear facilities," argued El Sayed.

"We have an even bigger advantage," the Mufti replied. "The Iranians are sending a fleet of 17 'merchant' ships through the Persian Gulf, the Red Sea and up towards Sinai. Right now they're less than a week away from being within range with their hidden cargo of Shahab 1 and 2 accurate, short range missiles. Unless the Americans are willing to risk war with Egypt, they're going to be very reluctant to attack these ships."

"What is the timing?" asked Al Mahainu.

"The attack on the 'Zionist Christian Center' southeast of Haifa will occur on the evening of the first day; the date of the Syrian advance. It will cause international outrage of course.

"Military preparation is ongoing in Syria," he said glancing at Al Mahainu. "The new regime claims to be cleaning out remnants of the ex-president's supporters in completing the democratization of the country. They, accompanied by the Army of Hezbollah, will attack Israel's northern border on the eve of their so-called Independence Day.

"Likewise, for the past month, the Egyptians have been having what they call 'exercises' along the northern Sinai." Al Sayed nodded in agreement. "The ostensible reason for these exercises is to remove, or at least control, the various gangs that have been wreaking havoc in the region. The Americans and Israelis, who have been spying on the activity with their satellites, have been told that this will actually make the region safer for innocent travel. Their surprise attack on Israel's southern border will commence shortly, the day after that of the Syrians.

"The attack on the Christian enclave will be brought to the attention of the UN as evidence of Israel's intolerance toward any non-Jews, including Christians who have been supporters of Zionism." The Mufti finished his lecture, looking with satisfaction at his impressed audience.

Chapter 13

After briefing both Hadley and David Peretz at the Israeli consul on what they had learned in Waco, Lara and Uri hurried to JFK where, unable to get into the crowded first class section of the El Al plane, they settled into adjacent seats in economy class for the eleven hour flight.

For Uri, being that close to her, yet not being able to be intimate in any sense of the word constituted torture of the worst kind. As for discussing the case, they feared even writing notes on the crowded plane. But each was mentally going over the facts in the case and contemplating various strategies to discuss once they arrived in Tel Aviv.

Lara tried to imagine what could possibly motivate people to disguise themselves as members of another religion, spend years in preparation, then murder dozens of innocent people who had become their friends. Of course, she had seen firsthand the lunatics who built bombs and placed them with the intent of killing and injuring noncombatants. But to spend years with people, masquerading as their friends, all the while preparing for their slaughter ... That was inconceivable.

She slept off and on, her head sometimes falling lightly onto Uri's shoulder. He made no attempt to remove it; and overcame the urge to put his arm around her shoulder. Instead he tried to focus on what they had learned and what they might be able to do.

Arriving in Tel Aviv too late to check-in with Shimon, they left a message with his service saying they would see him in the morning, took a taxi to a medium-priced hotel downtown and checked in, booking separate rooms. Now past 2200 hours, the hotel restaurant was in the process of closing. They cajoled some sandwiches and drinks out of the weary servers, ate quickly and, exhausted from the long day, headed upstairs.

The rooms conveniently shared a connecting door. Their luggage had been placed inside, courtesy of the hotel. As Lara opened her door, she looked at Uri; he nodded, then said "We need to talk" and followed her inside.

"Agreed," she said, "but do you realize we've been going non-stop for twenty-four hours? Give me twenty minutes to freshen up."

"You've got it," he said, and headed into his own room through the connecting door.

He showered, looked at himself in the mirror and decided to shave and remove the prosthetic eye that he had never quite gotten used to. Putting on his distinctive eye patch, he dressed in comfortable clothing, and knocked softly on the door. "Who is it?" she asked, laughing.

When he opened the door, she gave a little start, seeing his Moshe Dayan appearance. Then she quickly regained her composure, shook her head in amusement, and sat on the bed. "Forgive me, I thought for a second you were a pirate."

They both laughed, the tension of the last couple of days suddenly released. This was the first time they actually had been alone together in a relatively secure environment. Uri sat on the chair next to the bed and allowed himself the pleasure of looking at her. She had dressed casually, but not in bed clothing. "I think it's okay to talk in here," he said, "but let's turn on the TV anyway." He pushed a button on the remote, tuned to a music channel, and sat back down.

"So now we can talk, finally; who do you think is behind all this?" she asked.

"No doubt this is a large-scale operation," he said. "And I think I see the work of one particular terrorist, just devious and clever enough to set it all up."

"And he is ...?"

"An individual named Saleh Halibi, a so-called Palestinian, known as 'The Ghost.'"

"Who? I've never heard of him."

"He's always stayed behind the scene. You remember the suicide bombings of the Marine barracks in Beirut in 1983?" Lara nodded. "And the US. embassy there earlier that year?"

"Of course. I thought those were the work of that Sheikh Mughniyah guy. The one who was ... assassinated ... in 2008." She looked at Uri, questioning. "I always thought that you were the one who ..."

Uri gave her a little smile. "No one has actually taken responsibility, or credit, for that ... execution ... but let's say we weren't sorry to see him go."

Lara let that go for now, but she felt sure Uri was the one who triggered the car bomb that killed the Hezbollah terrorist. "So you're telling me that Mughniyah wasn't the one behind those incidents?"

"I'm not saying he wasn't involved, and there are a lot of other terrorist attacks he's been attached to, also."

"Such as ...?"

"Three U.S. embassies in Africa, on one day in August, 1998. Hundreds of Americans killed."

Lara stared at him, shaking her head. "I remember those vividly," she said. "I lost two friends in the Kenya Embassy. I was still in school but I remember it as if it were yesterday. It was part of the reason I wanted to work for the government ..."

Uri continued. "In Buenos Aires, the Israeli Embassy and the cultural affairs center were both bombed in the early 90's, killing hundreds of Argentinian Jews."

"Sure, I remember those. If nothing else, they showed us what could happen in the U.S. Unfortunately, we didn't do enough ..." Her voice trailed off as she remembered 9/11. "The same bastard got away with all that?" Lara's face flushed with anger.

"As a matter of fact, the new Pope, Francis, publicly indicted the whole bunch of Muslims who were responsible. He's trying to get them thrown in jail," Uri said. Lara nodded, thoughtfully, well aware of the Pope's declaration, she wasn't at all sure that Argentina would cooperate, even with the Catholic leader.

"There's even more." Uri went on. "In 1985, Hezbollah terrorists hijacked TWA 847. They tortured and killed a U.S. Navy diver. The Sheikh took the 'credit' for that too. He's even been accused of setting up the attack on the USS Cole in October of 2000 outside Aden."

"I know about all that, but I thought that was bin Laden's work."

"Oh yeah, no doubt he was involved. Also no doubt most of this stuff was financed by Iran."

As part of the JTTF, Lara was well aware of Iran's funding of terrorism, maybe even more than Uri. But she wanted to get back on topic. "So you're saying even though the Sheikh was involved in all this ... he wasn't the main 'operator'?"

"No, there's this other character, Halibi, behind the scenes. We, that is, the Mossad, have known about him since 1983."

"Why was he so hard to find?" Lara asked.

"The guy is obviously very smart. He knows how to change his appearance; he can look like an Arab, an Italian, even an Israeli. He has that olive complexion that could come from any mixture of Mediterranean and African genealogies; plus, he can change his hair, grow a beard, mustache ... He's had lots of identities—and passports. That's where he gets his nickname. You know he's around, you just don't see him. He's quite a hero with the terrorists. The more Jews and Americans you kill, the more famous you get, with that bunch," he said.

"One thing he can't alter," he continued. "... his eyes. His are like intense, black embers. They blaze with hatred."

"Why haven't I ever heard of him?" Lara asked.

"We didn't want him to know that we were after him. So we haven't said anything to anyone outside the Mossad."

"So you *have* seen him, I mean pictures of him. And you have good reason to think he's the brains behind all this terror?"

"Yes. We have a number of witnesses ... captured terrorists, injured victims. They all claim to have seen or heard of him. We just weren't able to get our hands on him until 2004. And we were lucky to get him then."

"And you let him go?"

"I was getting to that." Uri answered. "We picked him up in the sweep of the West Bank after a series of bus and restaurant bombings in Tel Aviv back in 2004. We held him, along with a bunch of his friends, until 2011. I'm sure you remember the famous 'prisoner swap,' when we gave back over 1000 terrorists in exchange for one of our young soldiers Hamas had captured."

He leaned back, paused, and watched for her reaction. She showed little, but he could tell she recognized the ambivalence in his remark. "Halibi was one of a few prisoners that Hamas absolutely insisted be part of the deal. He got a huge welcome back in Gaza."

"Haven't you been able to keep track of him?"

"Since then, he's been linked to at least ten suicide bombings, including the ones I just told you about, all aimed at civilians of course. We've picked up over 100 of his gang, but he always slips away. We've got his DNA though."

"You've picked up 'suicide bombers'?" It sounded to Lara like picking up live Kamakazi pilots.

"Well, obviously not the bombers themselves. But after the fact, they leave enough evidence for Shin Bet to track down the location of their camps. Clothing, cell phones, girlfriends, stuff like that. The pattern is really clear, hasn't changed much over the years. Basically, Hamas, Hezbollah, Islamic Jihad, or whatever name they go by, get families to sell their kids to the cause."

Lara reacted visibly. "What do you mean, *sell*? I thought they went voluntarily, to get, you know, girls in the afterlife."

"I know it sounds unbelievable, but that's really what they do. The local imam 'prospects' his congregation for likely donors: families with more teenage children than they can feed. He promises them, and generally delivers, $25,000 a head. The boys are guaranteed an everlasting life of pleasure in the grace of Allah, if they will sacrifice themselves in the virtuous killing of Jews and other infidels. And they get a bunch of virgins, like you said ... seventy-two is the usual number ... whom they can defile to their hearts' content."

"And they really believe that? Where does the money come from? What about the female suicide bombers, what do they get?"

"Yes, they really believe it. The money gets funneled from Iran or one of the Arab countries. And the girl bombers ...

they're promised to be able to choose a husband, a faithful one, from the myriad of blessed single men in paradise."

"I've heard of a lot of this, of course, but each time I hear of it, I find it difficult to absorb."

"Awful as it is, it's all true. We've found written *hadiths* that state exactly this. And it makes sense; everybody makes out. The kids get to heaven, the families get the money, and the imams become famous. Oh, and the world gets rid of a bunch of troublemaking Jews."

"Yes, it's hard to believe," she said. "But the facts are there, I can see that. Now what does all this have to do with your guy... what's his name?"

"Saleh Halibi. Shin Bet and the Mossad have tried like hell to recapture him, or better yet, eliminate him. Israel doesn't have the death penalty, you know. Sometimes, well actually all the time, I wish we did." He sat thoughtfully, and Lara could see the built-up anger he held back.

"But you've been able to recapture or 'eliminate' a bunch of those terrorists you had to release, right? Why can't you catch this guy?"

"That's what got him his nickname: The Ghost. And he's really proud of it, from what we hear. He always manages to get away just before we raid one of their camps. We're not really sure exactly what he looks like these days, the way he can change his appearance. Just the eyes, he can't change those ..." Uri stopped abruptly. "The eyes ... that one student ... Of course, that's him!" Uri leapt to his feet, his demeanor changed abruptly. He strode around the room, oblivious to anything else.

"Those pictures the Dean gave us-- you have them with you?"

"I have them here in my briefcase," she said as she hurriedly searched through her notes. "You think your Ghost is one of those students headed to Haifa?"

"Almost certainly."

"What makes you think he's masterminding *this* operation?"

"He got an engineering education in the U.S., courtesy of American foreign aid, went to several schools, never graduated. But he knows how they operate, how to get the faithful in, and get them to do what he wants. Can speak English, American English, like a native."

"But he didn't go to the U.S. pretending to be a Jew, did he?"

"No, but we've been suspicious of him since he returned from there in 2003 and disappeared. Of course, we couldn't have eliminated him while he was in the U.S., even if we had known where he was. Shin Bet keeps a record of all the Arabs in the West Bank who go to America to school. When they return, they usually can get good paying jobs, but he obviously slipped back using another identity."

"Can't you keep track of them, I mean when they go to the U.S.?"

"With the number of people going back and forth every year, it's virtually impossible to keep track of everyone, including Halibi. Don't think we didn't try," Uri said. "Ramallah and other cities in the West Bank are doing fantastically well, financially. They need technically educated Arabs. But he, Halibi, was known to be especially devout and determined, so we kept watch on him. When the attacks, the 'intifada', started again in 2004, our informers told us he was the leader. So we were able to pick him up and kept him in solitary for two years, hoping to get something out of him. No luck."

"Torture?"

"Call it enhanced interrogation. It's gotten us a lot of useful information, information that's saved lives. With him though, nothing. Then when Hamas demanded the release of all the terrorists we had captured, Halibi showed up near the top of their list. The government had to give him up or we wouldn't have gotten our soldier back."

"Seems like a big price to pay," she said, as she continued to search through her notes.

"That's the way we are in Israel. We say we don't negotiate with terrorists, but when it comes to a grieving family, we bend a little. Shows the world we're a step above our neighbors. Kind of like the U.S.; they would do the same sort of thing, and have..."

"Here they are!," she shouted abruptly, handing Uri the sheets of student IDs.

It only took a few seconds for Uri to spot the suspect. "Here he is!" He shouted abruptly. "Asher Singer," he said with disgust, reading the name below the picture. "Like I'm Yasser Arafat. Look at those eyes-- remember those eyes? Of course, that's him! We're going to see this murderer again," Uri said intensely.

"But what specifically makes you think he's involved in this business?" Lara asked, her heart racing.

"Mohammed el-Husseini, the so-called Grand Mufti of Jerusalem. He's the last in a long line of religious leaders who've fought for the elimination of Jews everywhere for over six centuries."

"You have got to be kidding!"

"No kidding," he said as he ran into his room to grab his satellite phone. By the time he returned he had already dialed Shimon's office in Tel Aviv. Lara heard him rattle off some Hebrew, his voice brimming with urgency. Within a minute he had terminated the call.

"I told his assistant," he said, referring to the phone call, all the pertinent details. Shimon will pick it up from there.

"Anyway," he said to Lara as he paced around, The last few Muftis spied for the Kaiser in World War I, made public deals with Hitler in World War II, and have done their best to stop Jewish immigration ever since. And Halibi is known to have been in touch with this latest one. To think we were that close…!" He slumped onto her bed. "Oh well, Shimon will figure out how to use this information to our advantage."

A Uri realized they had done all they could for the time being and should be thinking about getting some rest. "Sorry," he said, "I get a little carried away. I'll let you get some sleep."

She saw the passion in his eyes, even through the tiredness. "Don't go," she said simply, and reached out to touch his hand. He didn't need any convincing.

In the morning, they met with Shimon at the simple, indistinguishable Metsada building just outside Tel Aviv. "You've got an hour to brief me, then it's off again for you," he said briskly. Typical Shimon, no time wasted on small talk.

"You got my message last night about Halibi?," Uri said anxiously, in English, for Lara's benefit.

"Yes, don't worry about that," Shimon answered. "We've got our people in the States watching for him right now. In fact, it may turn out to our advantage, knowing where he is and what he's up to." He smiled at the pair of agents reassuringly. "The fact that the Ghost has slipped away for the moment may accrue to our benefit. He may yet lead us to the entire team of terrorists; the way it is, they have no idea we're on to them."

Somewhat mollified, Uri inquired of Shimon, "You've gotten our encoded reports through the embassy, haven't you?"

"Yes, and to be frank, they scared the hell out of me. We had no idea of the extent of their operation in the U.S. Now, thanks to your work, we think we've spotted the main training camp for the guys they send over there. They haven't realized we've been able to break their satellite phone codes. I don't know how long it'll last; we've got to make use of the information right now."

Uri saw the look of surprise on Lara's face as Shimon said that. He smiled and said to her, "Yes, I couldn't tell you before now, but Israeli military intelligence was able to use the algorithms you developed for handling those coded e-mails. The Arabs bought into an inferior satellite phone system, developed in the Emirates, which uses only the L band frequencies. This made it about ten times easier to disencrypt their signals than those on the U.S.-made satellite phones, where they use a mix of L bands and K hands."

Shimon, to whom all this was gibberish, saw that Lara understood. She smiled in appreciation. "Anyway," he continued, "there's a hit team ready to go -- they're just waiting for you." He saw Lara looking at him quizzically. "Both of you," he said, clearly to her. "I hope you're as good in action as you are on the range. This is going to be messy. I've already cleared it with your boss in New York, but you can always stay out of it if you want."

"Not a chance! We're in this all the way." She looked at Uri, who nodded approval.

"There's something I didn't put in the reports, just kind of suspected it," Uri said.

Shimon glanced up. "Yes," he said, "We've picked up one single conversation between the camp site, just northeast of Kiryat Shmona, and on the West Bank somewhere in the heart of Ramallah."

"The Mufti?" Uri asked. "You think he might be behind something really big; I mean, involving all our 'friends'?"

"It's too coincidental that the Syrians and Egyptians are holding exercises right on our borders. And the Iranians, we think, too."

"The Iranians!"

"Nothing is certain; keep that to yourselves. We should know more when you get back from your little expedition. Be ready to go over by this afternoon, 1500 hours."

Chapter 14

Near 1500 hours, as the Mossad raiding party on the training camp prepared to depart, Shimon looked at Uri and Lara grimly. "We have no choice I think. Our only option is to clean out the rats' nest while we have a chance. If these people make it out of the country with false passports, there's no way to control where they go, or what they do."

"But," Uri said, "if word gets out that we know about their agents already in the field, they'll know something's up and we'll lose the element of surprise."

"We have to assume the agents already out there have their orders and, if they can't communicate to their superiors back in Lebanon or Ramallah, they'll proceed according to their original plan. It's a better option to wipe out the camp and any future agents."

"But how could Hezbollah train Arabs to look and speak as if they were Orthodox Jews?" Lara asked. "It doesn't seem possible."

"You know of an American named Aaron Cohen?" Shimon asked. "He came here when he was about 18, learned Hebrew, joined the IDF, then became a Mossad agent and learned sufficient Palestinian Arabic to act like a Palestinian policeman in the West Bank. He was able to apprehend a number of dangerous terrorists and break up several of their planned attacks. Then, unfortunately for us, he went back to Los Angeles and started a very successful security agency. If an American Jew can, in a few years, masquerade as an Arab, I'm sure there are a few Arabs who can learn to act like Orthodox Jews."

"How do you think they would go about it?" Uri asked him.

"Well, say they have this camp situated just across our northern border in Lebanon in the area controlled by Hezbollah. They have their trainees—men, women, and children---slip across the border and start attending services in Orthodox synagogues in any one of a number of border towns. It may take a few years, but soon they will speak, and act just like the people around them."

"And may have secured forged Israeli passports..." Lara added.

"That's right," Uri said sadly, "and if no one suspects anything, those fake passports can easily get them into the U.S., where they can blend in just like true Israeli émigrés."

"So now what we have to do," Shimon said "is to break up that gang before they can send any more rats into your house."

"Do we know," Uri asked, "who or where their contacts are in Lebanon or the West Bank?"

"We have picked up some cell phone conversations, but they always use throwaway phones, so we haven't been able to ID any specific individuals. But we're working on it."

"So what's the plan? Are we going to be able to take part in the raid?" Lara asked.

"You'll be going along, all right," Shimon replied. "Like I told you earlier, I've already gotten permission from your boss."

"Then we'll be part of the attack team," she said eagerly.

Shimon looked somewhat sheepish. "I've re-thought this a little. You'll be along, but in a secure, protected position behind the primary attack troops. You might be able to pick up some important information that they miss." He paused. "Seriously, you do know how to handle a weapon? I know you're primarily an intelligence agent," he said, addressing Lara.

Uri laughed. "Don't let her good looks fool you, she can handle an Uzi or a Glock as well as I can."

The team crossed the border from Israel into Lebanon at about 0200 the next morning. Uri was quite familiar with this area in the Galilee. He had a pretty good idea where the training facility was located, and they had the record of the cell phone call placed from the camp to Ramallah. The team packed themselves into a U.S.-made Blackhawk SA-70 helicopter that carried both the troops and all their equipment. Nine of them in all: seven young Mossad agents well-trained in use of the sniper rifles and machine pistols, plus Lara and Uri, were dropped in about a mile southwest of the target.

Eyal, the point man and leader, a slender, taut young fellow with dark curly hair, and just the beginnings of a beard, had a small GPS, as did all members of the team. He carried one of the new Uzi sniper rifles which weighed less than 5 pounds but was accurate over 500 yards, when equipped with a special night vision scope. He had a brazen confidence, without being cocky. *This guy can't be more than 20 years old,* Lara thought.

The second man, a short, muscular fellow named Meir, glanced more than occasionally at his watch and fidgeted in his chair. Also equipped with a sniper rifle, he carried, as did most of the others, a 9 mm sidearm. The third man, Natan, was the youngest, probably about eighteen, with blonde curly hair and just some blonde peach fuzz covering his face. Chosen for his stealth and speed, his job, once they found the compound, would be to look for any rear escapes.

The others, the backups, Noam, Shai, Raviv and Ziv, had limited combat experience but were well-trained and eager. Uri and Lara, dressed the same as the troops, totally in black, their faces covered with camouflage paint, brought up the rear. Lara carried a short-barreled Uzi and the U.S. Army .45 caliber pistol, her favorite. Uri followed her, armed with an Uzi machine pistol and his .357 Magnum Mark XIX Desert Eagle.

Eyal checked his GPS, as the others spread out in a variant of a wing formation. Meir, the eldest, at about age thirty, had the most battle experience. They would depend on him for any rapid change of plans in the case of unexpected adversity. He was in charge of the sophisticated surveillance equipment they carried with them. It could pick up almost any electronic security defense.

About 500 yards from the suspected encampment, his silent alarm indicated a relatively crude infrared sensing system. Meir had an ultra-secret infrared disabling system developed by Mossad engineers, a spray that covered the sensors with a near–invisible coating which reflected the infrared heat their bodies generated. As Meir silently pointed out each sensor along the perimeter where the detectors were located, Noam quickly disabled each.

The team glided on silently. About 300 yards distant they detected human movement with their night vision goggles. At the same time Meir picked up the tiny signal indicating motion detectors. Raviv carried the Mossad's new electronic disabling device, which, in effect, confused the motion detectors with enough multiple signals so as to give the observer a null result.

The encampment now was barely visible. Under a rocky outcropping at the base of a hill approximately 50 feet in height, stood a structure cleverly built into the existing terrain. The front stretched to about 50 feet in length, constructed of wood, and camouflaged to blend in with the surroundings. The rock outcropping concealed the structure from any satellite or drone surveillance.

Ziv picked up floodlights hidden in some pine trees, also concealed well enough to be missed even by low-flying drones. The raiders crept noiselessly into the rocky brush to about the 100 yard point. From there they could see the movement of three sentries, carrying weapons, but looking relatively relaxed.

It was time for the attack.

Natan scrambled around the south side of the hill with orders to climb to the top and be prepared for any possible escape from the roof. The two designated snipers, Eyal and Meir, on a hand signal, fired simultaneously at the two most alert sentries. The blasts from their suppressed weapons, though relatively light, were still evident to the third sentry. He spun around just as the other two sentries' heads exploded like ripe watermelons. Meir was to take out the third sentry at that point; however his rifle jammed, and in the second or so it took him to shove in a new round, the remaining sentry set off an alarm, shrieking loudly through the still night. The target suddenly came ablaze with floodlights and groggy, but now awake, Arabs came quickly to their feet.

Dazzled by the sudden light, the team quickly flipped up their night vision goggles and stormed the compound. Meir belatedly took out the third sentry with a short burst of machine gun fire. The door in the middle of the structure flew open and three windows appeared, as lights went on in the building. Shai and Raviv, close enough now, fired multiple tear gas rounds through the open windows and door.

As the main team stormed through the door hoping to catch the terrorists, trainers and trainees in a state of confusion, Lara was sent around to the right, where a hidden garage connected to the main structure. Her job was to make certain no one escaped from it in a vehicle. The team's main job was to apprehend as many individuals as possible, but anyone in a vehicle would have to be terminated.

Ayel, Meir and Noam, their faces covered with gas masks, stormed into the building ahead of the others. Firing short bursts into the ceiling on full automatic, uncovering their mouths long enough to shout in Arabic: "Drop your weapons, hands in the air!"

Clearly trained to anticipate this sort of surprise attack, rather than surrender, a group of eight or ten fatigue–clad Arabs made a dash for a weapons cache in the middle of the room jumping over those writhing on the floor from the tear gas. Meir, Ayel and Noam, weapons blazing cut down three of them.

Now inside, the team encountered a space of about 2000 square feet. On the left were two closed off-rooms, most probably dormitory-like sleeping areas. A set of portable toilets filled the back of the enclosure and, along the right wall, long tables had been set up for eating. A stockpile of weapons and several computers occupied the center of the room. With hand signals, Ayel ordered Shai, Raviv and Ziv to sweep left. Ayel and Meir, still wearing their gas masks, covered the guards still on the floor, coughing and gasping for breath. They didn't want to kill any they didn't have to; the Arabs would be useful as prisoners. But as one reached out to grab a gun, Ayel didn't hesitate to shoot.

At about 30 seconds into the operation, the doors on the left side of the enclosure burst open. Groups of men and women raced out of the rooms behind the two doors, all either carrying weapons or running for the arms cache in the middle of the room.

The males could easily be mistaken for Orthodox Jews, the mature ones by the long curly earlocks and untrimmed beards; the teenage boys with the beginning of beards, also had curly earlocks. Shai shouted at them in Arabic, "Stop! Raise your hands! Drop your weapons!"

Images from World War II documentaries flashed through Uri's mind. SS troops holding guns on Jewish citizens roused from their sleep in horrified disarray. The sight, burned into his memory both by the documentaries and stories from members of his family, stories that woke him in the middle of the night, covered with sweat, filled with hate, and vowing for vengeance. *Why hadn't they fought back?* he often wondered, torturing himself. The oft-quoted phrase: *Never Again* stayed with him constantly.

The image quickly vanished as the males carrying guns fired wildly at the team members. Raviv caught one round in the leg and dropped to the floor before Ziv could cut down the shooter. The women, also carrying weapons, ran to the center of the room to try to retrieve their co-conspirators. A short burst from Ayel stopped them in their tracks.

The other males, still groggy from sleep, attempted to make a fight of it. Noam and Shai, with no option left, their weapons on single fire, dropped five of them with kill shots. They would not be bringing back wounded prisoners. Those remaining threw their arms in the air, dropping their weapons.

Only then did the team notice that the computers had burst into flame. Apparently the alarm had set off automatic charges to destroy any information that might have been captured. What they didn't notice was one of the Arabs sneaking to the back of the enclosure behind the toilets, scrambling up a ladder. A few seconds later, they saw him come tumbling down headfirst onto the floor, snapping his neck.

Natan, stationed up the hill at the top of the enclosure, had placed himself at a point where he could see any light that appeared. A trap door opened up, a man with an AK-47 came into view. Natan dispatched him with one shot, and he fell back into the building.

Four Arabs, unnoticed in the fray, had crept around the edges of the enclosure. One of them, behind one of the toilets, raised his weapon and fired a short burst at Raviv, still lying wounded on the floor. Uri and Ziv, fired simultaneously. The Arab's body flew backwards, a bloody mess.

A wild burst from beneath an eating table punctured some of the metal water-storage cans sending a cold spray around the room. From their guarded position behind some racks of clothing, Noam and Shai followed instructions the team had been given to use head shots whenever possible, as the Arabs were most likely wearing body armor. Using single fire from their Uzis, they aimed for the men's heads, sending a mix of blood, brains and bones splashing over the women crouched behind the tables.

The last two Arabs, throwing their AK-47's out ahead of them, now emerged from their hiding places. Noam and Shai lowered their weapons, motioning them over with the women. Instead, the Arabs pulled 9 mm pistols out from under their robes and began firing. Noam and Shai dropped quickly to the floor as the pistol shots thunked harmlessly into the wooden frame of the building. Simultaneously, Eyal and Meir jumped from behind one of the toilets; one burst from Meir's Uzi killed both terrorists.

From her position outside the makeshift garage, Lara listened to the noises of combat coming from inside. Transfixed, she wished she knew what was happening. Suddenly, she heard the exhaust from an all-terrain vehicle racing away, dirt spinning from under its wheels. Startled, she unleashed a burst from her Uzi at the cloud of exhaust smoke, cursing herself for her momentary inattention. From the light available from the flood lamps she saw a dark-colored SUV, most likely an older-model Nissan Patrol. She had no idea whether any of her shots hit home; however, the vehicle did not stop.

The fight inside was now over. All in all, nine Arabs had been killed, while of the team, only Raviv had been hit, mortally wounded by the second burst. Noam and Shai carried his body gently outside, while Natan and Ziv herded the surviving terrorists out to a clearing about 50 yards southwest of the makeshift cave. Ayel called on the sat phone immediately and requested two SA-70's to bring everyone out: the eight surviving team members, along with the 12 Arab prisoners, both men and women. Raviv's covered body would take a place of honor in the lead helicopter.

As always, Uri took this loss hard. Every one of these men and women were special; he hated to lose anyone to these jihadists, whose whole agenda consisted of murdering innocent civilians.

While Ayel was in charge of the military part of the operation, it was Uri's job to scour the remains of the encampment for any useful intelligence. Dismayed once again to see the burned-out computers; the hard drives and flash memories, trashed beyond repair, he shook his head and turned to the weapons. None were worth transporting out. They would be torched along with the dead Arabs. He turned and walked slowly back to wait with the others.

The helicopters arrived within 30 minutes, and the members of the team along with their prisoners were hustled aboard. Two men from Metsada, Mossad's fighters, were aboard to aid in the evacuation. They rode with the Arabs who had been searched, bound, and laid along the floor of the chopper. Uri suffered another attack of anguish as he looked at the Arab men, men who looked every bit their role as Orthodox Jews. The fight knocked out of them, they glared at their captors silently, hatred burning in their eyes.

Chapter 15

Grand Mufti Muhammad Al-Husseini slammed down the phone. The fool should have known better than to use a cell phone to call. There was, after all, a very good chance the Israelis were monitoring every call that came to his residence. But his agent probably didn't have a sat phone handy. The news he'd brought was catastrophic. Somehow the Israelis discovered their camp and destroyed it, probably taking many prisoners. Thanks be to Allah, someone there had been smart enough to destroy the computers before the Israelis could get to them. Perhaps his agent had been the one. Of course, he had to be the one. He had to be the one to save the plan that he was so instrumental in creating.

Steps would have to be taken to make sure operations were carried out ahead of schedule, before the Israelis could interrupt the grand plan. Let us hope and pray he makes it here to Ramallah; otherwise …

Gideon got the call about 0430. *"Apprehend and bring in suspect. Suspect will be driving medium age black Nissan SUV covered with dust from the Galilee area, and possibly with bullet hole or holes in the rear. No other passengers. Suspect dressed fatigues, camouflage style probably. Will be headed for Ramallah probably down Highway 60 and also probably in one big damn hurry. Best shot would be to get him somewhere around Beit El or al Bira.. Will have help for you on the access roads. Suspect armed, extremely dangerous. Terminate if necessary."*

This meant he had to hustle from his nice warm bed in the northern reaches of Beit Shemesh, and the cozy arms of Leah, get into his Jeep and make a mad dash on the dirt roads leading through Tira. None of these thoughts appealed to him at the moment, but he was used to these last-minute calls for action. As one of the Kidon, the certified lone-wolf assassins of Metsada, he knew this must be a high-value target.

Gideon drove his remodeled Jeep as fast as it would go. He had come around through the small villages of Dayr Dibwan and Beit El. As he approached al Bira, the smallest of the villages just northeast of Ramallah, dawn was breaking in the East casting long shadows on the dusty road known politely as Highway 466.

As he came around a bend just north of a grove of date palms, he slammed on his brakes when he saw an SUV lying on its side in the middle of the road. Coming to a halt some yards away from the wreck, he judged from the angle of the car, it was clear the driver had tried to take the curve at too high a rate of speed. He judged that the accident must have occurred just a few minutes earlier; the dust had not yet completely settled.

He saw no movement, no people, no animals, nothing. Gideon, however, was no fool. He was not going to jump out of his vehicle into an ambush. He parked his Jeep about 50 yards north of the overturned SUV, noting it was a Nissan, which at one time had probably been black. Now it lay on its passenger side, completely covered in dirt and scrapes, the driver's door flung open.

Gideon armed himself with his TAR 21 machine pistol with its 30 round magazine, and crept along the opposite side of the road from the wrecked SUV. The sun, directly at his back, would blind any survivors of the wreck. It took him fully five minutes to reach a point where he could see into the wreck from the driver's side. The front seat, littered with waste food and papers showed no sign of life. He searched the palm grove, but still saw nothing, only dust and rocks. He stood in eerie silence … not even a goat or donkey was to be seen or heard. He couldn't see into the back seat, but it appeared that whoever had occupied the car, had managed to open the driver's door and leave on foot. *Perhaps he has been picked up by someone driving by,* Gideon thought.

Torn by conflicting procedures, Gideon could take the more careful route, return to his Jeep, and call in for assistance. But as a Kidon, he chose the more direct approach, and decided to make a direct assault on the vehicle. His weapon at the ready, safety off, he charged across the road and ripped open the back door. Nothing. He noticed the trunk had popped slightly open from the impact of the crash, so he pulled it fully open. The spare tire and jack had come loose and rattled around inside, but he found nothing of import. *Well,* he thought, *whoever or whatever had been in the Nissan has somehow survived and now is gone.* Before calling in however, Gideon took one more look into the driver's seat, checking to see if perhaps some of the waste paper had any writing on it.

While Gideon stood carelessly in the sunlight, a single shot crashed through the rear passenger window. The shot, he realized immediately, had come from the east side of the road where he had just been. He had been so intent on the SUV that he failed to notice a small cluster of bushes about 100 yards from the road. The shooter must have seen him coming and hidden so that he now had the sun at his back. Gideon had violated one of the first rules of combat: check any location your opponent might use to his advantage.

With little choice now, he fired a short burst of about ten rounds at the bushes, then clambered under the overturned SUV, trying to scramble far enough toward the passenger side to be out of direct view of the shooter. He had just found a spot by the right front wheel when a second shot hit the tire, blowing it out. This shot must have come from a spot further north, but still on the opposite side of the road. *The guy is smart. He moved his cover at the same time I moved,* Gideon thought and then grimly added: *Either that, or there was a second shooter.* This latter option seemed unlikely, since that was the direction from which Gideon had come.

To put the SUV between himself and the shooter, Gideon scrambled around to the front of the vehicle and peered out from underneath. There seemed to be little cover from where the second shot had come. This puzzled him; the shooter seemed to be one step ahead of him. He had pulled back into the slim shelter of the blown-out tire, when a third shot from nearby on the same side of the road hit him directly in his left ankle. The shooter, he realized too late, had taken the opportunity to cross the road and had him directly in his sights.

In serious pain, and with no target in sight, Gideon desperately emptied his weapon vaguely in the direction from where the shot had come. Searching in the pockets of his armored vest for another magazine, he looked up into the smiling face of an Arab, dressed in fatigues, holding an AK-47 pointed directly at his head. Gideon never heard the shot that entered his right eye and left a gaping hole in the back of his skull.

It was near noon and the Mufti still had heard nothing more of the disastrous raid on the training camp. He did not want to notify any of the other planners until he had more information, and until he could come up with alternate ideas. Suddenly a visage appeared in his sitting room without having made a sound. He wore a black and white keffiyah and dust-covered fatigues, an AK-47 strapped across his back, a large grin on his dusty face, showing gleaming white teeth. *The "Ghost,"* thought the terrified Mufti. This must be the notorious Saleh Halibi. It came to him in a rush. He was the one who phoned from the camp and somehow had made his way here to Ramallah.

"You do not look pleased to see me, Mufti," said the smiling assassin.

"You surprised me, that is all. What happened up there, is anyone left, how did you get here, what …?"

"One thing at a time, my friend. Somehow the Zionists discovered our camp and destroyed it. Fortunately, I was able to take care of the computers before they could get their filthy hands on them."

"And our trainees, our soldiers …?"

"All lost, I'm afraid. The Jews may have even captured some. I was fortunate to get away; there was no chance to save anyone else."

And that is why you are called The Ghost, thought the Mufti admiringly, with a great sense of foreboding.

Chapter 16

Staunton Richardson drove home that momentous day two years ago, his mind blurred with a mixture of excitement and anxiety. He first had to decide what to tell Sally, if anything. If he accepted Dale's offer he somehow would have to explain his sudden increase in wealth. He had been totally honest in his 20 years with Sally, but there was no way he could tell her the details of the relationship with Simmons. He decided that, if he did go ahead and take the position as offered, he would have to explain it as a public-relations position: talking with students and prospective employees for Simmons. The job, of course, would involve some travel.

He continued to rationalize the positive aspects by considering the impact on their two children: Stan Jr., a senior in high school and Bailey, in his first year at Alabama. The costs of having two kids in college were substantial. With this new income, not only could he cover that, but also provide them the kind of luxuries he never had as a student: new cars and stylish clothing for example.

They could also afford a new house with a country club membership, somewhere in one of the affluent suburbs. In his position with the church, he had received several invitations from some of the wealthier members of the congregation, now he would be able to join. Sally could afford a cook, a maid, a gardener. The more he thought about it, the more he realized what he'd been missing.

Before he got any further though, he needed to check out Dale's story. As soon as he got home he went onto the Internet and looked up *Neturei Karta*. He could barely believe what he found. There were more entries than he could check. But what he discovered agreed with what Simmons had told him. Not only was the ultra-orthodox sect anti-Zionist, it was actually cooperating with the Arabs. His head whirled at the sight of photographs showing leaders of the Neturei Karta, in full religious dress, meeting with known terrorists; photos taken in southern Lebanon showed prominent Karta rabbis shaking hands with Hezbollah political and military figures!

Hezbollah, one of Israel's fiercest and most criminal enemies, thrived on the suicide bombing of civilian targets, most notably schools. Even though he was no expert on the Middle East, the thought of an organized militia deliberately targeting innocent children disgusted him. And here were religious leaders of their Jewish community greeting them like old friends. *Why hadn't they been thrown in jail?*

He remembered photographs he'd seen of ultra-liberal celebrities during the Vietnam War ... Hollywood figures seen greeting North Vietnamese leaders; even posing on the anti-aircraft guns the enemy used to shoot down American planes. Even that, did not approach the audacity, the perfidious behavior of these citizens of a country facing daily atrocities.

Well, Dale hadn't been lying; not even exaggerating. If these nut cases were capable of cooperating with Hezbollah, they were certainly capable of targeting institutions like Mount Zion.

Stan met with Dale in his Waco office. By this point, he had resolved most of the issues concerning the offer. One important point he had to address concerned his position with the church. Leonard Depew had been like a father to him. He'd given him the opportunity to expand the membership, a job in which he had been eminently successful. Richardson's natural "people skills" and fundamental Christian background had gone over well in the West Texas community. Because of his efforts, the church had been able to move ahead with their ambitious plans for an elaborate Zionist-Christian center in Israel. A center warmly embraced by an overwhelming majority of Israelis.

The Israelis, of course, did not believe in the "Rapture" as interpreted by the fundamentalist Christians in the book of Revelation. They did not expect to be consumed in flames at the second coming of Jesus. They did welcome, however, the financial and political support of this large American community.

Dale greeted Stan warmly. After a few opening comments indicating his favorable inclination, Stan brought up his present position with the church. "Stan," Dale said immediately, "that's a done deal. Of course you'll keep your job as director of membership. The way we'll deal with it is simple. You go to Len, and tell him that you've found a wealthy donor who wishes to give an extremely substantial donation to the church; an amount of several million dollars. As is often the case, this particular donor wishes to remain anonymous, but has found you to be a compassionate and trustworthy member of the church staff, and wishes for you to do whatever intermediary work is necessary. See that the money is properly handled, that sort of thing."

Stan had seen a few anonymous contributions before, usually from people who didn't want to be annoyed by the press or by other organizations in need of funds. "Wouldn't it be a noteworthy contribution for Simmons Oil?" Stan asked. "I would think you would get a lot of good press from something like that."

"I'll tell you Stan," Dale explained, "we would get so bombarded with requests from other churches, schools and the like, it would be more than we could handle. We already have an active program, handled by another office, that contributes to all sorts of worthy organizations. This program, the one we're talking about here, obviously needs to be kept separate. Any time you'll have to spend away from the church, to act as liaison with this donor, will be time well spent. This individual has friends and business associates in the same sort of situation. They are about to retire, or expire, and want to make sure their money goes to an organization like our church. Your lost time will be more than made up for by the new contributions that these folks will make."

Richardson, had in fact, run into people who didn't want their contributions to the church made public, for a number of reasons. He was happy to do as they wished, and Len had no problem with their anonymity.

"That will mean you'll need an assistant or two, to cover your less important duties, but the income from this new donation will more than cover that expense. Knowing Len, I think he'll be tickled to death," Dale concluded.

The two shook hands warmly and Dale handed him a folder containing a lot of paperwork. Richardson, who was used to these legal documents, quickly scanned them, and said they looked fine, but he of course, would have to take them home and examine them more closely. He did notice that one of the forms was for a "direct deposit" of close to $42,000 each month, into his bank account. Another was a "Letter of Transmittal"-- a copy of a legal document sent to the church's bank in Waco, saying the sum of $30 million was to be deposited in the church's account to be used "as the church sees fit." The source of the fund was not named, only the depositing bank. The size of the contribution was staggering to Stan, but he tried to hold his composure steady. He was in the big time now.

After a bit more conversation, Simmons suggested that Stan begin by meeting some of the students from Israel, who had already begun school at West Texas. They had also made preparations to start their affiliation with the church and the Mount Zion project. Dale would leave it up to Stan to "bring them into the fold."

Richardson started his new career by making contact with the Dean of Students at West Texas Poly, Dr. Amos Keltner. He arranged to meet the Dean at three o'clock that same afternoon. Keltner, a short, round sort of fellow, couldn't have been more delighted to see him. Clearly, Simmons had laid some groundwork. "Come in, come in, Keltner said, grasping Stan's hand. "Have a seat," he said. "Amos Keltner, right glad to meet you."

Richardson sat in the plush leather chair Keltner offered. "Staunton Richardson, but please call me Stan," he replied.

"I understand you'd like to meet some of these fine new students who come here to study, from the holy land, Israel."

"That's right," Stan replied, "I would like to talk with them, see how they're liking Waco, how they're doing in school, that sort of thing."

"I think that's great," replied the Dean. "I think you'll find they're a fine bunch. Very religious, Jews, you know. Most of them are here to benefit from our strong programs in science and technology," he said proudly. "We have over a thousand international students here, but these are some of the first from Israel. Be happy to see more like 'em."

This was terrific news to Stan. While he knew that part of the Dean's enthusiasm came from the fact that these "students" brought with them significant funds in tuition and fees, he was glad to see that they were maintaining a positive image on campus. This was going to make his job significantly easier.

"I'll be completely honest with you," Stan said. "I'd also like to see if they have any interest in our church." The Dean looked a little surprised; after all, these students were Jewish, and very religious. "You see, Dean Keltner, our church, as you may know, is one of the largest Zionist Christian congregations in the country. We have very strong ties to Israel. I think these kids might really be interested in the work we're doing."

"Well, now that you mention it, I did know about that Israel connection, and I think they very well might like to talk to you. Might even like to visit the church. You're building some kind of visitors' center over there in Israel, aren't you?"

The Dean was making his life easier all the time. "Yes, that's right," Richardson said. "You may not know that some of your Israeli graduates are already working over there helping with the construction. And I was hoping to show at least some of these new fellows our plans."

As a matter of fact, the Dean was quite aware of the Israeli graduates that had gone to work in Israel. He hadn't publicized the matter, being unsure of the effect that news would have in the mainstream Baptist atmosphere of the University. Texas folks liked to think their graduates were going to stay in Texas, and help their economy.

"Well," Dean Keltner said. "I think you'll find them a very smart, hard-working, receptive bunch. I can give you the phone number of the building they use as a kind of religious center, Hill Hall they call it. They use it to prepare their meals, have services, that sort of thing."

"That would be great; I really appreciate it," Stan replied, rising from his chair. "I'll give them a call, try to set something up real soon. You've been very helpful, Dean."

"Any time, Stan. And please call me Amos."

Things were going extremely well.

Richardson set up a meeting with a few of the Israelis for the next morning. Simmons had given him a list of the leaders, those already primed for their true mission. "Michael ben-Aaron," Simmons had said, "has been here the longest of this present batch, speaks the best English. He'll set things up for you."

Stan spoke with ben-Aaron on the phone over at Hill Hall. Using his campus map, it was easy for Stan to park in a visitors' lot, and walk over to Hill Hall at nine the next morning, a bright, sunny day, typical for Waco, with the usual brisk breeze snapping away at the American and Texas flags, ubiquitous on campus.

He found the ancient wooden structure, apparently an old classroom building, not on a hill, but rather named after the donor: "Texas" John Hill.

Three young men stood on the shaded terrace wearing religious Jewish clothing. Their heads, arms and legs covered with light, linen garments with fringe hanging out from beneath their jackets. All three smiled when they saw Richardson. The tallest of the three took a step forward and warmly took Stan's hand. "Mr. Richardson, I presume," he said, laughing at his little joke.

"Staunton Richardson, but please call me Stan."

"Come on into our humble quarters. My name is Michael, these are Sela and Hermon," the young man said, indicating his two companions, and led Stan into a small room that appeared to serve as a library. Various sorts of textbooks lay indiscriminately on the shelves and tables. Glancing quickly, Richardson noticed that most were in English, but a few appeared to have Hebrew lettering on their covers.

The four of them sat at a table, Michael closing the door behind them. The slight pause gave Stan a chance to look the men over. The leader, Michael, was dark complexioned, with curly black hair and sidelocks, and the beginnings of a beard on his young face. The others had similar appearances, clearly Middle Eastern in origin. They deferred to Michael, speaking only briefly.

Michael, Stan noticed, spoke English with the least accent. Without the religious garb and facial hair, the three would be barely recognizable as foreigners, perhaps only dark complexioned descendants of Central American families. "It's a pleasure to meet you, all of you," Stan said, breaking the ice. "I guess you know it's my job to make things easier for you around here. I'm membership chairman over at the church," he nodded, indicating eastwards across the river. "When it's convenient, I'd like to take you folks over there and introduce you to the Rev. Leonard Depew, our boss." He grinned conspiratorially, and added, "We'll go over just a few at a time. There's no rush."

Richardson understood that these 13 Neturei Karta had enrolled gradually, over the past four semesters. All had excellent academic records. Some had transferred from other American universities, while others, like Michael, had come directly from Israel. All were enrolled in technical programs: chemistry, mathematics, and engineering. The Computer Engineering Department here was highly thought of, and acted as a magnet for international students. Indians, Pakistanis, Chinese and Koreans attended as well as the Israelis. In fact, the international students far outnumbered the American-born in the technical disciplines. Richardson had learned all this in his brief perusal of the University's website, where he was pleased to find photographs of all the students, along with the disciplines in which they were enrolled.

The three students chatted casually about their experiences in Waco. Their tuition, fees, room and board, and other expenses appeared, to the University, to have been paid for by the Israeli government. Universities don't look too hard at the sources of funds; West Texas Poly was no exception. After about an hour, Richardson made plans to take the three over to the church as soon as they had time. He would, of course, have to check with Depew also. But he had no doubt Len would be delighted to have religious Jews on the team. It was something, Stan knew, he would be pleased to brag about to the congregation.

Things went along quite well for several weeks; Richardson, pleased with the progress he was making, felt confident he had made the right decision in taking this post. His wife, Sally, delighted with the increase in income, went ahead eagerly with plans for their new home. One day at one of his regular meetings with Simmons, sitting across from each other at Simmons' desk in his plush office, Richardson described with pleasure the ease with which progress was being made. Everything was going well: the students were contributing to both the college and the church, the Dean was pleased, and the patriotic effort toward America's strategic partner, Israel, was something to be proud of.

As he spoke, a figure appeared as if from nowhere. A man dressed in nondescript clothing, his olive complexion disguising his age—he could have been anywhere from 30 to 50 years old—smiled and approached the pair.

Speechless, Richardson stared at the apparition. Simmons stood and placed his arm around stranger's shoulder. "Stan," he said, after a brief pause, "I want to introduce you to someone. This is Saleh Halibi, sometimes known as 'The Ghost.'"

Richardson still couldn't speak; in fact he could barely breathe. What in the world was going on here?

"Stan, you've been doin' a great job, everything I could possibly ask from you. You know the goals we are aiming at, but I have to admit I haven't been completely honest with you about our methods."

Richardson's mind went into panic mode. What had he gotten involved in? He waited breathlessly for Simmons' next words.

"You know that our main goal is to disrupt the Zionist Christian influence in Israel, always has been. The only thing I've held back from you is the nature of our accomplices. They're not Neturei Karta. They're not even Jews. They're Hezbollah agents trained to look, speak, and act like religious Jews. But in fact, their goals are the same as ours: the return of Israel to its true owners: the Arabs."

Richardson could see the logic in what Simmons said. Still, his sense of betrayal was enormous. He had carried out this mission partly based on the fact that the Israelis themselves, or at least a sect of them, were acting to bring about the change in their country. Now, it turns out he was assisting an outside force, a devoted, murderous group of assassins to achieve their goal. A wave of nausea engulfed him as he considered his possibilities, his future. If he backed out now, or even tried to, what would become of him? Simmons would expose him for what he had done. Who would believe that Richardson had unknowingly gone along with this deception? He would be disgraced, dishonored, banished from his community, and bankrupted. His family would never forgive him.

On the other hand, he rationalized, as Simmons and Halibi patiently waited, if he continued on his current path, their final goal would still be achieved. And the deception, if it worked as well as it had so far, would never be exposed. Israel would be destroyed from within. American oil interests would prosper. The world would be a better place. He also realized he had little choice.

Richardson's capitulation was complete. His face and body relaxed.

"Tell me," Richardson said, almost as an afterthought, "Why do they call you 'The Ghost'?" His voice trembled slightly, like a fighter hit with a rabbit punch.

Simmons replied for Halibi. "They call him that because he appears and disappears as if by magic. I know I can tell you this because you'll find out as soon as you get to your computer anyway. He has been the brains behind some of the most audacious acts of bravery, or as the press may call them, 'terror,' the world has ever seen. He has been responsible for the military actions in the Middle East that caused our government to withdraw, ending our irresponsible support of the illegal State of Israel."

Richardson thought hard for a few moments. Could Simmons possibly be talking about the bombings of the U.S.

Embassies, the USS Cole? He would find out for sure once he could get to his computer, but he had the sickening feeling that this was, in fact, the case.

Before he left the meeting, however, he was in for one more surprise. After a bit more learning and discovery on his part, he was going to embark on a trip to the Middle East. He was going to meet the central figure in the upcoming battle: the Grand Mufti of Jerusalem.

Chapter 17

The spiritual leader of Iran, the Ayatollah, looked disdainfully at his newly re-elected president and said, "Cooperate with the Sunnis? Never."

"But, your reverence, the Grand Mufti represents more than just the Sunnis. When it comes to the destruction of the Zionist entity, he represents all of us, all Muslims," the president replied, exhibiting his usual deceitful grin.

"The Grand Mufti of Al Quds, or Jerusalem, as it is called by the Jews, has never represented the Shi'a. He has always been appointed by the Sunnis; he owes his loyalty to them only," said the aging cleric.

The diminutive president was not to be easily dismissed. "Remember the hadith that our great sheikh Qyaradawi always quoted when it came to removing the Zionists from our land:

"Allah's Apostle said, 'The Hour will not be established until you fight with the Jews, and the stone behind which a Jew will be hiding will say. 'O Muslim! There is a Jew hiding behind me, so kill him.'

"You know as well as I, blessed Ayatollah, that Allah meant all Muslims, Sunni and Shi'a alike, must unite against the Jew."

The Ayatollah sat thoughtfully, moved but not persuaded. "We have never accepted the Mufti as our leader; he is a Sunni, not one of us."

"But, great leader, his plan has been accepted by the vast Arab nations that surround the Zionist curse in our midst. Even now, huge armies of the Islamic Brotherhood in Egypt and Syria, are preparing to deliver the fatal blow. And, Your Reverence, Hezbollah has joined with the Syrians! Their forces will take part in the attack. Recall how Hezbollah protected our Shi'a villages in Lebanon when they were attacked by the Sunnis! It would benefit Muslims everywhere if we would be part of the onslaught."

"What would they want from us?" the ayatollah asked after a brief silence.

The feisty little president recognized victory. "We will aim our new long-range missiles at them. They will see them with their satellites, but be powerless against them," he said, grinning foolishly, as was his custom.

"You are forgetting their servants, the Americans. They will unleash all their weaponry against us, to save their Jewish masters."

"But you see, supreme leader, that eventuality has been taken care of. There will be an attack performed by pious Jews upon American interests that will turn the great Satan against the Jew bastards. The Americans will not come to the aid of the Zionist filth when they see this perfidy."

The Ayatollah was clearly impressed. "You seem very certain. It is a beautiful picture you paint. But our nuclear weapons are not yet ready, you know that. We could not retaliate effectively. What more is expected of us?"

"A great convoy is already on its way, carrying hidden weapons to destroy the infidels from close range. Once the Arab attack commences, we will support them with missiles from the Suez Canal and the Red Sea."

"Why was I not informed of this sooner?"

The president had been prepared for this question. "We did not want to trouble you, your Reverence, until we were certain the plan could be realized. This way you will never be held responsible, but can share in the victory. You will be hailed triumphant by both Sunni and Shi'a alike in destroying the Jew and recovering our sacred land!"

The ayatollah pondered this for a moment, appearing to see the benefits accruing to him, while leaving him blameless in the eyes of the rest of the world. "You say the Arab nations, Egypt and Syria, are preparing for the attack, but what of the other Arabs? What of the Saudis? You know of the hatred that exists between us. It has been so for countless generations."

"The Saudis will not interfere. They will be pleased to see the Zionists crumble, while retaining the Americans as slaves to their oil."

A smile crept across the religious leader's face. "You have planned well, my son. But tell me, what is the attack you speak of, that will so enrage the Americans? What could cause them to abandon the Zionists, to whom they have become so beholden?"

"It is best that you know nothing of this plan. It does not involve us or Iran."

The Ayatollah was silent, stroking his long, white beard.

"Then we may proceed with your blessing?" the president asked impatiently.

"And with the blessing of Allah: let us kill the Jew wherever he lurks."

Bowing deeply, the president then asked the Grand Leader, the Ayatollah, the question he had been leading up to: would he, the Glorious Religious Leader and Supreme Commander of all the Forces of Islam, cast upon him, his servant, the president and voice of the Grand Master, the humble designation as tactical chief of the Armed Forces of the Prophet? How could the ayatollah refuse? With a flourish, the president produced a grand-looking document granting him, the president, lifetime power over all the armed forces of the Islamist Republic of Iran. It placed him in the irrevocable position as the military leader of the nation.

Within hours of his elevation to supreme military commander, the president called an urgent meeting of his military chiefs of staff. Copies of the document, signed by the ayatollah himself, were broadcast on all the television stations and exhibited on all the public billboards.

Foremost among his minions was the minister of defense, Brigadier General Ahmed Vahidi, who sat at the center of the table. Among all his military leaders, Vahidi was the most practical. A short man, even among Persians, he insisted on maintaining an immaculate personal image. His hair had prematurely disappeared, but his small, angry features were outlined with a short, white beard and mustache. He was groomed to perfection. As with all members of the general staff, Vahidi was permitted his own design of uniform.

Vahidi outfitted himself with a light tan, short sleeved shirt, on which three gold stars decorated each lapel. Rows of campaign ribbons lavishly garnished each of his shirt pockets. Additionally, epaulets dressed each shoulder, no doubt intended to enhance his rather slight frame. He maintained his belligerent appearance so as to confirm his recent remarks belittling the military preparedness of Iran's enemies.

The titular commander in chief of the Army, General Ataleh Salehi, perched at Vahidi's left. In contrast with the other generals, Salehi wore an officer's cap similar in design to that of the U.S. Air Force, complete with a "50 mission crush," designed to make the wearer appear the embattled veteran. As head of Iran's regular military he was a member of Iran's Supreme National Security Council. Despite his bellicose remarks, aimed particularly at Israel, Salehi had no real battlefield experience. He had been particularly embarrassed by his stern warnings against the traversing of the Strait of Hormuz by the U.S. Fifth Fleet. The U.S. fleet commander paid absolutely no attention to his warnings, and the warships conducted their pre-planned war exercises throughout the Persian Gulf without incident.

Next in line was General Sayed Firizabadi, whose title was "Chief of Staff." This pudgy, little peacock gained his position mainly through the support of the president; he had no combat training. In fact, he was basically a coward, fearful for his life and position. He was, however, fond of making remarks to the effect that Israel would be "bulldozed" if it ever made an attack on Iran.

Finally, the head of the once-feared Revolutionary Guard, was General Hussein Sulami. Sulami often attempted to outdo Firizabadi in the nature of his grandiose remarks as to the ultimate annihilation of the West in the inevitable battle to come. However, in an actual recent battlefield situation, the attack by a small number of Sunni revolutionaries, nearly 100 of Sulami's vaunted "Guard" had been summarily disposed of.

It was this recent act of treachery by the Sunni minority in Iran that had most inflamed the ayatollah, leading to his outrage when approached by his tiny president, with the idea of a military alliance.

The commanders of the Air Force and Navy, Farzad Esmali and Mortez Safari, respectively, were "paper tigers" of the first-degree. While both had been commissioned to set up air and naval defense against an attack from the West, neither had actually been able to do so. Surreptitious tests by Israel and the United States had shown Iran had virtually no defense against a coordinated air-sea attack. Their defense system, obsolete and uncoordinated, had no viable chain of command.

At any rate, fumed the president, the military action begun so cleverly by the Arabs against the Zionists, demanded some sort of response. The Mufti, it seemed, spoke for both the Egyptians and the Syrians. If not, how could their coordinated attack on that Jew-infested bit of land have been prepared so well? Sometimes one must set aside regional conflicts in defense of the overall glory of The Prophet.

Killing Jews is a form of worship that draws us closer to Allah, was a phrase from the Qu'ran that never left the deepest confines of the ayatollah's heart; the president felt the same. The other principles for which he had fought, and would continue to fight—first, the removal of any traces of Christendom from Jerusalem, and second, the conversion of the tiny fraction of Muslims who still held to the Sunni doctrine—must wait until the total elimination of the Jews.

He realized, perhaps more than any of his contemporaries, how vital the actions of the present Mufti and his predecessors, had been in that pursuit. Both the Ottomans and the Nazis had been only a prayer away from the de-infestation of the world of the Jewish lice. Each of the Muftis had done his best in setting up alliances which would have brought world Jewry to an end.

It was difficult for him to explain to these mere mortals under his command what the chain of events must be. He knew his Revolutionary Guard would be fundamentally opposed to joining forces with the Sunnis; especially after being humiliated by them. It was his job, as the Ayatollah, the Supreme Leader of the Shi'a, to explain the teachings of the prophets in such a way that the true believers would understand the necessity of his Grand Coalition.

First, however, the new supreme military commander had to have a new and distinctive attire. He had planned ahead and instructed his personal tailor to fit him with a uniform in keeping with one of his favorite military heroes: Heinrich Himmler. In contrast with the other generals and admirals now under his command, all of whom were clad in standard brown or khaki, the new leader appeared in front of them for the first time dressed in his new uniform: all in black, complete with black leather waist-belt and cross-strap with nickel-plated buckles and fittings. He wore riding breeches, shiny black boots and the high peaked officer's cap made so popular by his Nazi hero. Instead of the lightning strike SS emblems on his lapels, were the Iranian coat of arms. On the peak of his cap stood the symbol of Hamas, the most fanatical expression of anti-Judaism. Hamas, of course, had the financial and military backing of Iran.

A red and black band adorned his left arm. In place of the Nazi swastika the president had chosen the Muslim star and crescent, to indicate his religious fervor.

In keeping with Himmler, he carried a leather riding crop in his right hand, with which he punctuated his remarks. All in all, he might well have been attending some sort of satanic costume party; except that here, his aims were all too real.

"I want to welcome you all to the first meeting of the Supreme Iranian Military Council," he began, smiling stupidly. Mouths, which had fallen open at the appearance of this visage of a figure from the last century, now snapped shut under the scrutiny of a creature from another world. Any impulse toward laughter soon dissipated as the supreme commander began his lecture, punctuating each proclamation with a smack from his riding crop.

He passed down each aisle, addressing each of the military chiefs in turn.

"First, and foremost, we must strike fear in the very heart of the devil. General Vahidi," he began, addressing the minister of defense, "the Shahab 3 missiles at Tabriz and Khorramad must be made ready to launch as soon as possible ..."

"But, Mr. President," began the clearly astonished Vahidi, "in the first place, they are not fully armed, and secondly ..."

"When I need your opinion I will ask for it!" the diminutive despot interrupted, punctuated with a slap on the table from his riding crop. "You were about to say, I believe, that the Americans will detect the activity around our missile silos. This is precisely what we wish them to see. With their megalithic political structure they will be unable to come to any sort of agreement on what action they might take." He smiled slyly.

"Were they even to consider a preemptive strike against us, the liberal factions in their government would become hysterical, accusing the military of criminal intent. Instead, they would claim, it was the action of the Israelis, whatever that might be, that caused the alarm among the Islamic nations." He continued striding around the room. "Instead, the initial response of the Americans will be to have an emergency meeting with the Zionists, pleading with them not to take any action that might be seen by the Islamic republics as a threat of war."

"Next ... Admiral Habibollah, while the world is anxiously waiting to see what we have in mind, you and Admirals Fadavi and Rastegari will prepare for an immediate seaborne invasion. Ships from our ports on the Gulf of Oman will form into flotillas that will make full speed southwestward toward the Gulf of Aqaba. The most rapid of our warships will head directly into the Red Sea at Sana'a. The American Fifth Fleet will, of course, follow us at a respectable distance. These are international waters and while they might make inquiries, they can take no action. I have calculated the trip to take no longer than five days, even accounting for loading of fuel and cargo."

The chief officer and commander of the Navy, Rear Admiral Safari, had little real knowledge of naval maneuvers; however, he had spent several years as Ambassador to Spain, and so had some experience dealing with the diplomats of the West. "I see several problems here, in addition to the repositioning of our Shahab 3 missiles," he said quietly. Safari was a small man, even compared with the president. He was immaculately groomed, with a white tunic and dark blue jacket, rather than the opulent uniform preferred by the others. He rarely spoke except when he felt he had something important to say.

119

"The movement of any number of naval vessels, especially those containing cargo of the size and shape resembling missiles is bound to attract international attention. The kind of attention we certainly do not need at this juncture."

The new commander-in-chief, grandly dressed in his SS-like costume was ready for this criticism. "You see," he said with his foolish grin, "special coverings are being constructed even as we speak. They will disguise the ships as carriers of grain and other foodstuffs. Should the Americans and their sniveling dogs object, we will simply bring the matter to the United Nations, saying we are conducting a humanitarian mission to the starving peoples of northeastern Africa. Even our Arab colleagues would not dare to come to the defense of the Americans."

A light buzz filtered around the room as the military council considered this argument. Everyone in the room recalled the tremendous international outcry that accompanied the incursions of the United States into the Middle East. Without more evidence on which to make judgment, the Western powers were unlikely to risk another adventure like Iraq or Afghanistan.

"I can tell you now: the Arab armies of Egypt and Syria are, even as we speak, preparing to launch coordinated assaults on the Zionists. I myself have been in direct communication with their commanders in chief."

The buzz in the room became a roar. "But, Mr. President ...," spoke out General Vahidi, who quickly changed his form of address to, "Commanding General ...," as the little man snapped his riding crop against table, "won't such an attack bring immediate retaliation from the Americans, not to mention some of their European allies?"

"That is where the brilliance of our strategy will shine in its most glory. There will be an event of such historic magnitude, that the American public will strike out against their government in a manner unseen since their ignominious defeat in Vietnam. Their government will have no recourse but to allow the Zionist entity to crumble under the weight of the Muslim opposition ..."

Major General Firizabadi, who held the title of "Head of the Armed Forces," immediately piped up with ... "Not a moment ago, you spoke of the 'Arab' armies. Now suddenly it becomes the 'Muslim' opposition! What has occurred that suddenly brings us into alliance with the *Sunni* nonbelievers?"

"Your point is well taken, my friend. Were it not for the audacity of this plan, the opportunity to obliterate the Zionist entity from our land once and for all, we would not have been so eager to be part of it."

The word "we" assured everyone in the room that the Islamic Republic of Iran was to join forces with the Arab nations of Egypt and Syria.

General Firizabadi continued, "Just when is this joint Arab attack scheduled to commence?"

"The plan is to have the operation underway in time to match the Zionist Independence Day," the president continued with obvious relish. "However, our participation, that is, the attack of our naval forces, will not occur until we are certain of the success of the Arab land campaign."

There was a murmur of satisfaction around the room. "How did you manage that advantageous strategy?" General Vahidi inquired jealously.

"I have been in contact, contact of the most clandestine sort, for the past several weeks, with leaders of both nations. Not even our glorious Ayatollah had known about it until just very recently. In fact, it was this masterstroke of military prowess that prompted him to place me in the position in which you now see me: Commander-in-Chief." He flourished his dashing new uniform in a style he had recalled from World War II movies of his hero, Heinrich Himmler.

Still curious, Vahidi asked, "But how did these transmissions take place? As far as I know, you haven't left Tehran these past few months."

"Correct you are, my friend. All communications have been conducted using our latest satellite phones, manufactured by our new friends in the Emirates," the little Commander replied proudly. "They are the very latest in technology: absolutely impenetrable. Why, even the Americans feel absolutely confident in their security."

Admiral Habibollah was still cautious. After all, it was his naval forces that would be in the most jeopardy. "But who was it, if I may ask, that initiated this bold move? The Islamic Brotherhood has only had control of Syria for less than a year. And their control of Egypt has been tenuous, at best."

"That is a most reasonable question. The leaders of these two countries were more than willing to enhance their positions with a victory over the Zionists. But it was a person whose hatred of that illegitimate state has festered through many generations; a man who has the same religious power over the Arabs that our blessed Ayatollah has over our people—the Grand Mufti of Al Quds-Mohammed Amin Al Husseini!"

General turmoil reigned throughout the room for nearly a full minute. It was Vahidi who asked the question on everyone's mind: "How could the Mufti conceive such an outrageous plan? What strategic experience did he have such that the Arab leaders would have confidence in him?"

The Commander smiled: "He has the aid of the greatest military mind in the Middle East, the man responsible for the elimination of more Americans than anyone else of our generation: *Saleh Halibi!*"

A moment of silence followed, then finally someone muttered the name that had struck fear in the hearts of the Zionists for the last four decades: "*The Ghost.*" Everyone in the room knew of his reputation. Everyone in the room knew that he had never failed. With his help, anything seemed possible, even this outrageous military undertaking.

Chapter 18

The Grand Mufti of Jerusalem, Muhammed Amin al-Huseini, met Staunton Richardson at the door of the Mufti's Ramallah apartment just after 1400 hours, as agreed upon. They had met several times during the past eighteen months.

"You're sure you were not followed?" the Mufti asked glancing hurriedly up and down the empty street. The only car in view, the rental Renault sedan Richardson had brought from the Jerusalem airport, as directed. He'd had no trouble entering the country, as he'd been there many times over the years dealing with Mount Zion. His passport showed the stamps of all the major Israeli airports.

"No, of course not, you think I'm an amateur," he said sharply.

"With an enterprise of this size, we are all something of amateurs. A cup of coffee perhaps," the Mufti offered, "after your long journey." He knew Richardson had used a tortuous itinerary, starting in Dallas, through New York, Paris, Athens, and finally Jerusalem.

Richardson knew only too well of the thick, syrupy Turkish coffee the Mufti was offering. He graciously declined. "Let's just go through where we stand now, all right?"

The Mufti leaned back in his cushions. "Things couldn't be better," he said with sublime satisfaction. "Aboud Al Agha has his Syrians primed and ready to go all along the border—over 700 tanks, 500 aircraft and 50,000 troops—all eager to attack. The Galilee will fall in 48 hours at most.

"The Egyptian leader, Rabiah Tariq Al Khalid, has 1200 tanks, 1000 aircraft and over 150,000 men lined up all along the sea from Port Said to Gaza through Al Arish and Rafah. What's more, the Saudis have promised an attack from the Southeast as soon as our initial objectives have been achieved," the Mufti lied.

"I think we have a pretty good idea how much we can depend on the Saudis," Richardson replied sarcastically. "You know how much they depend on the Americans."

"That, my friend, is where your attack on the Christian enclave becomes key. As we have discussed, any attack by Jews, on a fundamentalist Christian development in the 'Holy Land,' will bring a storm of protest the likes of which have never been seen. As you know, an underlying power of anti-Semitism is just waiting for an incident such as this. Not only will the Saudis be free to march into the Negev, the Iranians will have license to launch their long range missiles directly at Jerusalem and Tel Aviv."

"You mean their 'Sajjil 2' rockets are ready to go?"

"They are right now situated at Ahvaz, Dezful and Sanandaj, their targets firmly in sight. The launchers are disguised as oil derricks, and the American drones have shown not the slightest interest in them."

"You mean to say ...," Richardson started ...

"Wait, there's more! The ayatollahs are so eager to have an opportunity to destroy Israel, they have a fleet disguised as merchant ships sailing around Aden, and up the Red Sea into the Gulf of Aqaba."

"I wasn't told of any Iranian involvement!" Richardson exclaimed.

"You know only what you need to know; that's the way this business works, my friend," the Mufti told him, smiling at the man's naïveté.

"Do you have the map and list of saboteurs?" Uri whispered. He and Lara were hiding in the shadows of the nearly-complete Zionist Christian Center outside Haifa. This was it ... the night they were to sabotage the plans for its destruction.

"Yes, course, we're ready for them," Lara replied. She seemed calmer than Uri, even though he had been in this sort of situation countless times as part of the Mossad. Perhaps his nerves grew from his knowledge of how easily one simple thing could go wrong in a complex plan such as this.

The sun finally set in the shadows that had been creeping across the compound. They watched the disguised Arabs, many of them the same ones they had met at Waco, working surreptitiously around the support columns. Finally finished with their job, the imposters silently departed leaving only the temporary work lights to illuminate the visitor center and huge auditorium. With the map, Lara and Uri had constructed based on what they had learned from the "Orthodox recruits," they felt they had most, if not all, of the locations of the C-4 explosives. They also felt they knew which of the saboteurs would be in each location.

The Arabs had been surprised to see Lara and Uri. Uri, of course, had been cautious to have his prosthetic eye in place when they arrived at Haifa. Most of the Arabs they recognized from Waco. Others, newer recruits, had arrived since. None had expected to see the two strangers at the Haifa construction site, now nearly finished as the "Zionist Christian Center for Learning." The workers pretended, at least, to be pleased to meet with them again. They had left Waco on the best of terms.

Uri, especially, had shown interest in the details of construction back at the model of the Center in Waco. So it seemed perfectly natural that he would want to see the structural details now that the full-scale building neared completion. He and Lara spoke with the workers, still in their disguises as Neturei Karta, about the load-bearing elements of the structure, complimenting each on their engineering expertise. Lara carefully kept mental notes of the unconscious glances that sensitive places in the columns received. Such glances, she knew from her FBI training, were dead giveaways. Being careful not to appear to notice these "tells," kept the suspects at ease.

Now that the sun had set, and the work ended for the day, the two agents returned to do their job. Starting at the northwest end of the auditorium they crept silently to the first of the structural members. Sure enough, a yellow dot indicated the place where the concrete had been replaced with a gray putty-like substance. The spot, hidden behind a pot of artificial ferns; would have been almost impossible to discover accidentally.

Uri reached into his bag, hidden under a seat, and grabbed a trowel. The 4 inch diameter putty yielded after a modest effort. Underneath he found about a pound of molded C-4, more than enough to bring down the column. Tucked in alongside the C-4 he found a tiny detonator complete with antenna. Lara expertly disarmed the explosive by detaching one of the wires between the antenna and the detonator. Uri didn't have a chance to ask what she was doing; he might've gone into shock. "It's a little late to ask, but how did you know that thing wasn't going to blow up in your hand?"

"Quantico," she said. "This is one of the most primitive types of detonators. I could see it wasn't booby-trapped."

"Well, thanks for not scaring me with one of those Hollywood 'Let's hope for the best' routines, just before you jerked out that wire. I might have had a heart attack," he said and laughed while wiping his brow. Lara inserted a small batch of weak gunpowder in its place, then reattached the putty and detonator as best she could. Meanwhile, Uri put back the artificial fern. He stood there for a few seconds examining their handiwork. "Come on," she said. "Let's get to the next one, we don't have a lot of time."

As indicated on the map, at the next structural column they found a near identical lump of putty at its base, this time hidden behind an innocuous statue. They performed the same surgical routine as they had before and moved on to the eight columns supporting the auditorium itself. Still more supported the library and visitor center—getting them done before the saboteurs arrived seemed an impossible job.

They finished column number six, and everything was going according to plan. Uri began to breathe easier. *We're going to be successful after all*, he thought, when Lara poked him sharply in the ribs, gesturing up towards the visitor center building. There on the walkway was the one they knew simply as "Eli." He still had the beard and earlocks, but he had replaced the Orthodox clothing with camouflage fatigues.

Eli spotted them at almost the same instant. "What are you two doing here?" he shouted. In the stunned silence, Uri and Lara groped for a reasonable explanation. "I said, what do you think you're doing!?"

"We were making sure everything was ready for the grand opening," Uri said.

"Let's have a look at what you've got in those bags," Eli demanded. His shouting alerted the rest of the Arab team. The odd sight of Orthodox-appearing men in fatigues would have been laughable, had it not been so terrifying. They had no simple way out of this - the saboteurs would quickly see what they had been up to.

Hoping Lara had picked up on the ad hoc plan, Uri walked toward Eli. "Of course, I'll show you," She realized at once what he had in mind and she surreptitiously reached into the large canvas bag she was carrying over her shoulder.

Five or six other Arabs followed Eli's lead and began to dodge through the auditorium seats toward the agents. When they were within fifty feet of the pair, Lara and Uri simultaneously jerked their pistols out of their bags.

The saboteurs were initially startled into inaction. Uri fired first, his .357 Magnum Desert Eagle sounding like a cannon in the empty auditorium. Eli, struck in the middle of the chest, spouted a fountain of bright red arterial blood. The last sight Uri had of him was the startled look on his dying face, as Lara and he dived behind the nearest column.

After a moment of indecision, the other Arabs spread out, ducking behind seats. Luckily for Lara and Uri, the arms they carried were not automatic weapons. Poorly aimed pistol shots rang against the concrete columns where they had taken refuge. Lara, the expert marksman, even with her 9 mm pistol, fired at the flimsy wooden auditorium seat from which one of the shots had emerged. A cry of pain indicated she had at least wounded another of the enemy.

Not certain where any of the others had hidden, Uri knew the psychological impact of the .357 rounds. He fired three more shots from his 15 round magazine in the approximate direction he had seen some of the saboteurs hide. The huge slugs rammed their way through three or four seats each, sending out a shower of splinters along with the deafening roar the weapon emitted. The remaining Arabs emerged from their hiding places in abject terror, running out of the auditorium. They didn't even bother firing their pistols. Lara and Uri each took a couple more shots in the direction of the fleeing men in fatigues, as Lara pointed excitedly at her watch. It was nearly 2100 and the explosions were set to go off. They needed to get out of there...fast.

They ran toward the fire exit at the northeast end of the building, grateful for the lack of enemy fire. They tore out of the building and headed for the parking lot. Realizing they hadn't been successful in completely saving the structures, they hoped the IDF had gotten their message and sent some troops. Just as they crouched down in the parking lot, the remaining explosives went off with a deafening roar. The visitor center had enough structural integrity to withstand the diminished load of C-4, but the auditorium and connecting hall had not. They crumbled, and in the aftermath, terrified screams and sobs came from amid the wreckage.

The two agents hesitated, not sure whether to try to attend to the survivors. That hesitation cost them their advantage. Five heavily armed men emerged from two of the parked cars. Uri and Lara dove behind a bulldozer at the edge of the lot and began firing. The futility of their position quickly became apparent. They were outgunned and outmanned, but at least they were close to the pine grove. If they could distract the Arabs ... "Fire at some gas tanks," Uri said. Lara responded at once and one, then two, then a third vehicle exploded into flames, illuminating much of the parking lot. They ran for the pine forest. One of the Arabs detected their movement and gestured to his colleagues. A gesture that cost him his life, as Uri dropped him with a single shot.

Both he and Lara took the opportunity to reload with fresh magazines. They continued to fire, but the enemy outflanked them. Between them, they dropped three more of the Arabs, but remained in an untenable position. As their magazines emptied, and they struggled to find replacements, they found themselves looking into the muzzles of three AK-47s.

128

"So, you are the traitors!" said the apparent leader in highly-accented English. Even in the dim light from the parking lot, his was an imposing figure, over 6 feet tall, bearded, and clothed in camouflage fatigues. He wore the black and white checkered keffiyah, common to Hezbollah. "I should kill you now, but that would be too easy. We have some more useful plans for you. Come on, move!" He and the two remaining Arabs shoved Lara and Uri hard in the back with the muzzles of their rifles.

"What do you think you're doing?" Lara asked, trying unsuccessfully to present a position of authority.

"You will refer to me as Yasim, you stupid Jew bitch!" he said, spraying them both with khat-laden saliva. The odor of his breath was similar to that of a farm animal. While Uri was used to it from years among the Palestinians, to Lara the smell was near overwhelming. Her reaction was obvious to Yasim and the other two terrorists; the two inferiors broke into laughter at her discomfort. Yasim spoke harshly to them in Lebanese-accented Arabic. Uri could not quite understand the entire order, but it had the effect of immediately sobering the other two.

"Just come with us. You will find out soon enough what we have in store for you," Yasim ordered. Lara and Uri moved as quickly as they could under the prodding of the weapons. The darkness and the rubble-covered ground made walking difficult. But the rush of adrenalin provided by the terrorists' AK-47's and foul breath kept them moving. After about twenty minutes, they arrived at a structure where building supplies and machinery were stored.

As the other two filth-covered Arabs held Lara and Uri at bay, Yasim searched through some keys and unlocked the door. The two thugs pushed the agents up a flight of stairs near the entrance of the building. At the top of the stairs Yasim unlocked a door that opened into a large, empty loft. He flipped a switch illuminating the room with the light from a single, bare bulb, hanging from the ceiling.

The hooligans, Tariq and Yusuf, grabbed Uri and Lara, throwing them to the ground in the empty loft. Tariq was the worse smelling of the two; Yusuf the bigger and bulkier. After seeing them in operation, however, there was no doubt about both their strength and their stupidity.

"Don't you realize the IDF is going to be here at any minute?" Lara warned them.

"Sure, and the New York Police will be right behind them," Yasim laughed. After a moment's consideration, the two cretins laughed along with him, even though it was clear their knowledge of English was rudimentary at best.

"I'm not joking," Lara persisted, "we've known about this operation for months; they were just waiting for you to make your move."

"You stupid Jewess," Yasim spat, slapping her hard across the mouth. "At this very moment Israel is being destroyed by a combined attack from all sides."

"What are you talking about?" Uri interjected.

"You'll find out soon enough; that is, if you live long enough," Yasim said with a cruel grin. In Arabic, Yasim ordered his henchmen to handcuff each of the captives around a two-inch steel pipe that acted as a ceiling support. He then instructed them to strip their prisoners of their belts and shoes. "I thought you Jews weren't supposed to wear leather."

"Only on some holidays, asshole." Uri spat back.

"Thanks for reminding me, Jew bastard. "Take their jewelry too," Yasim ordered his men. "You never know, we might be able to get good money for the stuff."

The two louts roughly pulled off Uri's belt and shoes, as well as his watch and wedding ring. They took his Desert Eagle pistol, admiring it, before Yasim grabbed it from them and thrust it into his own waist-band. This was a real prize. The goons then moved to Lara, pulling off her belt and side arm, while taking the opportunity to grope her between the legs; Lara shuddered violently. They then removed her bracelet, looking her over for anything else that might be of value. Finding nothing, they turned Lara and Uri so they were back-to-back against the pole, cuffed by both arms and legs. The agents found themselves in a standing position, totally helpless.

Yasim took one last look around the empty room, decided it would make a proper burial ground, laughed at them one more time, and said, "Don't be embarrassed to shit on each other; no one will ever know." He then jerked his hand at Tariq and Yusuf, gesturing for them to leave, took one more look around before following them, and locked the heavy door behind them.

Chapter 19

"Well, here's another nice mess you've gotten me into," Uri said in his best Oliver Hardy imitation.

"Is that all you can think about, gags from old American movies?" Lara replied. Then she suddenly remembered: "These are American-made cuffs, aren't they?"

Uri thought about this for second, trying to figure out what importance it might have. He looked down at the edge of his left handcuff. "Yeah, I think so, why?"

"Can you see if they have a brand name on them?"

Uri craned his neck and looked down at the cuff on his left hand. They were the old-style with about a four inch chain between them. "'*Peerless*?'" he said. "Mean anything to you?"

Lara trembled. "Could mean the difference between life and death. Can you possibly reach around with your mouth and grab my ear?"

"You're joking right? You pick the craziest time for romance. Any particular ear?"

"Okay, look," she said, "'Peerless' handcuffs are made so they all work with the same simple key. That's so any officer can operate any set of cuffs in an emergency."

"Fine. But I'm not following you; you happen to be carrying around a set of keys?"

"I'm wearing a pair of small hoop earrings; our raghead friends didn't notice them; they were too interested in my crotch."

"And who could blame them ... besides I thought the Bureau taught you guys not to use those old stereotypes. Who knows, deep down they could be very nice family men with strong religious convictions. We're just seeing their 'sharia' side. You know, where you kill, maim, and torture anyone who doesn't agree with you ..."

"Listen, doofus," Lara said, trying to ignore his attempt at humor, "if you can get one of those hoops out of my ear, I may be able to make a crude key out of the wire."

Uri considered this for second, figuring, *What the hell it's worth a try.* "All right, what do you want me to do?"

"First, bend your head around as far as you can to the left." Uri did as she asked, and could barely brush her hair with his face, as she twisted to her right. "Okay," he muttered, "now what?"

"See if you can get my ear lobe in your mouth."

He considered a wisecrack, then thought better of it. Craning his neck as far as he could, he could barely feel her right ear lobe between his lips. With his tongue he could feel the hoop earring.

"Okay," he muttered through the side of his mouth, "now what?"

"See if you can pull the hook out of my earlobe with your teeth."

"You're kidding, right?" Uri asked with as much incredulity as he could muster. "I've got more of your hair in my mouth than I do earring."

"Just give it a try. We haven't got all day, you know."

Uri gathered up his nerve, bit down on the parcel of hair and earring, and jerked his head around forward.

"Yikes," she cried, as Uri ended up with the earring, a good bit of hair, and a mouthful of blood. "Now, for God's sake, don't try to say anything, just see if you can spit the earring into your hand without losing it."

"Sorry about your earlobe," he muttered, as the tiny wire hoop dropped onto the concrete floor. "Oops, now what? I just dropped the little guy on the floor."

"I do have one more ear," she said through gritted teeth. "But that's my last one. Can you try to be a little more careful this time?"

Uri swallowed once to get up his nerve. "Okay, let's give it one more try."

"Tell you what," she said. "This time I'll put my hand right under my ear and try to catch the thing as you pull it out. How does that sound?"

"Better than anything I can think of at the moment." Uri gathered up his nerve, took a deep breath, and turned his head as far as he could to the right. She could feel his breath on her cheek as he reached for the earring with his teeth. He felt a slight resistance as he tore her ear, pulling down on the earring a little too hard.

Trying her best not to move or cry, Lara said bravely, "Don't try to talk, but did you get the damn thing!?"

Uri nodded.

"Now, I've got my hand right under your mouth. Can you try to gently drop it?"

Uri took another deep breath, and as gently as he could, moved the tiny bit of wire to the tip of his tongue, and as lightly as he could, spit the contents into the approximate location of her hand.

Lara let out a happy sigh and said, "I've got it!"

"All right, now what do we do with the damn thing?"

"If I give it to you, can you get both hands on it?" she asked hopefully.

"I can try, but your hands are smaller. Besides, I assume you know what you're doing."

"My hands are shaking too much," she said, "Can you make the key if I give you the instructions?"

"*Your* hands are shaking? Can you feel mine?"

"It's still our best shot," she replied. "Will you give it a go?"

"I can certainly try," he said with a gulp.

Lara touched his hands with hers and gently placed the bloody earring into his palm.

"Got it," Uri replied, as he spit out a mouthful of hair and blood.

"All right!" she said. "Now see if you can straighten out the wire part into something about two inches long."

"You sure you know what you're doing?" Uri asked doubtfully.

134

"I learned this at Quantico; I thought you were a spy, you didn't practice this stuff?"

"No women in our class, and the guys didn't wear earrings. OK, I've got something resembling a straight wire, now what?"

Lara said carefully, "Stick the end of the wire into the lock on my right handcuff, as far as it'll go. Then bend it at a right angle to the left. Then bend it again, so you have kind of an S-shape."

"You're sure about this, right?" Uri asked, more doubtful than ever.

"If you did it right, it should work."

"Should?!" Uri was getting less and less optimistic.

"The manual says it might not work the first time, but keep at it," she replied remorsefully.

"Great! What do I do now?"

"Press the wire down as far as it will go into the lock, and it should spring open. It worked at Quantico," she added.

"Well, that's certainly reassuring," he muttered as he pushed the wire down into the lock and twisted back and forth. "This'll be good practice for us, so the next time ..." Suddenly there was a sharp click and Lara shook her hand loose of the cuff. She turned and looked at him. "Nice work for a beginner," she laughed. "Tell me, do all you Mossad guys turn into amateur comedians in stressful situations?"

"It's something we Jews learn as children; our parents encourage us," he said with a grin.

From then, it was short work to remove the other cuffs from their hands and feet and consider their next move. The lone door to the room was securely locked, though not with a deadbolt. For the first time, they could smell smoke and hear a commotion outside. They could also hear men running down the corridor, speaking urgently in Arabic.

"We need a plan, and quick," Uri said.

"I have an idea!"

Uri looked at her, expectantly.

"The Krav Maga front knee kick." Uri knew she referred to the special kicking style used in Israeli martial arts. "We stand at the iron post the way they left us. They won't be expecting us to have our hands and feet free. They'll want to take us somewhere to use as hostages; otherwise, they would have killed us already, right?"

The Arabs had arrived at the door; Lara and Uri could hear them trying to unlock it. "All right," Uri said, as they moved over to the post, hiding their cuffs behind their backs. "If only two of them come in, we've got a chance. Maybe. If they put down their guns to unlock our cuffs ... we'll have to play it by ear. The guy bends over, kick to the throat. Otherwise, front knee kick, got it?"

Lara nodded just as the door sprang open, Yasim and Tariq rushing in. Yasim yelled something at Yusuf; Uri got enough of it to realize he was telling Yusuf to stand guard outside. Yasim smiled broadly as he saw his two "prisoners." "I hope you've been enjoying yourselves while we left you alone," he said laughing. "Here," he said to Tariq in Arabic, "hold this while I unlock him."

Uri understood enough of this as Yasim handed his AK-47 to the other terrorist. Tariq, however, had other priorities. He laid the weapons down on the floor and headed towards Lara. "I want to see if the Jew bitch has wet herself," he said, his eyes gleaming.

When Yasim got within four feet of him, Uri lashed out with his left foot, striking out and down at Yasim's right knee. As the Arab crumpled to the floor, Uri struck his cuffs sharply across Yasim's face, driving him into Tariq. Lara was now in the perfect position to kick Tariq sharply in his groin, while slashing him across the face with her cuffs.

As he fell, Lara struck him viciously in the neck with her right foot. He rolled helplessly on the floor while desperately clutching his throat, gasping for air. Simultaneous with this action, Uri pounced on Yasim, gouging both his eyes. Then he struck him with the cuffs directly in the solar plexus, briefly paralyzing him.

All this action had taken place in less than ten seconds. The dimwitted Yusuf, hearing the commotion, briefly left his post and looked in to see what was going on. Totally unprepared for the jumble of bodies on the floor, he gaped at the strange scene. Lara had grabbed one of the AK-47s, flipped off the safety, and ripped Yusuf nearly in two with a short burst. They heard no other noise from the hallway, so were able to relax somewhat.

"You've done this before, I take it," Uri said with sublime understatement.

"Quantico," she reminded him. "Now what do we do with these guys?"

"We cuff 'em and drag 'em along out of here. I imagine the Marines have landed. I'm guessing that's why all the commotion outside." Before leaving, the two agents roughly searched the terrorists, retrieving their clothing, jewelry and sidearms. No way was Uri leaving behind his beloved Desert Eagle.

The two surviving Arabs followed along unresisting, one nearly blind, dragging one leg uselessly, the other barely able to breathe, and bleeding heavily from the wounds inflicted by the enraged Lara. Both needed to be supported to make it down the stairs. Stained with his urine, the front of Tariq's fatigue trousers added to his already disgusting odor.

Outside the building they found small groups of IDF troops patrolling around, apparently looking for survivors. Uri hailed one, a sergeant with a short-range radio. The sergeant and his two mates dropped down into firing position and asked for identities. Uri spoke quickly in Hebrew, apparently with sufficient detail to bring the three soldiers over to them.

Uri introduced the team to Lara, and told them in a brief, very brief, discussion of what they had been through. He also introduced them to the two injured Arabs, who were not interested in conversation.

"Can you take care of these two prisoners?" Uri asked. Seeing the sergeant nod, he then asked for transport for himself and Lara to military headquarters. He needed to make sure the surviving "suicide bombers" were properly identified and placed in secure imprisonment.

Chapter 20

Lara and Uri followed two IDF soldiers to the makeshift headquarters tent. There a major with an identifying tag "Shenhav" filled them in on what had gone on during the past few hours. Tel Aviv had received advance warning of the upcoming terror attack on the Center, but couldn't get troops there in time to prevent it. About half the attackers had been killed in the explosion, most of the others captured. Unfortunately, two American women visitors had been killed and a number injured.

The captured terrorists insisted they were members of Neturei Karta, and were hustled off to imprisonment in Tel Aviv. The rest of the IDF detachment were on a "search and rescue" mission. With battles raging in the North and South, no troops were available other than these few reservists.

Major Shenhav also told Uri that a small number of attackers, appearing to be Hasidim dressed in fatigues, had managed to make an escape. They were last seen headed toward a rock-covered hillside to the southeast. Unfortunately, he had no men available to make an adequate pursuit. However, he said that two of his young men, Daniel and Shai, could be spared if Uri and Lara had enough energy left to chase down the terrorists.

"When do we leave?" Uri answered immediately for them both.

The four of them: Lara, Uri, Daniel and Shai, made their way up the rocky slope, each carried a machine pistol as well as a side arm, with ammunition for both. Their backpacks held water and food for two days, along with smoke and fragmentation grenades. Uri carried the sat phone from which they'd gotten the coordinates of the last transmission to the Mufti. It had come from somewhere on this south-facing, brush covered mountainside. Exactly where was another question.

The setting sun illuminated the slope, but the trees and boulders casting long harsh shadows, made it difficult to see details. The four hunters spread out in nearly a straight line, just within shouting distance of each other. Suddenly, Shai, a young slender man barely eighteen years of age, assigned to the far right, waved to the others, pointing straight up the hill. Trees and boulders obscured their view, but Uri, at the far left, scrambled straight up and motioned for the others to encircle the area that Shai pointed toward.

Shai dropped to the ground, pulling his machine pistol into firing position. At the same time, puffs of dust appeared all around him, the sound of rapid fire followed a second later. From their positions, none of the other three could see the position of the shooters, so could not return fire. The result was inevitable: Shai screamed out in pain as at least two of the heavy rounds found their mark. They were now just three against an unknown number of enemy combatants.

Using his intercom, Uri told Lara and Daniel to hold tight to their positions hidden behind boulders, until twilight fell. Then he and Lara would attempt to come around from the west, while Daniel came straight up under the cover of the rocks and cedars. He surmised the enemy fire had come from a jumble of large boulders directly above them. He guessed some sort of enclosure lay hidden within those rocks. If Daniel and Lara could lay down some distracting fire in the gloom of the twilight, Uri might be able to toss smoke grenades in from above. It seemed their best opportunity as he got confirmation from the others.

The sun rapidly began its dip behind the hills to the west. As it disappeared, Uri made his move around to his left and up the mountain, keeping out of sight behind the cluster of rocks. Lara fired in short, quick bursts straight up the slope, expecting any moment to hear the staccato sound of an AK-47. Suddenly she could see the shape of a man, outlined in the twilight, moving from one boulder to another directly ahead of her, but aiming his weapon to her right. The terrorist must have spotted Daniel, who was moving in that direction. She radioed him to take cover.

The three of them were now less than 50 yards from the enemy position hidden among the rocks. Darkness was coming swiftly now, and it seemed to Uri the best opportunity to attack. Daniel and Lara, at Uri's signal, fired into the enclosed area. To Uri's surprise, it attracted no return fire. Uri took the opportunity to belly crawl to the top of the boulder from which the earlier fire had come. From there he could see a makeshift structure hidden by the large rocks below him. He immediately lobbed in a smoke grenade, a prearranged signal for the other two to move in.

After a couple of short bursts from their machine pistols, Daniel and Lara charged toward the structure. One of them had killed the disguised Arab Lara had seen moving. His body, clad in camouflage fatigues, lay in a pool of blood at the entrance to the plywood structure. Seeing the others, Uri dropped down from his position, and at his signal, they emptied their weapons into the hut. To be certain, Daniel tossed in a fragmentation grenade. They held their hands over their ears against the defining sounds in the enclosed space. In a few seconds, the smoke cleared, and the three carefully entered. Daniel, who had pulled out his sidearm, stayed at the entrance, as the others started to reload their machine pistols.

"Welcome, my friends!" came a voice from directly behind them. "Be so kind as to drop your weapons—slowly, please." Daniel, like Shai a young reservist with no battle experience, misread the situation, dropped to his knees swinging his pistol around. Gunfire struck him from two directions, tearing the weapon from his hands. His head exploded in a mushroom of blood and brains.

Uri and Lara, their weapons not yet reloaded, dropped them and turned. Holding AK-47s and powerful flashlights, two grinning Arabs emerged from their cover in a deep rock crevice. Having discarded all remnants of their Hasidic dress, only their sidelocks remained as mementos of their former disguises. One of them kicked Daniel's lifeless body aside, spitting on it.

"Come in and make yourselves comfortable," said one of the Arabs in surprisingly unaccented English. He motioned with his rifle toward two wooden chairs near the center of the small room. The other Arab laughed crazily and shoved them down. Uri now saw clearly how they had been baited into this trap. The Arabs sacrificed one of their soldiers to bring the three down into the hut, while the other two Arabs waited, hidden in the shallow rock cover. Uri felt more stupid than he ever had in his life. He had sacrificed two good men and put himself and Lara in a position to be the victims of some unspeakable tragedy.

While the first Arab held them at gunpoint, the other searched them roughly, admiring their IMI machine pistols. He tossed them aside along with Lara's handgun. He then came upon Uri's Desert Eagle. "Give me that," the one with the gun commanded. "You'll have no use for this anymore," he said to Uri, stuffing it into his fatigues. "I've always wanted to kill a Jew with one of these."

Uri saw that they had a pair of handcuffs and remembered that he had saved the key he had made from Lara's earring; it was in his pants pocket. Figuring he might need it, he reached in his pocket with his right hand and stuck it between his third and fourth fingers.

"What are you doing there?" the first Arab shouted at him, "take your hands out your pockets, let me see them!"

Uri showed them his hands, carefully hiding the wire between his fingers, in the dim light. Meanwhile, the other Arab lit a camp stove on a small table in the middle of the space. Dancing images of the bizarre scene floated crazily on the rough walls.

"Sit there," the first Arab commanded Uri, shoving him into a rough wooden chair that he placed at the foot of a bed. Uri got his first clear look at him; there was no doubt who he was: The Ghost. Nearly six feet tall, clothed in fatigues, with relatively short black hair and only a light beard, Uri realized he had been shaving to modify his appearance. His complexion, only moderately dark; he could have passed for any of a number of Mediterranean heritages. His eyes were the distinctive feature that Uri remembered from the university pictures he had seen in Texas and recalled from his imprisonment photos. Dark and penetrating, the very essence of evil lurked in them.

"What are you staring at, Jew?" Halibi, The Ghost, shouted at him, shoving him down into the chair. "I know who you are, your glass eye doesn't fool me." He held his rifle pointed at Lara and ordered the other Arab, whom he called Ahmed, to handcuff Uri behind his back in the chair. He walked over to Uri, grabbed him by the hair with one hand, and swiftly plucked out his prosthetic left eye with the other. "You have no need for this anymore, either," he said, laughing, throwing it across the cave.

The Arabs then turned their attention to Lara. Halibi pushed her down onto the wooden bed, and ordered Ahmed to tie her hands onto the two wooden bedposts. "Leave her legs free; we're going to have some fun with the Jewess before we kill her," he said, keeping his eyes fixed on Uri. He produced a straight razor from his pack, eyeing it with obvious anticipation. Uri took the opportunity to slowly move the wire handcuff-key down into his right thumb and index finger.

Halibi roughly grabbed Lara's right leg and pulled it to the side, as Ahmed did the same with her left. Lara, fearing the worst, screamed out, "Don't; I'm not clean!"

"A likely story, Jew whore," Halibi shouted at her, slapping her face. They began tearing at her fatigue jeans, using the razor to strip them down to her knees.

Uri slipped his makeshift key into the cuffs behind his back, hoping that in their excitement the Arabs wouldn't notice his movements. Lara lay terrified, immobilized on the bed. Uri's heart slammed hard into his chest, one rapid beat after another, as he desperately maneuvered the key into the lock. He knew he would have only one chance.

"You go after me," Halibi said to the wildly excited Ahmed, as he dropped his fatigue trousers to the floor. He then used the razor to easily tear Lara's underpants away from her body. "Hold on to that leg," he commanded Ahmed, as he pinned Lara's other leg to the bed. Uri noted that, in their frenzy, they had put aside their AK-47s. "Unclean?" Halibi said laughing, as he looked at Lara, helpless on the bed. "Perhaps we need to do a little touching up," he said, grabbing the razor.

Uri felt the lock click open finally, and freed his hands. He was able to just catch Lara's eye and give her a slight nod. The Arabs were too intent on their immediate purpose to notice.

"You'll have the pleasure of knowing two real men before you plunge into hell," the Ghost said, his dark eyes gleaming. He then pulled down his filthy undershorts, showing himself to be totally aroused. Ahmed was himself nearly senseless with excitement.

At this instant, Uri caught Lara's eye and gave her a second nod, and leaped to his feet, rushing at Halibi, holding his open handcuffs as a weapon. Halibi, caught completely by surprise, reached for his pistol, forgetting his pants were down around his ankles. Ahmed, also caught completely off guard, let go of Lara's leg for an instant. The movement gave Lara all the time she needed to launch a perfectly placed kick onto the Arab's nose, smashing the bone into his brain. He crumpled to the ground.

The Ghost stumbled attempting to avoid Uri's charge; his feet hopelessly tangled in his trousers. Uri hit the Arab with the handcuffs directly in the jaw, paralyzing him for an instant. At the same time, he smashed his foot into the Arab's knee, sending him crashing to the floor in agony. Pinning the helpless terrorist to the ground, Uri picked the straight razor up off the bed. He saw the terror in the man's eyes. Before tending to him further, Uri first used the razor to quickly slash Lara's right hand free of its rope. He then turned his attention back to The Ghost, who lay trembling on the ground.

Lara untied her other hand. She found the weapons the Arabs had thrown aside and smashed the butt of an AK-47 into Ahmed's face, but it was unnecessary. He was already dead, his lifeless eyes staring into space, bright red blood covering the ground around his head. At the same instant, she saw Uri bent over Halibi. The Ghost emitted a bloodcurdling shriek that came to a sudden halt. His back still to Lara, Uri pulled the filthy blanket off the bed and threw it over Halibi's body.

Realizing she was in need of a covering for her legs, she pulled her clothing together as best she could. Fashioning a crude belt from a piece of the rope they had tied her with, she managed to hold them onto her slim hips. Uri helped her rip a blanket into a makeshift skirt also tied at the waist. It wasn't Vogue, but at least it gave her a modicum of dignity.

They looked at each other just a moment. Then Uri said, "Let's collect our stuff and get downhill. If you can grab the packs, I'll get the lanterns." They made a quick search of the cave, looking for anything that might be of value. Uri made sure to retrieve his beloved Desert Eagle, along with their machine pistols. Finding nothing else, they headed out of the crude hut and down the slope, with the help of the kerosene lamps.

It took them about 30 minutes to reach a fairly flat area, one that could accommodate a helicopter. Uri found his sat phone in his pack, punched in a few numbers, waited a moment, and then barked some quick Hebrew into the instrument. Hearing what he was waiting for, he put the phone down. The two washed their hands and faces with the water in their packs, each taking a long drink from the remainder. Still breathing hard, they tried to put together all that happened.

Uri finally looked at her, grabbed her and held her hard, as they laughed with the release of what seemed like endless anxiety. They placed the lantern out on the center of the flat plain as a marker, then moved to the edge and sat down against their packs. After a long moment, Lara asked, "What did you do to him? That shriek, I didn't..."

"Let's just say The Ghost didn't enjoy his last meal."

Chapter 21

Lara and Uri watched as the two helicopters approached, circled and landed, their lights playing out over the deserted landscape. The pilot of the first chopper flashed a greeting to the two exhausted agents as they touched down.

"Everything all right, sir?" The commander of the rescue mission asked Uri. Uri noticed him glancing at his left eye, or what was left of it.

"It is now, Lieutenant Friedman," Uri replied, glancing at the airman's name tag. He realized he had forgotten to replace his eye patch, and rummaged through his trousers to find it. "Listen, Lieutenant, I lost two of my men in the fight. You'll find their remains in a little hidden structure just to the right of a couple of big cedars standing by a large boulder." He pointed up the slope as Friedman directed his second-in-command to shine the copter's searchlights in that direction. They spotted the landmarks about 1000 yards up the hill. "That's the place," Uri said.

"I'd go with you, but in the shape I'm in, you'd probably have to carry me."

The lieutenant got four of his men together and gave them instructions. They brought two stretchers and began to move in the direction of the hut. "Just a second, lieutenant," said Uri in rapid Hebrew. "There are three Arabs up there; you can search the bodies, but leave them there. Their buddies need to see what we've got in store for them."

Friedman looked at Uri for just a second, then nodded and had a brief discussion with his men. The five rescuers headed up the hill with the stretchers. The pilot of the second helicopter, the smaller of the two, asked if Uri and Lara wanted to head back to base. Uri repeated the question to Lara, who nodded in the affirmative. They both needed a hot bath, a meal, and a good night's sleep. Their debriefing could wait till morning.

The two exhausted agents sat side-by-side for the noisy, bumpy 30 minute ride back to Tel Aviv. Uri forgot decorum and draped his arm over Lara's shoulder. To hell with it, he thought; this has been one of the toughest days of my life. He could only imagine the terror that Lara had felt. Suddenly she sat up with a start: "The Ghost; how can we prove we got him?"

"DNA, I took a sample."

"Oh," Lara said, settling back. Jumping up again a moment later, she said, "You didn't...!"

Uri laughed and said, "No, I just took a piece of an earlobe."

At the base, a car was waiting for them. "The general has rooms set up for you in the guest barracks," the driver said as they climbed in. They found that Shimon had thoughtfully provided them with kits of fresh clothes and toiletries. They stuffed them into their packs, thanked the driver, and wearily made their way up the steps into the hotel the IDF maintained for VIPs.

"I've got two rooms set up and ready for you," the desk sergeant said, recognizing Uri immediately; he had replaced his eye patch. "Let me get somebody give you a hand with your things," he said. Uri made a quick gesture, indicating they would take care of themselves, and held his hand out for the keys.

The rooms were on the second floor, but Uri didn't bother opening both. The two exhausted warriors fell into one room, but Lara warned Uri to stay off the bed. "You're a bloody mess you know," she said. "I'll take a quick shower and get in bed. You follow," she commanded. Uri didn't argue. He did however, call the desk and ask for whatever food was available.

"Just leave it on a tray outside room 206, okay?"

Less than twenty minutes later, the food arrived, they had cleaned up, and were sitting up in bathrobes, greedily gorging themselves. Until that moment, they hadn't realized how long it'd been since they'd had any real food. It didn't take long for them to clean the tray. He reached for her, and pulled off her bathrobe. His own flew to the floor an instant later, as they climbed under the covers.

"My God," she said, finally able to relax. "Did you ever really think we'd get out of there?"

"To be honest, I was too damn scared to even think about it. The only thing on my mind was getting your little earring into that lock. By the way, where'd you learn that kick, Quantico?"

She nodded, nuzzling into his shoulder. "Amazing what you remember when you need to, isn't it?" She reached up and gently caressed the area around his left eye. "You're gonna need a new marble," she laughed. Then she kissed him there, and tousled his hair. "How are we going to explain the fact we only used one room?"

"I think of all the things we're going to have to explain to Shimon, that's the one least likely to come up," he teased, kissing her lovingly on the mouth. "Want to watch TV?" They both laughed as he turned off the light.

\Chapter 22

Nizar al-Kuzhani, the new military chief of Hezbollah, sat cross-legged on his newly-acquired oriental carpet, dining on his evening meal of roast lamb, mixed with chickpeas. His eldest wife, Yana, had prepared it for him, as usual; while he preferred one of the younger, Zeinah, or Kamar, to satisfy his other desires, Yana was still best at feeding his ample belly.

The events of the past few weeks had been spectacular, to say the least. Savoring the remains of his meal, he thought back on the unparalleled successes of the Muslim Brotherhood.

Egypt had come back into the fold, the world's largest Arab country, now ruled by sharia law. In Syria, the militant, fundamentalist *al Nusra Front* had finally taken control after eliminating the former president.

Abu Mohammed al-Jawlani, al Nusra's political leader, had gone on record supporting the Al Qaeda chief, Sheikh Ayman al-Zawahiri. After the unfortunate death of the great and revered Osama bin Laden, Zawahiri, hunted in vain these many years by the vaunted American military, had become the symbol of the Islamic Revolution.

Under his spiritual guidance, the huge forces of the Muslim Brotherhood were about to embark on the greatest of all the triumphs since the start of the Arab Spring: elimination of the Zionist entity known as "Israel."

Now that the great campaign was about to begin, Abu Mohammed al-Jawlani had come to al-Kuzhani to ask for an alliance: He requested that the Hezbollah forces join the new Syrian army in removing the Jew from the Middle East.

Al-Kuzhani's Hezbollah army would join up with al Nusra's magnificent Syrian forces in removing the Zionist stain from the Nation of Islam. Their combined forces would strike, without warning, from the North, using the Lebanese border, the Hezbollah stronghold, as their launching point.

The plans, though talked about for months, finally came to fruition two weeks ago at a meeting in Nabatieh, at the southern end of the Beqaa Valley. There Al-Kuzhani met Yaman Al Mahainu, who brought word from the Mufti. Of course, in attendance also was the head of Hezbollah, Mustafa Bader al-Din. But the most important figure to appear was Sheikh Aboud Al Agha, the leader of al Nusra itself.

There was no doubt now: the entire operation was in order. Al Mahainu, the Mufti's trusted confidant, confirmed the coordinated attack. The forces of Hezbollah and Syria would strike the northern border of the Zionists at sunrise May 14. The forces of the Muslim Brotherhood in Egypt, fortified by their new allies in the Sinai, the Takfir, would assault into the south of Israel the next day. The Israelis would be overwhelmed by the combined surprise attacks.

In the North, the Syrian al Nusra Front and Hezbollah, would impact at key points along a twenty mile front. The attack would reach from Quazzani in the East, overwhelming the Israeli town of Kiryat Shmona. These troops would be comprised of Hezbollah from the Beqaa Valley, training ground for fighters for the past forty years. From there the front would stretch westward to the village of Rmaich. Here there was known to be an outpost of young Israeli reservists, untested in battle.

The Syrian soldiers of al Nusra would simultaneously attack the scattered Zionist forts on toward the coast. All of these Israeli settlements and military forts had been under surveillance for some months. The comings and goings of the soldiers, occurring on a regular basis, had been carefully recorded.

On the other hand, the Muslim forces would move with deliberate speed into position the previous night, which they knew would be moonless.

They would drive southward on the first day to the village of Nahariya, on the coast, eastward to Safed in the Galilee. The Israelis, always anticipating an attack into the Golan, well to the east, would be totally unprepared for this strike into their heartland.

By sheer force of numbers, the Syrians would overwhelm the unprepared Israelis. Thousands of Soviet built T-72 tanks, along with a similar number of artillery pieces, consisting mainly of 130 mm guns, would be moving along the entire front. In the air above them would be the formidable force of hundreds of Russian-built MiG 26 and MiG 29 fighter jets.

Of course, all these numbers had been drastically reduced by the Civil War that had overthrown the regime of the former president. Still the sky and land would be trembling with their advance, striking terror all along the front.

The main advantage they had was the sheer force of troops. The combined forces of Hezbollah and al Nusra would number over 100,000. If things went as planned, the Israelis would be on the run by the end of the day, through the fertile Galilee plane toward Haifa. The next day, the Egyptians would strike at least as far into southern Israel.

The success of the entire plan, of course, depended upon the lack of assistance to Israel from the United States and their allies. This was assured, according to Al Mahainu, by a provocative action concocted by the famous "Ghost," Saleh Halibi. It was rumored that he had somehow put together the wondrous destruction of the synagogue in New York, killing an untold number of Jews on their holiest day last Fall. That event caused celebration all through the Muslim world.

No one doubted the large number of Israeli surveillance drones and satellites; however, Hezbollah and Syria had both been conducting exercises, called "war games," in the region for several weeks now, and the distances involved in the cross-border attack were not great. So, in the span of one moonless night, hundreds of tanks and thousands of men would be moved without causing undue alarm; however, up to this time, the Arab agents planted amongst the Israeli troops had not reported anything at all unusual in the way of planning for defending against a surprise attack.

The morning of the blessed day began with a cool onshore breeze, always considered a favorable sign. At precisely 0500, the rumble of tanks and other heavy machinery, including the towed artillery pieces, broke the silence. Al-Kazhani could only imagine in his mind's eye, the stunning mass of arms and men stretching across from the sea to the heights above Kiryat Shmona. The sky suddenly filled with scores of Russian-made

MiGs, headed south in a protective shield above the troops. This must have been what it looked like on September 1, 1939, as the massive Nazi blitzkrieg poured over the border into Poland. Al-Kazhani had never been so proud of his men and his heritage. His heart pounded with anticipation as he saw his own two brigades of men striking southward toward the border.

As the sun rose, from a hilltop near the border, they all could see the Syrian aircraft strafing what must have been the enemy's northernmost outposts and villages. Al-Kazhani had expected at least some minimum resistance in the form of surface-to-air missiles or antiaircraft fire, but there was none. Apparently the attack had indeed come as a complete surprise to the Zionist intruders.

The combined Arab forces advanced steadily along southward as the day progressed. Al-Kazhani receiving updates on his satellite phone from the brigade commanders further east toward Quizzani. They also reported no enemy action, and continued to move steadily southward. At 1000, Al-Kazhani checked in with Aboud Al Agha, the acting Syrian army chief, to find that his forces also had encountered little to no resistance. Skirmishes of small-arms fire occurred, but the enemy melted away to the south without any serious engagements.

The largest battles of the day had been expected at Kiryat Shmona, the heavily-occupied town at the northernmost tip of a beautiful valley. Lately, it had become a favorite tourist destination with a luxurious hotel and observation tram. In prior decades, dating back to the 1920s, however, the village had been known as the target of terrorist assaults from Arabs dressed as Israelis. Their prime objective had been children, clearly the most effective means of inflicting pain.

Al-Kazhani had especially looked forward to hearing of massive numbers of civilian casualties, as the Syrian forces overran the town and slaughtered its defenders. He was surprised to the point of bewilderment when he heard that Aboud's forces had met only scattered resistance, and that the entire population had been evacuated. They saw no need to destroy the structures built by the Israelis; they would make fine residences for their new Lebanese occupants.

Still, as wonderful as this news was, it triggered a worrisome thought. How had the Israelis known to evacuate the town, and why was it that they had put up virtually no resistance to the Arab advance?

The negative thoughts quickly dissipated in the thrill of victory, and the march through the Galilee of its rightful owners continued. The military commanders quickly decided to forgo their first day's goal, and move more rapidly southward, covering ground as quickly as their troops and armor were able. The Arabs poured through villages of Hurlesh, Jish, Ma'alot Tarshiha and other small farming communities. As in Kiryat Shmona and Rmaich, all were nearly deserted, and the only resistance the troops encountered was small arms fire, meant only to slow their advance.

By 1500 hours, they had more than doubled their anticipated first-day's goal, and all across the front, the troops had stopped for some well-deserved celebration. They prepared to bivouac, enjoy some food, rest, and dancing.

And that's when all hell broke loose. The skies above, which had been filled with Syrian MiGs, suddenly exploded in balls of flame as surface-to-air missiles, seemingly from nowhere, splattered the planes across the landscape. Those that escaped the initial onslaught, raced northward, seeking to escape across the border, however; there they were met by what seemed like 100 or more Israeli planes, equipped with the modern American long-range, MRAAM, radar-guided missiles. All along their newly acquired front, the Arabs on the ground were horrified to see their Air Force disappearing in clouds of smoke and flame. A few pilots did manage to escape their burning aircraft, only to plunge headlong into the ground below.

Al-Kazhani and his fellow commanders only now recognized the trap into which they had fallen. In the ecstasy of the rapid forward movement through enemy territory, they had far out-reached their supply lines. In less than thirty minutes, they saw the inevitable: a huge mobilized Israeli force approaching them from the south. Phalanxes of Israeli Sabra M60 tanks bombarded the old Russian-built Syrian T-54 and T-55 tanks with their unprotected ammunition supplies. The Syrian tanks exploded like children's toys under the onslaught.

The Arab commanders' sat phones lit up constantly with wild, urgent messages from all along the front. The troops, without any experience or guidance, dashed hopelessly around, looking for any sort of cover. Only their 130 mm guns provided them with any sort of protective fire. Even that wilted under the barrage of the Israeli M109 155 mm cannons.

As the sun began its rapid descent into the Mediterranean, the troops on both sides withdrew for fear of causing casualties among their own men. Al-Kazhani finally got through to Mustafa Bader al-Din back in Beirut. The background noise at Hezbollah headquarters was stupefying. Apparently they had been getting reports from both the Hezbollah and Syrian brigade commanders in the Galilee. From what Al-Kazhani could tell, it was near chaos. Both Mustafa and Aboud Al Agha, head of the Syrian forces, in near panic mode, were at a loss as to what to do, neither of them having any real battle experience. Leading terrorist attacks on groups of unsuspecting civilians had not given them any sort of experience in battle against organized armies.

"It is essential that our reserves be brought in at once!" Al-Kazhani screamed into the phone. "Where are they now?"

"They are being held back at the border!" shouted the overwhelmed al-Din.

"You must rush them down here overnight to support us!" Al-Kazhani yelled in return. "Our lines are less than ten miles south of you. You must send at least 50,000 troops to us, along with more of your long-range guns, and all the F-16s at your disposal. Otherwise the Israelis will overcome us at first light. The pathway is clear all the way from the Lebanese border. The reinforcements will not run into any hostile action!"

"But my dear Al-Kazhani," came the distressed reply, "the Syrian reservists are as fearful as we are of leaving Southern Lebanon and the Beqaa undefended!"

"Can you please point out to Aboud that our entire force down here will be lost *for certain* without reinforcements? We will have to gather together enough of the civilian population to protect the Beqaa. At any rate, the Israelis will have their hands full fighting the Egyptians. They could not possibly spare any troops to attack our homeland."

It was a powerful argument, one that Mustafa Bader al-Din could not refute. He knew there would be, hopefully, a raging battle going on soon in the Negev, in southern Israel. Surely the Zionists could not have anticipated this two-front war.

"All right, you will have your reinforcements before first light," Mustafa shouted above the din surrounding him. "At least we have the advantage of another moonless night; we should be able to move rapidly without fear of engagement."

Hearing this encouraging news, Al-Kazhani instructed the Hezbollah and Syrian brigade commanders to form a protective perimeter. By first light they would have enough reinforcements to regain the advantage and drive deep into the Israeli heartland.

Chapter 23

News of the Arab attack in northern Israel spread swiftly across the world. CNN and the Arab network, the most watched international news networks, broadcast vastly different accounts of the situation.

CNN reported that they had been given aerial reconnaissance photos from the Israelis, showing massive movement of troops across the Lebanese border. According to the Israeli news source, the attack consisted of a combined force of Hezbollah and Syrian Muslim Brotherhood commands. They had encountered little resistance, according to the Israeli source, and had advanced several miles into Israeli territory.

The Arab network, in its quiet, authoritative manner, had quite a different assessment of the situation. They said their sources on the ground reported a surprise Israeli attack on civilian populations in southern Lebanon. This prompted an urgent plea from the Lebanese government for help from both Hezbollah and Syria.

In reply to the aerial reconnaissance photos showing the massive movement of unprovoked al Nusra military into Israel, the Syrian attaché had merely shrugged. Had they not heard of "Photoshop?" he replied. The so-called satellite pictures were merely fakes; totally credible sources on the ground had verified the initial Israeli incursion. The combined Arab forces had driven the cowardly Zionist attackers back across the "1967" border.

When asked by the Arab network reporter how far Hezbollah and Syria were prepared to move southward, the attache's answer was simple: "Until the land of Palestine has been returned to its rightful owners."

The reaction across the Arab world was swift and universally gleeful. In Cairo, Tripoli, Damascus, Ramallah and other Muslim capitals in the region, people literally danced in the streets. News cameras set up quickly in their broadcasts to a

155

waiting world; to capture the outpouring of triumph and excitement. Exuberant crowds, similar to those after the Brooklyn synagogue bombing, filled the streets. Television cameras caught images, not seen since 9/11, of the youthful crowd, nearly all male, as they triumphantly stomped on U.S. flags, spitting upon them and setting them afire, and gleefully doing the same with photos of the Israeli prime minister and the U.S. president.

In Western cities, the reaction was muted; in fact, viewers watched in widespread disbelief. CNN continued to show on-the-ground photographs taken by their own reporters. In addition, military analysts verified the assembly of satellite reconnaissance photos, a mix of U.S. and Israeli aerial and ground images. The experts didn't doubt that the images were genuine. Time-stamped views showed unequivocally that there had been no Israeli incursion. They also verified that there had been little to no resistance as the Arab troops poured across the border.

The reports of CNN and other Western news media had no effect on the wildly enthusiastic Arab crowds. Government and religious leaders lent their support to the version of events being widely accepted in all the Muslim countries. Iran gave atypical encouragement for the Arab attack. Iran, almost completely Shi'a, seemed proud of the accomplishments of their mainly Sunni Arab neighbors. Wild celebration filled the streets of Tehran, celebration of a type normally discouraged by the ruling ayatollahs.

In Washington, officials shared widespread anxiety over the apparent encouragement of the public demonstrations. The reaction in U.S. and other Western cities was skepticism. People seemed more inclined to believe the CNN reports than those of Al Jazeera and the other Arab networks.

In comparison, the Middle East governments showed no doubt as to the advance of the Arab forces. Official statements came from the Arab capitals in Libya, Tunisia, Egypt, Syria, and a host of others decrying the "Israeli aggression" and applauding the "brave Arab resistance."

The jubilation in the Middle East continued for nearly the full day, until the television reports from the Western media could not be easily dismissed. Footage showing Israeli F-35's shooting down the Syrian MiGs was just too real to be rejected. The battle on the ground appeared to grind to a halt as the Arab forces no longer had their complete air cover. Both sides, Arab and Israeli, seem to be consolidating their positions for the evening.

The Arab media continued their campaign of misinformation as long as possible; finally, they had to give in to the reality that was apparent to everyone. However, rather than broadcasting the actual events as they unfolded, they turned to other topics, such as the unrest in Yemen and other outlying Arab states.

By dawn on May 15, two of Egypt's four armored divisions, and three of its infantry divisions started their movement through Sinai, headed for the Israeli border. Each division had four infantry brigades, each with 1000 men. Egypt's Air Force was powered mainly by 100 F-16s, purchased from the United States, the money given to them, of course, by the United States. Their 2000 tanks mainly Abrams A-1s, purchased in the same manner.

The main thrust of this force drove eastward in what they officially called "military maneuvers," but observers in both the United States and Israel clearly understood it as preparation for an attack.

In Cairo, Rabiah Tariq al-Khalid, the new supreme leader of Egypt, met with Merira ibn El Sayed, his military adviser. El Sayed had finalized their plan with the Grand Mufti, and the Syrian, Yaman Al Mahainu.

As the great day approached, al-Khalid grew nervous. "How certain are you that the Syrians will keep their word?"

Al-Khalid was a strongly built man of 45 years, with a hawk-like nose and prominent chin. His thick, dark eyebrows met to form a solid ridge over dark eyes with thick, curly, black hair completed the picture of a terrifying predator. He had gained the seat of power as the Muslim Brotherhood in Egypt had overwhelmed all of their opposition in the aftermath of the revolution in 2012. Reputed to have killed more than fifty men with his bare hands, a legend that carried a great deal of weight with the illiterate Egyptians, his appearance and bearing added to his mystique; his leadership was unchallenged.

"I am absolutely certain," replied El Sayed. A tall, slender man, with calm demeanor, El Sayed exuded confidence. His gray-green eyes complemented his olive complexion, giving him a rather noble bearing. Clearly of mixed ancestry, he nevertheless was accepted as fully Egyptian. He had a reputation of being quite a military scholar, studying both in England and the United States. Amusingly, both countries had paid for his academic training. Considered an ally of the West in any oncoming hostilities, he nurtured that supposition on their part, realizing the recent campaigns against Iraq and Afghanistan had left the West feeling vulnerable to any extremist military leaders.

"After our meeting with the Mufti, we spoke by secure satellite phone," El Sayed continued. "He assured me they have 1100 tanks and 150,000 men deployed along the Galilee already. The American television station, CNN, has gotten hold of American satellite photos showing near that number. The Syrians have assured the U.S. State Department that they are merely holding military exercises."

"Does that seem odd, considering we are doing the same thing in the Sinai?" said al-Khalid.

"Yes, of course. But when they spoke with our General Al-Falani, he assured them that this was standard practice for us each Spring around this time."

"And that satisfied the television reporters?" al-Khalid asked nervously.

"Well, of course he had to point out that Israel is our common enemy. He reminded them that the Zionists have attacked not only Egypt and Syria, but also the helpless Palestinians, whose land they still occupy. And because they have attacked us not once, but no fewer than four times, we must remain prepared. He pointed out that our preparations are strictly defensive in nature."

"Well, then we must keep up the pretense a while longer. If our attacks seem coordinated it will be difficult to explain, even to the United Nations," said al-Khalid with a sly smile.

As it is common knowledge that the United Nations had become nothing more than a front for the Muslim-controlled countries, the Western governments fear retaliation for any action that might be considered "aggressive." After all, the threats of terrorism and stoppage in oil flow hold the so-called democracies totally at bay. No matter what the provocation, the UN Security Council would vote to reprimand Israel or the United States for any paramilitary activity that led to loss of life. Vetoes by the United States would make no difference, as the UN has no power anyway.

"Precisely," replied El Sayed to al-Khalid's point. "That is why our attacks will not be simultaneous. To show their good intentions, in answer to your earlier question, the Syrians will attack the day *before* we do—and they will be accompanied by several garrisons of Hezbollah fighters. They will pour across the Lebanese border, destroying the Israeli forts and villages."

Al-Khalid smiled and relaxed somewhat. *I have chosen well,* he thought as he gazed at El Sayed. His commander-in-chief had selected excellent generals, men who would be ruthless when the time came to finally evict and eliminate the Jews.

Victory in Egypt for the Brotherhood had not come easily. As had been the case in Syria, much turmoil and bloodshed preceded the takeover. And, as in Syria, the Muslim Brotherhood claimed control over the people and the military.

El Sayed, for his part, was pleased to see the faith that his supreme leader exhibited in him. It suited him well to be second-in-command. In the newly-freed Arab lands, power was an uncertain thing. If one didn't show merciless authority, one might not see the morning sun. Others waited like jackals for the first sign of weakness.

After being dismissed by Al Khalid, El Sayed returned to his office in the building formerly occupied by Hosni Mubarak's police chief. He quickly got on the satellite phone and attempted to reach his old friend, General Saleh Ibn al-Falani, who had been given the title, "Commanding General." It was al-Falani who would lead the troops in the upcoming campaign. It was absolutely necessary that he have generals whom he trusted and were respected by their men. The slightest signs of weakness were fatal among the hordes of willing, but poorly trained men. The first few months since the complete takeover by the re-organized Muslim Brotherhood had seen a great deal of change in the government. Elections did not produce the desired result, and were deemed invalid by Al Khalid. His imposing stature and uncompromising nature insured little dissent. *Might assumed right* in the Arab countries, and he had the large, but disorganized Egyptian army solidly behind him, at least for now. Those officers who showed any vacillation simply disappeared during the night. This became quite clear to the others, and to the enlisted men.

As in Nazi Germany or Stalin's Russia, one followed the orders of the supreme leader or risked harsh consequences. Life in the army wasn't so bad after all, especially compared with life on the streets of Cairo. Immigrants from around the countryside arrived daily, with neither skill nor money, begging for scraps of food. At least in the army, one received something resembling two meals a day, and a uniform. The latter might have been worn by one or two others in the times before, but it kept out the cold of the nights and the harsh, blowing sands of the day.

El Sayed reached his commanding general after about 15 minutes of conversations with illiterate recruits. "Saleh, my friend," he shouted into the phone with relief. "Give me an update on our position."

"Splendid, my commander!" Al-Falani replied with undisguised glee. "Our first line of tanks, the third, seventh, and 110th brigades, are in position for attack all along the border with Gaza and Palestine. Two infantry divisions are with them, all awaiting your orders for the advance."

"And the rest of our forces?"

"As you have ordered, the other two armored divisions and four infantry are in place, hidden in the dunes near El Arish."

El Sayed relaxed in his chair, a plush remnant from the old regime. He picked up his cigar, a wonderful rich Cuban, and took a puff. Things were going well, just as planned. "And our air force?"

"We have 300 of the American F-16's ready at Almazzi, Abu Suwayr, and Al Mansurah. They will be flying support over the initial thrust of tanks and infantry as we discussed."

"We will wait until the day after the Syrian attack, as planned, and then our initial line of tanks and infantry will move across the border."

"Exactly, my commander! We will crush the enemy in just a few days. Are our compatriots ready as well?"

Al-Falani paused slightly as he considered their untested new allies, the forces of the "Takfir," under the leadership of the feared religious fanatic, known as Abu Ahmed. Abu Ahmed had not achieved leadership of the Takfir through adherence to the teachings of the Qu'ran alone. He, like many other Arab leaders, had shown his disregard for human life, and had ended the lives of many with his own hands.

The relations between the ruling Muslim Brotherhood and some of the gangs roaming the Sinai desert were tenuous at best. The Takfir were the fiercest fighters in the region, and Al-Falani was pleased, or at least relieved, to have their support. He knew their main allegiance was with Al Qaeda, and they considered all but the most fanatic of Muslims to be nonbelievers. Even the Bedouins, who had roamed the Sinai for thousands of years, feared of the Takfir, but couldn't be counted upon for any aid in the upcoming fight.

El Sayed had just about given up on the status of the telephone communication, when Al-Falani finally responded.

"I am just about to make doubly certain. Before I contact them again, I want to be able to assure them that our own forces are in place and prepared to strike. We can count on the Takfir to drive across the border as we have discussed. May Allah be with you and all of us."

With that, El Sayed shut off his sat phone and took another satisfying puff on his cigar. Things really were working out splendidly. The Zionists' days were numbered.

At that same moment outside Tel Aviv, an IDF Sergeant, a member of Aman, the Israeli army intelligence service, shut off his receiver. He then completed his memorandum and sent it off immediately to headquarters, labeling it "most urgent."

Chapter 24

In Khan Yunis, in western Gaza, the Takfir second-in-command, Hishem Al Sa'adam, met with Mumtaz Daghmush, titular head of Hamas. Hishem, known for his tactical experience in battle, was a small, thin, religious man, with a scraggly beard, who had little physical presence. Daghmush, on the other hand, was a brute of a man, large and muscular. He was clean-shaven in disregard of the rules of Islam, rejecting other laws of personal behavior as well. He was reputed to take orders from no one.

Both men were sought after by the Egyptians as well as the Zionists for their crimes: each had been responsible for murdering hundreds of infidels, praise be to Allah. Now they had a chance to participate in the historic restoration of Palestine, and the return of Al Quds as the center of all Islam. For too long had Al Quds been known as "Jerusalem," the name given to it by the Jews and their infidel Christian collaborators.

Each of them, Hishem Al Sa'adam and Mumtaz Daghmush, had little trust in the other. Both were extreme Sunnis, and hated the Shi'a almost as much as the Jews. But both also knew that liberating Palestine came above all other conflict. Their internal fight for control of Gaza would have to be put aside for the ultimate victory. At least that was the plan.

Hishem had other worries. In addition to pleasing his superior, Abu Ahmed, and the Al Qaeda agents who watched their every move, the Bedouins could be a problem. They had never associated themselves in any way with the Muslim Revolution. The Takfir did not permit anything but the strongest ties with Islam. In a confrontation, his men might just as easily begin firing upon the Bedouins as the Jews. The Israelis had allowed the Bedouins easy movement across the border, thus avoiding any animosity. This was not going to be a simple operation.

163

El Sayed could barely sleep the night before the Syrians were to attack. Even before dawn he flipped his television between CNN and the Arab network, waiting for any news of the burgeoning hostilities. Finally, at nearly 0600, both channels interrupted their normal scheduling to announce that major fighting had begun on the Lebanese-Israel border.

The Arab network had several reporters in the field; one, a female, completely covered except for her eyes. As El Sayed watched, she described the action occurring somewhere behind her. She described it as an Israeli attack on Lebanon, being repelled by a coalition of Syrian army regulars and Hezbollah fighters. In the background, El Sayed could see motor-driven howitzers firing at an unseen enemy.

In the camera's eye, a multitude of troops fired their rifles and screamed, "Allahu Akbar!" as they raced forward. Those closest to the camera waved their fists in the air, smiling triumphantly. The reporter was in a village called Ma'alot Tarshiha, the northern Israeli border town where the well-known "Stone in the Galilee" International Sculpture Symposium was held. Her cameraman panned over some of the stone sculptures to evidence the fact that they were indeed a few miles south of the disputed southern Lebanese border.

Another reporter for the Arab network, this one male, showed ecstatic Syrian troops running through the Zionist town they called Kiryat Shmona. Signs testifying to that were nailed on deserted buildings and shops. The jubilant soldiers fired their rifles at nothing in particular, breaking store windows, as they made their way uncontested through the town.

No enemy combatants, that is, Israelis, could be seen in the reporters' views. Interviews given sporadically with field officers of the Muslim Brotherhood, verified that the Zionists had been routed. The Israelis had attacked Lebanese settlements, the officers stated, just before dawn, and had been driven back. The forces of the Brotherhood were now advancing all the way west to the Mediterranean, pushing the cowardly Jews southward towards Tel Aviv.

El Sayed got a somewhat different analysis when he switched over to CNN. According to them, it was the Syrians, along with Hezbollah volunteers, who initiated the hostilities. Satellite photos, apparently obtained from U.S. sources, showed troops, tanks, and motorized guns moving southward, all along the Lebanese-Israel border; however, no Israeli forces could be seen. No evidence of the Israeli incursion, as reported by the Arab sources, was apparent.

Interviews with U.S. State Department officials confirmed the fact that the Arab troops had indeed invaded northern Israel; however, they stated categorically that there was no report of any Israeli military action. El Sayed relaxed; things were going exactly as planned.

Just then, his cell phone rang. Checking the caller, he saw that it was Abu Ahmed's second-in-command, Hishem Al Sa'adam. Ahmed had full trust in Hishem, he had assured El Sayed. Although small in stature, he had the heart of the lion, Ahmed maintained; however, there was no reason Hishem should be telephoning.

In the first place, any communication should have come from Abu Ahmed himself, not his lieutenant. Secondly, the forces of Takfir and Hamas should be preparing for imminent assault. They must have seen the television reports of the initial victorious Syrian offensive. This should have removed any remaining doubt as to their battle plan.

Accepting the call, El Sayed, alarmed to hear a nearly incoherent babbling from the nervous little Hishem, ordered, "Calm down, you fool, and speak rationally. What's going on?" He tried to keep any suggestion of fear from his voice, "and why isn't General Abu Ahmed himself calling?"

He heard rapid, shallow breathing at the other end of the line, and could picture the small man trying to gather the courage to deliver some news; clearly news that was not good.

"General Ahmed has been shot! There has been a violent disagreement!" Hishem paused, apparently trying to pull himself together.

"Calm down! Just give me the facts," El Sayed ordered, his heart sinking. His part in the grand operation had not yet even begun, and his command was falling apart.

Hishem began again: "There was a dispute at the time of evening prayer. The forces of Hamas, they are completely irreligious. They were drinking, whoring and smoking hashish when they should have been at prayer! Abu Ahmed immediately sought out their leader, whom you may know: Mumtaz Daghmush."

El Sayed of course knew Daghmush, a fierce, violent man, veteran of many battles with the Israelis in their raids on the Hamas rocket bases within Gaza. El Sayed's fears of allying the Takfir with Hamas had been quelled after the first meeting between Daghmush and Hishem. He realized now, too late as it turned out, that he should have sent Abu Ahmed himself. He could picture the violent scene even before Hishem related it to him.

"The trouble began immediately, as soon as we entered Gaza and saw the immoral actions of the Hamas soldiers. It looked like a scene out of a Hollywood movie, the drinking, the display of flesh ..."

"Never mind that," interrupted El Sayed, "What happened to cause the injury to Abu Ahmed?"

"Well, of course, as soon as the general saw the debauchery, he asked for Daghmush," continued Hishem. He paused to take a few more breaths.

"Go ahead, man, get on with it!" shouted El Sayed,

"The two men met outside one of the cafés," Hishem continued. "Daghmush appeared to be inebriated. He laughed when our general demanded that the Hamas troops cease defiling the Prophet and prostrate themselves in shame for their hideous behavior ..."

"And did they?" asked El Sayed, fully knowing the answer.

"No. The two just stood there, face-to-face. As you know, both are very large, fearsome men."

"And they began brawling, I suppose, right out there in the street, in front of the men?" El Sayed asked. He feared the worst.

"No, sir. One of the Hamas, who was on the roof of the café, shot general Abu Ahmed once, in the abdomen."

El Sayed gasped, "What then, did your Takfir return fire?"

"No, sir, we saw that we were outnumbered, and so I ordered our corpsmen to retrieve the general, and move him outside to our encampment," Hishem replied somewhat shamefacedly. He, after all, was next in command.

Almost as an afterthought, El Sayed asked, "and Abu Ahmed …?"

"He is resting; the wound was not fatal. But I'm afraid our troops may not now join in the battle against the Zionists."

"It is up to you now, Hishem. You must show your leadership skills, make contact with Hamas and demand a full apology from Daghmush. Otherwise—and you may say this comes directly from me—the Hamas will not share in the fruits of our victory. The Syrians will be told of their treachery."

A full fifteen seconds of silence passed as Hishem considered his dilemma. Finally, he answered. "It shall be as you command. I will contact you tomorrow before our forces attack."

El Sayed cut off the connection and slumped dejectedly into his chair.

In Damascus, the new Syrian leader, Aboud Al Agha, strolled anxiously around his palatial office. For the hundredth time he browbeat his Chief of Staff, Yaman Al Mahainu. "How can you be so certain the Egyptians will attack the day after we do? I don't trust that dog Al Khalil."

"I tell you, your Excellency, at the meeting with the Mufti, El Sayed swore on his mother's grave that he would contact me if anything went awry. You've seen the satellite photos yourself; the tanks and infantry divisions ready to strike in the Sinai," El Mahainu replied. He knew whose head would fall first if the Egyptians were not true to their word.

Al Agha had not arrived at his office easily. Many thousands had perished in the internecine struggles that followed the destruction of the former president and his last loyal followers. The civil war between the Muslim Brotherhood and the former president had taken years and cost nearly 100,000 lives. Once the Brotherhood had taken full control, the internal bloodletting continued. In all, five contenders to the throne had been executed. Only one remained: Aboud Al Agha.

167

Although he had inherited the post from his father, it was only a matter of time until the former president had been overwhelmed by the wave of Arab nationalism that swept the region beginning in 2010.

In the bloody aftermath of the former president's removal from office and assassination, it was all but certain that it would be Al Agha who replaced him. The remainder of the Syrian armed forces fell into place behind him, grateful for a strong leader who would bring Syria back to its rightful place as the focus of Arab strength.

Al Agha was a tall man, like the father of the former president. But there the resemblance ended. His son had been tall and slender, weak-looking. Al Agha was the manifestation of evil from head to toe. He dressed always in the manner of an Arab warlord, wearing the standard "didashah," or "dishdash," and three-piece keffiya. He carried an AK-47 and full bandolier across his shoulder, with a bejeweled *jambiya* in his belt. The weapons were almost unnecessary; his visage was enough to bring fear to most men. He had a massive head, adorned with an uncommonly large nose and ears. But his mouth was most menacing of all: his large teeth, which appeared whenever he smiled evilly, were that of a primitive carnivore. His large, pointed canines looked capable, at any time, of ripping out the throat of anyone who displeased him. He terrified the mostly-illiterate Syrian Arabs.

Indeed, Yaman Al Mahainu was terrified of him now. Yaman was not a large man. Barely 30 years old, he had spent his life in the army. Not strong physically, he had an uncanny memory for names, faces, and numbers. This made him sought out by each of the pretenders to the throne. He had chosen to ally himself with Al Agha more out of fear than anything else. Al Agha needed someone like him to organize and control the brutal, but illiterate mass that constituted the Syrian army.

He himself had doubts of the Mufti's ability to hold the tenuous coalition together. He was well aware of the disasters that had occurred in each of the wars the Arabs had started against Zionist interlopers. In each: 1948, 1967 and 1973, the Arab coalitions seemed to be unstoppable, overwhelming the

Jews in manpower, armor, and air power. Yet every time, the Arabs had been humiliated in combat: their men running away, their tanks destroyed, their planes incinerated. All recorded by those accursed newsmen for the world to see. The Arabs had been the laughingstock each time.

But always in the past, he had been told, it was the United States that made the difference. The Americans always came to aid the Zionists just when their defeat had been imminent. At least that was what he had been told. This time, the Mufti assured him, the Americans would be loath to aid the Jew. Not when it was the Jews who destroyed the expensive, palatial Christian enclave outside Haifa. And without the Americans to help them, the true faith of Islam, with the help of Allah, will prevail.

Aboud Al Agha came close to him, looked down upon him from his great height, and smiled that terrible smile. "I hope so my friend, for all our sakes." It was all Yaman could do to hold his water.

169

Chapter 25

Hadley Parkinson finally got a call through to Lara. It had been almost impossible to reach her. She and her Israeli friend, Uri, had been sent to try to find a Palestinian training camp somewhere near the Lebanese border. He hadn't had word from her in more than two days. Now with the ongoing conflict, their normal channels of communication were considered too dangerous for him to try to reach her directly. In desperation, he went through the Israeli Consulate in New York, and spoke to David Peretz. He knew that if anyone nearby knew of her whereabouts, or how to reach her, it would be David; she and Uri had consulted with him before they went to Waco, and after they returned.

He got Peretz on the phone rather quickly. Peretz recognized the calling number as belonging to the JTTF. Hadley had never met him in person, but he knew of him through Lara. "Mr. Peretz, this is Hadley Parkinson. I have a matter most urgent. Would you please call me back on our secure line?" He knew that the Israeli Consulate had access to the JTTF secure landline.

"Yes, of course, and please call me David. I'll call you immediately." The line went dead.

It seemed an eternity, but actually it was more like two minutes, when the phone in Hadley's top-right desk drawer rang with its distinctive double tone. Hadley picked it up at once. "Parkinson," he said sharply.

"David Peretz here, Mr. Parkinson. What's going on?"

"Please call me Hadley, David. It's about Lara Edmond and your man, Uri. I need to get in touch with them ASAP. I just got a call from the top—Washington. They want us to get the two of them in place, at once."

Peretz, had of course been following developments in Israel, both in the popular media, and through his direct line to Jerusalem. The American Embassy was in Tel Aviv, but he had no secure line to them. It made things a bit complicated, but the prime minister or defense minister could contact Tel Aviv without fear of interception. "Can you tell me, Hadley, what exactly you need from us?"

"Yes, of course. With the situation escalating as it is, we need to put the two of them into the battle zones. The government here is getting very edgy about what our role is going to be. The guys in Washington are quite aware of the part those two played in the nuclear threat a few years ago. They have more confidence in the information they can get from that pair than from our CIA operatives. Don't ask me why specifically, but I think our spooks there don't have the direct contact that Uri and Lara do."

"And of course," David replied, "they were right there when we busted up that Hezbollah training camp ..."

"And this business in Haifa—we just don't know how all this ties up with the action on your northern and southern borders."

"I'm getting the picture that your president and congress are somewhat uncertain about who ...," David began.

"Exactly," Hadley said, cutting him off. "That's why we need some certifiable information directly from them. We need to know who's responsible before we can decide what to do. There are certain elements in Congress that are becoming hesitant about our place in all this, if you get my drift."

"I do. I'll get through to Jerusalem and find out exactly where they are and what they've been up to. I frankly don't know myself."

"Thanks," Hadley replied, "and if you can figure out a way to get Lara through to me on a secure line, that would be great."

"I'll get right on it. It's the middle of the night there right now, but I know I can get somebody. I'll be back in touch this afternoon."

"Thanks again. I know you understand the urgency of the situation, to us and to you. Goodbye." Hadley terminated the conversation. He knew he could count on Peretz. Israel's very existence hung in the balance.

In less than an hour, Hadley received a call. By this time he was sweating profusely; he wiped his bald head with his handkerchief. Peretz informed him that he had contacted his government, and they had found Lara and Uri. They were being transported to Tel Aviv from Haifa. The pair had been directly involved in the incident at the Zionist Christian Center, but had managed to escape without serious injury. Peretz would arrange for direct communication via this secure line, as soon as the IDF in Tel Aviv could reach them. Hadley relaxed a bit, but his hand still shook as he poured himself a glass of ice cold water.

"Lara, are you alright?" were Hadley's first words. "What's going on, what's happened over there?"

"Yes, boss," Lara replied, knowing her use of that term for him would let him know that she was indeed alright. "Listen, we were in on that explosion at the Center. We're pretty sure at least a couple of Americans were killed. But they caught the bunch of Hezbollah who were responsible. They're part of the same gang we found at Waco. You know the ones pretending to be Orthodox Jews."

"Right. I got you. You actually recognized them?"

"Affirmative. They had all intended to die in the blast, but we managed, that is Uri and I, managed to interfere with their plans ... listen, there's a lot more to the story, but tell me, what do you need from us?"

"The State Department wants you two to get in place, embedded, with the Israeli forces at the northern and southern fronts. They want direct information, not through the embassy," Hadley said.

"Just how are we supposed to go about this?" Lara asked.

"The embassies will work out the details between them," he stated sharply. Lara could tell he was just short of frantic. "I think State wants you at the southern front, near Ashkelon. That's the more sensitive area, and they trust one of our own to give them the straight scoop. Uri is going to be needed in the North, in the Galilee. What we want to know is what the immediate situation looks like. Do the Israelis intend to push back? Are they going to be able to push back? Furthermore, and this is going to be tougher to find out, are they going to push through all the way back to the Suez? Uri's job is to tell us as much as he can about the Galilee and the Golan Heights."

Lara could hear him breathing heavily as he finished this discourse. She could imagine him sitting there in his chair, damn near having a heart attack.

"That's a big order," she replied. "You think the Israelis will let us in?"

"I can't see that Uri is going to have a problem. We're counting on him to be candid with us. Of course, we'll have confirmation from our satellites as to troop movements. But what we really need are first-hand, on-the-ground reports. They're sort of obliged to let you in, considering what you guys did in the nuclear scare business a few years ago,"

"Who will we get our orders from?" Lara asked.

"The embassies will set that up. What's at stake here is the U.S. action, or I should say, reaction. The president, of course, wants to help out with at least arms and other tactical support— no troops. The problem lies in Congress. There are two factions: the liberal left and the Christian right, who are afraid to give any support to Israel right now. The left, course, has always been on the side of the Arabs. It's the bombing of the Center in Haifa that's the issue with the right wing, southerners especially," Hadley explained.

"The information we've got, and the captives, should clear up who's responsible for Haifa. They're going to be bundled up and set up for extradition, is what I've heard."

"That will help a lot, but it will take some time—to get them over here and get them to trial," Hadley said.

At that moment Uri came into the room and got on the line. "I heard what you need, and I'm sure we can get it done," he said, glancing at Lara. "I happen to know the general in charge of the first brigade down near the Egyptian border. His name is Alon Sharon. He's a nephew of the ex-prime minister, and a straight shooter, just like his uncle Ariel." He squeezed Lara's hand. "As long as we can be sure of secure voice transmission, she'll have real-time information for you."

"And you, can you get us the real story on what's going on up at the Galilee?"

"You bet. I know the guy in charge up there, too. He's Dov Zahavi's top man in the field, Chaim Levitsky. He's familiar with the area, veteran of a lot of the action against the Hezbollah. We're a pretty small nation; a lot of us know each other. I'll find out what's going on and what our plans are. I'll tell you this: I know we're going to need all the help we can get—surveillance as well as hardware. If we have that, we can do the real work on our own. "

Uri's confidence rubbed off, at least somewhat, on Hadley. He sat back in his chair and breathed a little easier. He knew now what to tell the guys at State. They could handle things from there.

Chapter 26

Extreme tension filled the dark-paneled room in the Senate office building. The unmarked room was used only in cases of extreme national emergency, when no press was even aware of the meeting itself. The presence of two Secret Service officers outside the door presented the only evidence that something was occurring. Its location, three levels below the main floor, offered the advantage of little foot traffic. To anyone aware of the circumstances, presence of the Secret Service was a pretty good indication that the president himself was involved. He sat at the center of one side of the long oval table. No cameras or monitors of any kind whirled in the windowless room, adorned only with flags of the United States and pictures of past presidents on the walls. The Secret Service had screened the room thoroughly for electronic bugs an hour before the meeting had begun.

To the president's left sat the vice president, former senator from Ohio, James Kirkpatrick, a purely political choice as a running mate; winning Ohio had been a necessity. Even though Kirkpatrick's career had been undistinguished, he hadn't made many enemies either. To the president's pleasant surprise, Kirkpatrick had turned out to be thoughtful and prescient. His advice had often been successful in achieving legislative goals; yet he rarely sought the limelight; another valuable asset.

Secretary of State Wright occupied the seat to the president's right. The decision to choose Laney Wright also had political overtones. She had been ambassador to both India and Pakistan, and had proven herself to be the ideal diplomat. While not specifically condemning the nuclear arsenals of either country, she had been able to achieve the previous president's goal of showing preference to neither; on the contrary, each country felt it had the president's favor. Armed conflict between the two vicious enemies had been avoided. Being a former member of the House of Representatives from California gave Laney's selection additional political weight.

That position had assured her approval by the Senate. California, however, was an unusual state, to say the least. Comprised of some of the most radical legislators on both sides of the aisle, the rural areas were home to some of the most outspoken advocates of the Second Amendment who, when at home, walked around with loaded pistols on their hips.

On the other hand, much of the urban population was hysterically ultra-liberal. They tended to vote in exactly the opposite manner as their rural neighbors, no matter how absurd the cause. For example, some communities had passed laws forbidding the de-clawing of cats. Veterinarians who performed this surgery were subject to a fine and loss of license. Ms. Wright, or "Ms. Wrong," as she was often referred to by her detractors, was more often in the liberal camp. As such, she almost always opposed overt aid to Israel. Although never public in her disapproval, she was still quite popular with the Arab States. Using her as a shield, the president was able to quietly pass legislation favorable to the small, isolated democracy, the only ally the U.S. had in the region, in his view.

The president himself, former governor of the state of Vermont, Leland M. Seymour, had been a compromise candidate. Certainly not a distinguished leader, his fiscal responsibility, lack of scandal, and middle-of-the-road approach to matters both domestic and foreign, earned him a hard-fought victory over his radical opponents in the primary. After that, he had a relatively easy time defeating his wild-eyed, and not very intelligent, opponent in the general election.

Going around the table, the secretary of defense, General Frank McHenry (ret.), a Texas native, sat next to Secretary Wright. General McHenry had been head of NATO's forces in the Middle East, and was a quiet, but steadfast supporter of Israel. The president relied heavily on McHenry's views on weaponry. For example, his decision to continue funding the F-35 stealth fighter program has been based primarily on McHenry's advice. He correctly saw that the U.S. would need aircraft superior to the F-15's and F-16's supplied to countries being overrun with Islamic radicals.

Others around the table included the secretary of energy, Roy Blankenship, a Texan, like McHenry, but with totally opposite views; the two could not be further apart when it came to issues involving Israel. The only way the president had gotten McHenry into his cabinet was by accepting Blankenship.

Completing the picture were the head of the Joint Chiefs of Staff, Admiral Jason "Hawk" Donaldson, and the Chairman of the Senate Armed Services Committee, Lawrence J. Jefferson. Of this latter group, Jefferson was the most able and least loquacious; he was also the only person of color.

Finally there were all of the "Service Secretaries;" civilians appointed by the president, the commanding generals of the Army and Air Force, and the commanding Admiral of the Navy. Seated in chairs along the walls were senior members of both the House and Senate. The only person taking notes was the president's private secretary with her electronic notepad, seated discreetly to the side.

At precisely 1400 hours, the president began the discussion. "As you all know, a major conflict has begun in the Middle East. The press of course, has already gotten wind of it, and rumors are flying faster than we can keep track of them. Most of what they've broadcast, naturally, is exaggerated, distorted, or totally erroneous. We do know from our own sources that major invasions are beginning both from the Egyptians along the Sinai border and the Syrians north of the Galilee. In the north, the Arabs are apparently meeting only token resistance from the Israelis. In the south, the Egyptians appear to be consolidating with some extremist groups in the region.

"If this weren't bad enough," he continued, "our satellites show the Iranians aiming their long-range missiles situated on their western border, in the direction of Tel Aviv. Further, there is a suspicious convoy of Iranian cargo vessels headed up into the Gulf of Aqaba. We have reason to suspect they are concealing their short-range missiles on-board. As you know, these are considerably more accurate than their long-range weapons." At this point the president paused to take a drink of water.

"Why the hell weren't we made aware of this sooner?!" demanded the Speaker of the House, Buford M. "Red" Riggs, an outspoken member of the opposition party, and longtime representative from Georgia. The president, inured to the ungracious behavior from the portly, loud, red-faced gentleman, replied without raising his voice:

"I understand your concern. I wanted to make absolutely sure of the facts before I brought you all together. You can be certain that the vice president and the secretary of state have been kept constantly aware of the situation." McHenry, the secretary of defense, may have noticed the slight, but, as was his manner, said nothing. He would have more than his share of responsibility before this thing was over.

"And what do you propose to do about it?" Riggs demanded. "Our resources are stretched pretty thin as it is, what with active-duty troops in Pakistan and Afghanistan. Not to mention our not-so-secret involvement in Egypt, Syria, and Libya!"

Chairman Jefferson, in his usual quiet, but knowledgeable manner, added without flourish, "We have maintained an adequate reserve of both troops and logistics to carry out whatever military mission is decided upon. I'm sure Frank will back me up on that," he said, nodding at McHenry. The secretary of defense said nothing, just nodded in return.

They all turned to the president for his answer. "Israel is, and always has been, our only true ally in the region. We cannot and will not allow our common enemies to overrun them. I can tell you, and this is to go no further of course, that the prime minister has asked only for logistical support from us; that is, absolutely no participation in any hostilities by our armed men and women."

"By 'logistical support' I suppose you mean aircraft as well as arms," Riggs interjected. He had good reason to be interested; his state was a foremost supplier of all sorts of military hardware, including fighter planes.

"That's entirely correct, Mr. Riggs," the president replied. "I've spoken with the Joint Chiefs," he nodded toward

Donaldson, "as well as the heads of all the armed services. They all assure me that we are quite ready to protect our ally."

A quiet, if concerned, murmur spread around the room, as they waited for the inevitable input from Secretary of State Laney Wright. She had been a known critic of U.S. involvement in armed conflict almost everywhere in the world. This posture had kept her re-elected as Representative from coastal California, before taking her present post.

She did not disappoint them. As the president looked over to her, giving her tacit approval to make a statement, she took a sip of water, adding to the drama of the situation.

"As you all know, I'm sure," she began, "I am not, and never have been, an advocate of the use of force as the solution to political quarrels."

The military men in the room tried to maintain their composure at the use of the word "quarrel" for the unbridled aggression going on in the Middle East.

"However," she continued, taking another sip of water, allowing the room to come to a deathly silence, "the actions of the Islamic radicals, including Al Qaeda, in attacking, without provocation, a nation which has attempted to come to a peaceful resolution of the conflict in the region, are completely without justification."

The room practically exploded in sounds of approval from all quarters. Except perhaps from some of the civilian "Service Secretaries," several of whom did not consider the Jewish state an ally worthy of U.S. aid, let alone military intervention. "You think she might actually be Jewish?" whispered one woman, just loud enough to be heard.

The president abruptly regained control of the meeting. "We do not take this action lightly. I think we all remember 9/11, as well as the attacks on our embassies, aircraft, and shipping. We have every reason to believe that the attacks on our ally, Israel, are being planned and carried out by the very people who were responsible for all of these reprehensible acts against the United States of America."

These sobering remarks once again brought the room to silence. This restrained gentleman from Vermont was not known to be a "cowboy" itching for action. They had just heard from the secretary of state, who decried even the dissolution of antiwar protests, no matter how violent they became.

"Does this mean," Speaker Riggs asked, "we will be supplyin' fighter planes to the Israelis?"

"That's right," McHenry said, without elaboration.

"But we won't be supplying troops on the ground, is that correct?" Lawrence Jefferson asked, for clarity.

"That is correct, Senator," McHenry added.

Speaker Riggs, from Georgia, the source of much of the military's hardware, asked: "Can we assume the fighter planes we're sendin' include some of our new F-35's?"

The president answered this time. "That is correct, Mr. Riggs. We have sent, and will be sending more to the Israelis. These new military-ready, stealth fighters are essential to their survival. We will, of course, not leave ourselves vulnerable to a surprise attack from any quarter."

The speaker beamed with pleasure as he realized the voters of his state would credit him for the lucrative contracts. Some of his political enemies had fought against the F-35 since the moment it had been introduced as the next weapon in America's air arsenal.

Laney Wright added, "We obviously would not be considering this action unless we thought it was in the urgent interest of the United States. We, and I take the liberty of speaking for the president and the other members of the cabinet, consider the situation most dire. The aggression of our sworn enemies, the Muslim extremists, including Al Qaeda, cannot be allowed to succeed ..."

"Thank you Madam Secretary," the president interrupted politely. "I might add, that the Israelis have not asked for any of our troops. Our aid, at this time, is limited strictly to aircraft and armaments; however, we have our eyes and ears open for any developments. By that I mean specifically, any entry into the conflict by Iran or other nations who have shown animus, to us or our allies." He looked around the room, and seeing no immediate negative reaction, closed the meeting. "That's all we have for now, ladies and gentlemen. You can be sure that you will be kept apprised of any developments as soon as they become available. Naturally, everything I've told you here today must be considered top secret."

The president and his cabinet rose almost as one, and just before they left the room, leaving a stunned audience, he added, "Not that the news media aren't right on top of this. Whether they get any of it right or not is another matter." This remark, whether meant to be humorous or not, elicited little reaction. Everyone in the room was frantically taking notes.

Chapter 27

On the afternoon of the second day, Uri went to meet General Mordechai Zamir at the Israeli headquarters on the northern front. The Syrians, aided by some Hezbollah, had penetrated through Lebanon several miles south into Israel. They had however, been stopped by an onslaught of Israeli tanks and planes. Uri met General Zamir at a temporary headquarters near the small town of Safed in the upper Galilee.

A large, bulky man, Zamir had a bald head, barrel chest, and thick, hairy arms that stuck out from under his rolled up sleeves. His headquarters amounted to little more than a large tent set up near a small grove of trees on the rocky plain. A corporal stood guard outside, carrying an IMI machine pistol. A large map rested on an easel to the left of his makeshift desk. A large cardboard box full of Manila folders sat to the right of his desk. He had a satellite phone and tablet computer along with an oversize monitor.

When he saw Uri, he leaped up and grabbed him in a powerful bear grip. The two men had not seen each other in several years. They met during the second intifada, in 2002. Uri had been an infantry sergeant, serving his time in the IDF. Zamir had been a colonel, in charge of a full squadron of tanks. They met during an especially fierce battle with the Palestinians. It had been the first time that Uri had seen, firsthand, the use of human shields by the Arabs. Zamir had cleverly driven his tank squadron through a field of rubble, deftly separating the terrorists from the young children they were using to protect themselves.

That action, saving dozens of innocent children, lionized him in the Israeli press; however it was virtually ignored by the Arabs. Uri would never forget meeting him afterwards, as the Arab children were brought to safety.

The Syrians had attacked the Israelis in the Golan Heights from the northeast in the 1973 Yom Kippur war, bringing their tanks down upon the Israeli positions from higher up in the mountains. Uri had been a young school child at that time, following the progress of the battles on the radio.

In classical warfare, the advantage always lies with those who hold the higher ground; however, in this case, the Syrian tanks found themselves looking down upon the Israeli tanks from elevated cliffs. Zamir, a young tank commander in those days, had wisely lined up his armor below the cliffs, such that the Syrians could not lower their guns to an elevation from which they could fire down on the Israelis.

On the other hand, the Israeli tanks had been perfectly poised to fire upwards at the exposed Syrian tanks, knocking them out, one after the other. The Syrians turned and fled. Those whose tanks had suffered mortal damage were forced to run on foot or surrender. That battle ended the Syrian attempt to regain the Golan Heights, lost to the Israelis in the famous Six-Day War of 1967. Those victories over the Syrians, along with the rout of the Egyptians in the Sinai turned the whole Yom Kippur war around. Eventually, of course, it led to the famous peace treaty between Egypt and Israel in 1979.

The two men shook hands. "It's been many years since the second intifada," the general recalled. "I've heard a lot about you, my friend. You're almost a legend, what with your dismantling that Hezbollah gang in the U.S. a few years ago, and now this business at Haifa ..." He shook his head and smiled broadly, clapping Uri on both shoulders. "We need more like you."

Uri colored under the praise. He was absolutely astonished that the general remembered him. "I'm sure my 'legend,' as you call it, far exceeds the truth; however, General, I've read many stories of your exploits in the tank battles in the Golan in 1973."

As Uri related those battles, it was the general who became embarrassed. "Like many war stories, those too were overblown." He said. The action of many brave tank commanders and their troops pulled that one off. But that was a long time ago. We're up against a new enemy here, with new weapons and tactics. We've got our hands full, I can tell you that." The general leaned back in his chair and looked up at the map thoughtfully. "These attacks appear to be well coordinated and planned." He paused as he continued to gaze at the map.

"So tell me, Uri," Zamir said, "... I can call you that, can't I?" Uri nodded and smiled, delighted to be in the presence of this great hero. "What exactly can you tell me about this business at Haifa?"

"I'm glad to say that I can tell you everything, I've been cleared to do so." Actually, Uri felt extremely comfortable discussing these things with Zamir, considering their history, more so even than with the defense minister.

"What it looks like, and I can't say this part for certain, is that Hezbollah has had a long-term training mission at a base not far from Kiryat Shmona across the border in Lebanon. What they've been doing is training their most zealous individuals and families to act like ultra-religious Jews from northern Galilee. They've spent a long time at it. One family at least, was placed in New York years earlier, and blew up that synagogue a few months back. They got away with it too. The Americans believe it was carried out by Jewish extremists, immigrants from northern Israel." Zamir held his head in his hands and moaned in despair.

"We have no definite proof of this yet; I'm just speculating from other information we've uncovered." Uri added. "Lara Edmond and I—you probably remember her name—from the nuclear incident in America—we tracked some of these characters down, from a college in the States. They came here, to Haifa, ostensibly to help build that Zionist Christian Center, then tried to blow it up. Luckily we were onto them by then, but they still managed to kill some Americans."

Zamir looked at him in disbelief. "All this going on right under our very noses?"

"I'm afraid they were exceptionally good at what they were up to. It's just lucky we managed to disrupt their plans enough to keep it from being an even greater disaster — Haifa, I mean."

"Were you able to capture some of these *momserim*?" the general asked sadly, using the old Yiddish word for "bastards." This was especially amusing, since they were speaking in Hebrew.

184

"We did. What's more, we're pretty sure they're part of the same bunch we captured a few weeks ago near Kfar Chouba. There was a big firefight; I'm sure you heard of it."

"Yes," Zamir said sadly. "I knew we were holding them in detention."

"It appears the whole thing, the attacks by the Syrians and Egyptians, and the attack on the Center at Haifa, were all coordinated," Uri explained.

"Yes it seems so, but by whom?" Zamir asked, concern darkening his features.

"Let me get to that," replied Uri. "The attack on the Christian Center was designed to enrage the Zionist-Christians in America. The idea was to force the American government into withdrawing any support for Israel."

"And this group, or organization, the Zionist Christians, they have enough political clout to derail our friendship with the U.S.?" Zamir asked.

"As you may know, America is split when it comes to supporting us. Many of the far left think that if they just let the Arabs do whatever they want, they'll leave the U.S. alone," Uri said.

"Unfortunately," Zamir agreed, "I do follow enough American politics to know you're right. I just wouldn't have thought so much of our support came from the American Christian community."

"From what I understand," Uri said, "things have been touch and go for a while now. When the American satellites showed conclusively that the Syrians and Egyptians had coordinated their attacks on us, the 'hawks' in the American government had enough firepower to convince the rest of the leadership that we, Israel, needed their help to survive. They even allowed us to use their new F-35's, as long as it was for our defense."

Zamir brightened up considerably; out here in the field he had a job to do, and didn't need to be hamstrung by politics. "With those planes, we'll have a tremendous advantage in the skies. And if you control the skies ..."

"That's when things got complicated ... just like the Arabs intended," Uri added. "They figured, and correctly as it turned out, that the Christian leadership, especially in the U.S. House of Representatives, would be hard-pressed to support a government whose citizens were totally opposed to having a Christian presence in the holy land."

"But there was no proof ...," Zamir began.

"The overall mood of America is distinctly anti-war," Uri pointed out. "And when you can show, or even intimate, that their allies are anti-Christian ..." Uri didn't even have to finish.

"So when a bunch of ultra-Orthodox Israeli Jews blow up an American-Christian visitor center ..." Zamir shook his head. "This story you're telling me has taken a happier turn of events, I take it."

"I think so; at least I strongly hope so. If we prove these people masquerading as Neturei Karta, are actually Hezbollah in deep cover, the Americans will allow us not only to use the F - 35's we have, but will send us another squadron right away."

Uri paused, hoping for some information from the general. But, he realized first he would have to finish his story about the attack at Haifa.

"So," he said, "to get back to your initial question; that is, who is it that put this whole strategy together against us?" He saw he had the general's complete attention.

"Not to bore you with all the details, but we were able, that is, Lara Edmond and I, along with the IDF, to keep the Hezbollah operatives from completely destroying the Christian complex. As you know, the IDF were able to capture the surviving Arabs masquerading as Neturai Karta ..."

"Yes, all right," the general said impatiently, "but surely they're not the ones who put together this whole plan?"

"No, not at all," Uri replied. "I was just getting to that." Uri took a deep breath, remembering the ferocious battle in the loft. "A few of their leaders managed to escape. We put together a makeshift team and chased them up into the hills. To make a long story short, it was Saleh Halibi and his bodyguards ..."

"The Ghost!" exclaimed Zamir.

"We're waiting for DNA confirmation from the Americans, but I'm sure it was him. I realized afterwards he was the one running the operation at Waco, where the masqueraders were insinuating themselves with the Zionist Christians. I just didn't recognize him at the time."

"I take it you ..." Zamir drew his finger across his throat, "finished him off?" and waited patiently for the rest of the story.

Uri nodded. "We realized that when the Arabs finished their training in the U.S., they came over here to 'help' build the Haifa Center ... and then blow it up. Luckily we caught them in time ... Or at least before they killed even more ..."

"But the overall strategy ... what's the connection with 'The Ghost'?" Zamir asked.

"There has been an ongoing cluster of communications between Cairo, Damascus, and Ramallah. We'd been able to intercept enough of the conversations to know that something big was going on," Uri explained.

"Ramallah!" Zamir practically leapt out of his chair. "You mean the PA is in on this too? We're hardly ready for an attack from the East!"

"No," Uri said calmly. "The Mufti. We know he's been shuttling between Ramallah and Amman. As you know, I'm sure. The IDF has decoded a lot of the transmissions, but not all of them. And while we don't know the precise location of the Ramallah intercept, we do know it's not the PA."

It was clear from his face that Zamir had put it all together. "So the Mufti's right-hand man, Halibi, The Ghost, has been the one keeping the plot going, is that it?"

"Almost certainly. At least that's the way I see it," Uri replied. "He's the only one who has the credibility to make believers out of both the Egyptians and the Syrians. After all, he's the one who put together the other successful attacks against the Americans all these years."

"Then what's the Mufti's role, as long as we're taking it this far?" Zamir asked.

"I'm not completely sure; I'm just guessing. But he's their so-called religious leader, foremost for the Sunnis. But he does have some influence with the Shi'a, mostly in Syria," reflected Uri.

"And now that the Hezbollah, who are supported almost totally by the Iranians, have joined up with the Syrians ...," the general began.

"... how better to get the Iranians involved? What better chance could they have to eliminate Israel once and for all?" Uri finished the thought.

Uri had told the general his thoughts on the matter, knowing full well the influence Zamir had with the ministers, especially Defense Minister Micah Eitan. Micah was a nephew of the most famous Israeli fighter from the War of Independence, Rafi Eitan.

Indicating he had finished his part of the debriefing, Uri asked, "What's our strategy up here?" By this he meant the action against the Syrians in the Galilee.

Zamir grabbed a big black cigar from his upper right desk drawer. Biting the end off with his teeth, he lit it with a wooden kitchen match, drew in a deep breath, and blew out a huge cloud of blue smoke. "What you've just told me, my friend, makes my orders a lot more reasonable. I can see why the PM wanted to wait and get this news to me in person. That is, via a carrier he has complete trust in." He leaned back in his camp chair and blew out another large, contented plume of smoke.

"You see, Uri, our plan here in the Galilee, some of which you may know already, is to allow the Syrians to believe they have a strong foothold ..."

At that moment, there erupted an enormous barrage of artillery fire that caused a general commotion in the camp. Fortunately, the concussive blasts hit more than a mile away. "The Syrians are still using those Russian ATMOS 130 mm guns, I see," Uri observed, as the high velocity shells whistled overhead.

In less than a minute, return fire came from behind their lines, as some old Israeli M109 155 mm cannons blasted away back at the enemy. Uri recognized the familiar roar, and the rattle of the metal treads as the mobile units altered their position. "And we're still using those ancient tank-mounted howitzers."

"Right. Very good," the general commended him. "You'll notice we haven't got our self-propelled missiles here yet. So it's kind of a standoff. For now," he said, smiling. "When the air battle begins, and that's not going to be very long now, it's going to be a different story altogether. Those *golems* will wish they had never started this … as usual."

Uri noticed, again with a smile, the old general's use of the Yiddish word for "dumb brutes." A *golem* was a monster from the underworld, a staple of ancient Jewish folklore. It was the basis for Mary Shelley's "Frankenstein's Monster."

"Bring me up to date on what's going on," Uri asked. "From where you've got your camp set up it looks like the Syrians didn't come down through the Golan, like they did in 1973."

"Right again, Uri," the general said. "We had expected them to come through and attack us at Yesod HaMa'ala."

"So you mean," Uri asked, "you were all set to let them take the Golan?"

"I know it seems crazy, but this is not 1973. We have satellites and drones and all kinds of missiles. We did have contingency plans for whatever path they were going to take, but our sat phone intercepts—you know about those I suppose?" he said, glancing over the desk. Uri just nodded, not wanting to interrupt the general's train of thought. He knew he was referring to the sat phone dis-encryption the IDF's Aman had developed from Lara's computer algorithms.

"At any rate, we fully anticipated they would go through Lebanon this time. After all, Hezbollah controls Lebanon these days, and they're firmly in bed with the Muslim Brotherhood in Syria, if I can mix metaphors," he said, smiling. The news Uri brought him of the F-35's had clearly lightened his mood.

"But tell me more about The Ghost and his alliance with the Mufti," the general inquired.

"We're pretty sure now that Halibi had been orchestrating this whole attack, using the Mufti as his cover. He'd been shuttling between here and the U.S., using various passports. As you know, he was a master of disguise. As I said, I didn't even recognize him when we were at Waco. It was just those eyes … I should've spotted him immediately."

"Don't beat yourself up over that, my friend," the general said paternally. "The important thing is you eliminated him. If what you say is true, and I have no doubt that it is, his absence will throw a monkey wrench into their plans." He leaned across the table and added with a grin, "How do you like my American idioms?"

Uri laughed at the little joke. "A lot is going to depend on how the Hezbollah spies do at their trial. I am really hoping our courts will allow the extradition. It ought to be a spectacle rivaling O.J. Simpson's."

The general leaned back thoughtfully, taking a huge pull on his cigar. "I'm betting the Mufti is going to hightail it to Amman, once he hears about his buddy, Halibi. He can't pull this off on his own. And we're going to pound the crap out of the Syrians and Egyptians, just as soon as we get the reinforcements from the Americans."

"And that is going to depend mightily on how that trial goes in New York," Uri added with a note of finality. Uri grabbed his field pack and made for brigade headquarters. As darkness fell, turmoil reigned all across the Galilee.

Chapter 28

News of the Christian enclave bombing and the death of American civilians hit the U.S. hard. The arrest of Orthodox Jewish volunteers as the perpetrators made headlines everywhere. Their statements were broadcast worldwide: "We want to keep Israel for Jews only. Christians are not welcome," the TV commentators for both CNN and Al Jazeera said. The captured "students" insisted they were Orthodox Jews from settlements in the Galilee, who had gone to the U.S. to study. Commentators had no time to get confirmation. At the time, "the students" were being held in an Israeli prison.

Beauford "Bo" Ogilvy, senior Senator from Alabama scanned through his e-mails and tweets with a worried frown. "What're we supposed to do?" he asked his longtime friend and colleague in the House, Thornton Frye. "We give the Israelis $3 or $4 billion a year, then they go and blow up a Christian church?"

"Now, Bo, we don't know that for sure," Frye replied.

"Dog blast it, Harry," Ogilvy said, using his friend's old school nickname, "they caught them guys with the earlocks and whatnot, tryin' to blow the place up! Caught 'em red-handed."

"I know, Bo, but that's all we know about them yet. We're tryin' to get the Israeli government to extradite them. Then we can have a proper trial over here and get the facts out ..."

"Trial, my rear end," retorted Ogilvy. "What we oughta be doin' is waterboardin' those suckers down at Guantánamo!"

"Well, you know that's not gonna happen. Not now, not with it all over the TV," said Frye.

"Did you see all them Arabs shoutin' and dancin' around?" Ogilvy retorted. "You'd think they just cleared Israel off the map!"

"Well, they have made some pretty solid advances up there by the Galilee."

"All I can see from these e-mails I'm gettin' is that folks are real burnt up about Jews blowin' up a Christian church, or enclave, or whatever they call it. This was a Zionist Christian church! Christians helpin' the Jews, and look what they get for it," Ogilvy said, ignoring Frye's point. "How are we supposed to defend our multibillion-dollar aid to Israel when they pay us back like this?"

"It's worse than that," Frye answered. "I hear the Israelis want more planes, arms and other logistical support to fight off the Arabs who are invading. I should say, have invaded."

At the White House, a similar mood prevailed. The president had received urgent messages from the Israeli Embassy, as well as influential Jewish groups across the country. They were asking for immediate aid to the small nation. But an equal or greater number of demands flooded in to the president from groups requesting a complete cutoff in aid to Israel. They based their demands on the attack at Haifa, as well as past transgressions, such as separating Orthodox from non-Orthodox students in Israeli school playgrounds.

Angry letters from Zionist Christian groups mirrored these demands, especially in the South, where people were angered by this apparent treachery: militant action by the very people they were trying to help.

The president was confronted with one of the most difficult decisions in his time in office. On the one hand, Israel had been his most formidable ally in his attempts to quell Islamic Fundamentalist terror around the world. All through Asia and Africa, as well as the Middle East, the Islamists were wreaking havoc among civilians, both Christian and non-Christian. The so-called "Arab Spring" of just a few years ago had turned into a religion-based terror campaign unseen for over a thousand years.

On the other hand, his European allies, even those in NATO, urged him to let the Israelis fend for themselves. He knew they feared unrest among the millions of Muslim immigrants they had accepted in the last decade or two. Now, to add to *their* animosity towards Israel, he had the turnaround of a large number of American Zionist Christians. Without the support of their representatives, he was unlikely to be able to grant the Israelis any aid at all.

He closeted himself with his secretaries of state and defense, and the vice president. They had to figure out something to do, and fast. The resistance of a number of ultra-left organizations, including even a few Jewish groups, added to the confusion. They opposed any aid to Israel as a matter of course; the fact that Israel was being invaded from two sides appeared to make little difference to them.

The president gave little weight to their opposition. After all, these were the same groups who supported the Arabs while they slaughtered innocents in Chad, Sudan, Somalia, Ethiopia, and numerous other locations. Even while the Muslim Brotherhood in Egypt killed unarmed Christians, these liberal groups turned a blind eye. They had an ultra-liberal agenda, and the facts made little difference to them.

The Israelis' most important needs at the moment involved warplanes. The enemy countries surrounding them all had some version of the F-16, the latest of which had been sent to Egypt in 2011. The plane could fly at a speed of 1,500 mph over a range of 2,000 miles. A formidable weapon; it carried a 20 mm multi-barrel cannon with 500 rounds of ammunition, up to six air-to-air missiles, air-to-surface munitions, and electronic countermeasures.

Israel, in its favor, had the same basic model of the F-16, with a few upgrades the Arabs didn't know about. But the Israelis also received from the White House, as requested, the delivery of the newest model F-35 Lightnings, the super-sophisticated fighter-bombers with better armaments and performance than any other combat plane in existence, including the F-16.

In addition, the F-35, built with stealth technology, used the most advanced carbon fiber material ever invented. This outstanding fighter boasted a radar "signature" just slightly larger than a metal marble; in other words, almost invisible. In combat, neither ground radar nor an attacking F-16 would be aware of its presence.

The F-35 carried a four-barrel, 25 mm cannon in addition to air-to-air missiles of both long-range and short-range capability.

It could turn tighter, fly faster, and fire its weapons more accurately than the F-16. In short, it was the most feared aircraft system in the world.

While the F-35, at least a small number of them, had been promised to Israel within the next four years, they desperately needed at least some of the radical new planes at once. They needed to control the skies above their country.

The president immediately consulted with the secretary of the air force. The ex-airman, General William K. Ernst, nicknamed "Krab," vigorously argued for the immediate delivery of a sizable number of the new planes, in agreement with the Joint Chiefs of Staff. He wanted to see the F-35 in action against F-16's, in real combat situations. After all, it was the success of the Israeli "Iron Dome" ballistic missile defense system that led to congressional approval of the newly accelerated U.S. program. Israel, in his view, was not only a staunch strategic ally, it also had proven itself a superb testing facility for new arms; arms to be used against known foes of the United States.

His advisory group had originally been split two-to-one in favor of granting Israel's request. The majority, consisting of the vice president and secretary of defense, agreed that defending Israel against annihilation was the prime concern. Additionally, they pointed out that the atrocities committed by the Muslim Brotherhood and their associates—Hamas and Hezbollah—required immediate action; otherwise, it appeared tacit acquiescence by the United States. This was really a test of will: if the U.S. allowed the terrorists to achieve their aim in this one arena, they would see it as license to escalate and broaden their genocide.

The lone dissenter had been Secretary of State Laney Wright. She initially argued that our European allies, even members of NATO, would see any action like this as amounting to war against Islam. She argued that we could expect no cooperation from these, our allies. The European countries not only were fearful of rioting among their Muslim immigrants; their almost total dependency on oil and gas supplied by Muslim-ruled countries remained an additional consideration.

Wildly escalating energy costs would create economic havoc, not to mention almost certain electoral disaster.

The president saw this opinion as factual; we needed our European allies; however, it lacked the very essence of humanity on which our country was based. If we stood by while a small, democratic nation was destroyed, how would history see us? Furthermore, what sort of blackmail would we be subjecting ourselves to? Ruled by unelected mobs and guided by religious fanatics, the Arab leaders had shown themselves to be nothing more than medieval, theocratic gangsters, anathema to the sort of world order he so fervently wished for.

Subsequent to her original dissent, the secretary of state came into line with the president and the others after the first word of invasion by the Arabs. Now in agreement with them on the delivery of the F-35's, she even spoke out vigorously in support of U.S. action.

But that was *before* the bombing of the Zionist Christian complex at Haifa. This news had brought her political supporters, predominantly left-wing, into a frenzy. She was obliged to air their concerns.

"What about these Orthodox Jewish 'terrorists?'" she asked. "What if it turns out that there is a large contingent of Israelis who truly do not want any Christian influence in their country? We would be seen then as siding with Jews against both Christians and Muslims."

It was time for the vice president to speak. In his numerous meetings with the Israeli prime minister, the issue of the Zionist Christians had come up frequently. In addition, he had spoken with rabbinical leaders in Israel, who had almost unanimously applauded the ecumenical efforts of the Christians. True, the holdouts were those few of the extreme Orthodoxy. But even they, he knew, would never even *consider* violent action; they even eschewed violence against their sworn enemies.

"Mr. President, these terrorists are going to be unveiled as frauds," the vice president said firmly. "The government of Israel is complying with our request for extradition. We'll put them on trial and expose them. Meanwhile, we have to give Israel all the help we can, short of putting boots on the ground."

As the president thoughtfully considered his decision, he reminded his colleagues of a similar situation in the late 1930s. Had the free world stood up to fascism and Nazism as soon as Czechoslovakia fell, the lives of some 30 million or more might have been saved. "It's regrettable, but sometimes, military action is the correct, in fact, the only, action to be taken, especially in drastic situations such as these," he said.

He informed his entire cabinet of his decision and, expectedly, his secretary of energy, Roy Blankenship roared his protest. "Military action! That's exactly how the world will see what we're doing. It will be compared to our invasion of Iraq, not to World War II." He stopped for breath. "I reluctantly agreed to our supply of limited warplanes and armaments, but that was before this terrorist activity against American Christians on the part of Israeli Jews ..."

"I can see now that I misspoke," the president replied quickly. "Israel is not asking for military intervention, only logistical support. I don't think they even want our pilots engaging in any of the action. If you wish to make historical comparisons, think back to our 'lend-lease' program when England was in dire straits in 1940. Sure, some well-meaning, peace-loving citizens resisted even that small intervention by the U.S. against Hitler. I would argue that our supplying Israel with the needs for its survival more closely resembles that situation." He paused briefly to assess the impact of his words.

"And," he said, glancing at his secretary of state, "I repeat, the perpetrators of the attack at Haifa will be tried in the U.S. and exposed as enemy agents, misrepresenting themselves as Orthodox Jews."

As the president looked closely at the faces of his colleagues, he could see that the matter had been settled. The vice president, secretary of defense, and secretary of state nodded their approval. Only the secretary of energy fumed with disapproval.

Knowing of the Texas oilman's severe anti-Israel mind-set, President Seymour had been reluctant to offer Blankenship a position in his cabinet, despite the other assets he might bring to the job. The decision, however, had been made; he, the president, would stand by it.

"In view of this discussion," the president said, "I'm going to ask the secretary of defense to immediately supply the Israelis with as many F-35's as possible. If I'm not mistaken, we have at least 100 at Ramstein Air Force Base in Germany." Frank McHenry, the secretary of defense, nodded, impressed with the president's acumen. "And I'm sure we can dig up another 50 or so at bases on our East Coast. They can hop to one of our mid-Atlantic bases, refuel, and be in Tel Aviv in 24 hours."

McHenry's eyebrows went up just a bit, but he nodded, and jotted a few notes quickly on his pad. The president knew he could count on this man. The secretary of defense had been a strong advocate of the F-35 program even when strong voices opposed it. The fact that he had been a Representative from Fort Worth, the base of the main assembly plant, only helped the situation.

The secretary of state did not say anything at first; the assurances the president had given about the true nationality of the terrorists still gave her pause; however, knowing her as he did, the president felt certain she would support his decision, just as she had earlier. She was a firm advocate of freedom, personal as well as political. She was, of course, laying her political future on the line. Everything hinged on the identity of the Haifa bombers. If they turned out to be, in fact, imposters, her actions would be vindicated. If not, well, that was a chance she had to take.

She did, however, have one last issue to present. "Won't U.S. pilots be needed in combat? How are the Israelis supposed to fly planes they've never seen?"

Secretary of Defense McHenry came quickly to the president's aid. "The Air Force has been training Israeli pilots at Maxwell Air Force Base in Alabama. Just in case the situation ever arose. It hasn't been widely disseminated; in fact, we didn't expect the need to come up so soon."

The vice president and secretary of state nodded thoughtfully. Only Secretary Blankenship exhibited a swell of disapproval so intense his face flushed dramatically.

The president, on concluding the meeting, considered what the vice president had said earlier. A lot depended on the extradition and trial of the men apprehended at Haifa. It could mean the difference between appearing to aid a friend, or be considered treasonous, and be open to impeachment.

Chapter 29

Lara climbed into the rear of a Jeep, carrying her small duffel bag with only essentials. The short hop from the military base at Tel Aviv to the port took only 20 minutes, even though the port area was bustling with residents and tourists. Apparently it took a lot more than the threat of an Arab invasion to keep the Americans and Europeans away.

A small craft, about 30 feet in length, with inboard engine, waited at a wooden dock near the north end of the harbor. The two young Israeli soldiers who had accompanied Lara took her duffel and tossed it into the waiting arms of the sailors on the boat. One of them, a young man of about 19, offered his arm to help Lara on board. The engine, already running, let out a low, throaty rumble from below decks. They were eager to get started.

The three sailors, trim, tanned young men, similar to the soldier, were friendly and courteous to her, and all spoke English, with that distinctive Israeli accent: a mixture of Middle Eastern and European throatiness. They saluted her with a smile, as though they knew she was not quite military, but still a person of great significance.

They all donned helmets and goggles as they strapped themselves into the two rows of seats in the open vessel. Blue and white camouflage paint coated its hull. Lara saw a 25 mm cannon mounted aft of the seating area; she hoped they wouldn't need it.

The trip to Ashkelon harbor, a distance of only 35 nautical miles, took less than two hours. They arrived at the breakwater about 1100 hours and turned into the tiny marina, which housed only two rows of docks. It looked to be set up mainly for pleasure craft. One of the sailors hopped up nimbly and tied the craft to a dock in an area painted with vivid red and white stripes. The message was clear: official boats only.

Lara was met at dock side by another Jeep, driven by a young Russian immigrant who called himself Oleg, accompanied by a 30-ish master sergeant armed with an IMI automatic rifle. They drove about thirty minutes over a dusty road to a temporary camp outside the village of Nehora, which, according to the map she had been given, was just west of the town of Kiryat Gat. She got the impression that the Israelis expected an attack from the south, either by Hamas, or more frighteningly, Egypt itself.

Oleg pulled the jeep up to what appeared to be a hastily built barracks, with a sign on it written in Hebrew. Oleg translated for her: "Women's Officers Quarters." While Oleg held the door open, the master sergeant, whose name she never quite got, brought her duffel bag in and set it inside the door. "You are to meet with General Sharon at 1400," he said in heavily accented English. "You may freshen up here and he will send for you." With that, he nodded and headed back to the Jeep. Lara found quite a clean, if not fancy, restroom and shower. She also found a rudimentary kitchen with coffee, tea and snacks of all sorts. At that point she crashed on the nearest bunk, certain she would be awakened when the general sent for her.

A few minutes before 1400, a knock on the barracks door brought her to a groggy wakefulness. She hastily dressed in the fatigues she had received in Tel Aviv, and grabbed a notepad and pencil. A patch on her left jacket pocket proclaimed the name "Edmond" and a glaring white patch identified her as "PRESS," ensuring against anyone casually releasing sensitive information. Oleg took her to another temporary barracks with a name on the door in Hebrew lettering which he told her meant "Headquarters Building." He escorted her inside where a female lieutenant sitting at a small wooden desk, looked Lara up and down, then got up, turned around and knocked on an unmarked door and, opening it, motioned Lara inside. Behind another rough wooden desk sat a stocky, mostly bald man of about 55 years, with very little decoration on his open collared shirt. Just a name tag sewn over the pocket: Sharon. The resemblance to his uncle Ariel, the famous ex-prime minister, was apparent. He smiled broadly, jumped up with surprising grace, came out from behind the desk, and grasped Lara's hand with both of his beefy ones. "Shalom, hello," he said warmly. "I've been looking forward to meeting

200

you. I know what you did with those Hezbollah *chazerai* in your country a few years ago. We owe you."

Lara had a vague knowledge of the Yiddish word he used; it meant something like "pig food." She was charmed, and slightly overwhelmed to meet this formidable military figure. She had been prepared to have to deal with a military leader reluctant to deal with outsiders.

"We also heard that your guys got a positive match on the DNA from, you know, Halibi, The Ghost. Luckily the IDF takes samples from all its prisoners. You know we had him imprisoned for a few years, but he was released in that prisoner swap ... he paused for a moment ...

"Yes, Uri gave me the history ..." Lara recalled those terrible days at Haifa and shuddered noticeably.

Sharon nodded. "Anyway, having him out of the way is going to help a lot. I have a feeling he's been in on this all along, maybe even instigated it."

Lara looked at him quizzically. "You think that he, a single terrorist ...?" Uri was of the same opinion, but Lara had always silently questioned his conclusion.

"Yes, I see what you're thinking. But he has some friends in high places, or I should say 'had.' We know he's had contact with the Mufti ..." Sharon saw her appreciative look. "You've heard of him, I see: The Grand Mufti of Jerusalem—Mohammed Amin al-Husseini, the somewhat self-appointed religious leader of the Sunni Muslims. He comes from a long line of hate mongers. Similar to what the head cleric in Tehran does for the Shiites. At any rate, with The Ghost out of the picture, it does make it a little easier for us. I must say we're all delighted you were able to find him and take him out, along with a bunch of his gang."

"But there hasn't been any public resolution of the identity of the gang that attacked the Christian enclave at Haifa," Lara argued.

"That's true," Sharon said. "However, we have confidence that their identity will be revealed within the next few days—in New York. The plan, as you may know, is to try them in federal court and expose them as Arabs, posing as Jews. That should convince the Americans to continue aiding our effort."

Sharon paused for a second, as if not sure if he could share the next bit of information. After a moment, apparently considering what she had been through, he decided he could.

"You see, getting the Iranians in on this multi-pronged attack, we figure, was nearly a necessity for them. With this set back it's less likely."

Lara thought back on the last couple of days with a mixture of pride and revulsion. If she had contributed even a bit to keeping Iran out of the conflict she considered it a major success; however, the horror of the events would never leave her.

"Well," he said, trying to get her mind off that incident, "have a seat and I'll give you our latest assessment."

He eased himself into a more comfortable position, as if to begin a lecture. "As you probably know, the Muslim Brotherhood, who now rule both Egypt and Syria, are basically Sunni in their beliefs. They split off from the Shi'a about 700 or 800 years ago ... something about who the true successor of Mohammed is. I'm not exactly a professor of Islamic studies.

"The Iranians, of course, are strictly Shi'a, and have nothing good to say about the Sunni, except when it comes to the Zionists and the Devils of the Western World. Recently we've received word, I guess you know about our sat phone intercepts, that the Mufti has played the part of sort of an intermediary. We believe he's convinced the ayatollahs that, with their help, the triumvirate can 'wipe Israel off the map,' especially if they can divorce the Zionist Christians from the Israelis. But you know all about that."

"This is the latest word," he added grimly, "it's strictly for your FBI boss in New York; not for publication. He must be discreet in what he tells your Defense Department. It is essential that what I'm about to tell you does not leak to the press. They will find out about it soon enough. For now, we need all the help you can give us."

Lara grabbed her notepad and pencil and sat down. If Sharon was going to object, he would do so now. Apparently, he trusted her to just use the notes for her conversation with Parkinson, because having seen her action, he did nothing to stop her. "Here's the situation," he began. "The Egyptians have begun an attack on our border with Sinai." Lara's mouth dropped open. Sharon smiled and stopped speaking for a second or two.

As she regained her composure, he continued, "We will allow their forces to move across our southern border. They intend to move as far north as Be'er Sheva in the Negev, and through the Gaza border crossing. We evacuated the civilian population a couple of days ago. "The Egyptians have at least six brigades of ground troops in addition to thousands of tanks and F-16 aircraft." Lara felt dizzy as she scribbled down some notes. What she had thought was already a full-scale war in the Galilee was about to escalate dramatically.

"Adding to our problem," Sharon added, "they have been joined by the militant Takfir, and a ragtag bunch of terrorists in Rafah, on the border with the Sinai. We fear they will enter Gaza from the south and recruit Hamas into their strike up the coast." Lara wrote all this down; she would have to check her maps when she got back to her barracks. Sharon could see that she was a little overwhelmed by all this detailed information, so he said, "In sum, this means that various factions of radical elements in Gaza and the Sinai have apparently joined forces with the Egyptian Army. As you know, their army has now defected to the Muslim Brotherhood."

Lara's head whirled. She knew that the official position of the Egyptian army was to keep the Takfir under control, and not allow them to smuggle arms through their border crossing into Gaza. A vast array of tunnels exists through which food and medical supplies is purportedly transported; however, it's well known that arms and other supplies for the Hamas terrorists is the main cargo. To maintain total control of the Sinai, the Egyptians had attempted unsuccessfully to close all of the tunnels.

What she was hearing now meant that Egypt had totally dropped any pretense of maintaining the border. In fact, what they were doing in allying themselves with the most radical terror groups in the region, meant they were abrogating any and all peace agreements. It meant war on Israel's Southern front as well as the North.

"Why are you allowing them to do this?" Lara asked. "Surely you must have been able to stop them or at least slow them down."

General Sharon sighed deeply. "We, that is the ministers and the general staff, concluded it would be better to allow them to make the first transgression. That way, the world would not accuse Israel of being the aggressors."

"And in the north?" Lara asked.

Sharon shook his head sadly. "There we have a similar situation, as you must know by now. Same strategic objectives: let them make the first move. And they have."

"So your forces, they're holding back, waiting for the proper moment to …?"

"I'm not in on our grand plan, only in achieving our objectives here in the south." Actually he had been given permission to share much of the strategy the IDF intended to use against the Egyptians, but not knowing Lara at all, he felt uncomfortable going into too many of the details for both fronts. "When we get orders to move against them, we will. What we're hoping, you see, is that the aggressive moves by the Egyptians, along with Hamas and the other terrorists, will tilt world opinion in our favor. The attacks by Syria and Hezbollah into the Galilee must have had an impact already. You're probably aware of the hostility against us, especially in Europe," he said.

"You don't think, then, that the European countries will come to your aid?" Lara asked.

Sharon laughed bitterly. "Not hardly. Not with the fear they have of their North African immigrants. What we hope is that at least the Americans will help us, with logistical support, anyway. Without that we're in big trouble."

"But you have a huge reserve army, I understand." Lara said.

"True. But we need them for our long, porous Eastern border. If the PLO, excuse me, the Palestinian Authority, the 'PA,' decides to enter the fray, it will be like 1948 all over again. And we'll already have our hands full in the Galilee and Sinai. The Mufti has some considerable influence in Jordan and the

West Bank. He might be able to convince them to join the assault."

He paused for just a moment and stroked his chin as he considered whether to burden her with the next political maneuvering. "The next step we expect them to take, that is the Arabs, is to make a formal appeal to the United Nations Security Council seeking help against what they will call 'Israeli aggression.'"

Lara looked at him in frank disbelief. "How could they expect the Security Council to act once they've seen the satellite photos, at least of the Syrian border crossings?" The general remained silent. "Surely the Israelis have that information as does the United States. They certainly would allow the UN access to it, no?"

"This is not a question of facts, my dear. The UN has been under total political domination by the Muslim world for more than two decades now. Countries that used to be our friends are now in fear of their energy supply, as well as their very lives. It's unlikely that more than a scattered few will vote in opposition to a condemnation of Israel's 'aggression.' Your country, at least, will stand behind us. But we may need more from you than just talk."

She considered his last remarks. "And you think Iran may enter the fray?" she asked.

Once again Sharon considered just how much he should share with this American. True, she had proven herself a trustworthy ally; however, he knew she would be sharing much of the information he gave her with American intelligence. Ever since the Jonathan Pollard affair, he didn't have complete faith in their relationship.

The prime minister could not forget the infamous spy scandal involving a U.S. government employee who gave top-secret information to the Israelis. While no damage was done to the U.S., they were outraged that one of their allies would deceive them in this way. Repeated attempts to gain his release had so far led to nothing.

The Americans would already know a certain amount from their satellites and drones. This much he could confirm. "We know from our intercepts that the Iranians are planning to aim their long range Shahab 3 missile launchers at Tel Aviv. That alone constitutes an aggressive act. One which we're hoping Washington will retaliate against."

"Oh, and by the way," he said, adjusting himself again to a more comfortable position, "we owe you a huge debt of gratitude for the algorithms you developed in deciphering electronic communication. It was a great benefit, you may know, to Aman, our military intelligence, to their success in the dis-encryption of the Arabs' sat phone conversations."

Lara did know this, but still appreciated hearing it from the General. She blushed graciously and said, "No, I wasn't aware of that, but I'm delighted that it was helpful to you."

What he did not feel comfortable in telling her, was that the Arabs had discovered the leak and since used a more protected communications system. If the Americans didn't already know this, he didn't want to be the one to spill the beans.

"Anyway," he said, "even beyond their long range missiles, we still have a problem with a convoy or two of Iranian ships steaming up toward the Gulf of Aqaba. They are trying to maintain the pretense of commercial shipping. But, as I'm sure the Americans are as aware as we are, these ships carry a significant number of their highly accurate short-range Shahab 1 and 2 missiles. We suspect the main thrust of this fleet is towards Aqaba, but some of the smaller vessels may be headed up the Suez Canal. These could be used in support of any campaign in the Sinai."

"You know we have our 5th Fleet based in and around Yemen?" she countered. "A contingent is also in the Persian Gulf. That combined firepower would surely dissuade the Iranians from taking any overt action."

Impressed with her strategic knowledge, Sharon said, "Yes, you're exactly right, the Americans have the ability to knock out any Iranian involvement in the situation, but the problem is political, not logistical. It comes down once again to what America sees as the global impact of their actions ..."

"At least we don't have to worry about the Saudis," she offered. "From what I know, and I agree it's not much, the Saudis would be pleased to see Iran lose some of its global hegemony." Once again Sharon was impressed with her knowledge of the region. "Quite so," he said. "The Saudis would just as soon stay out of any military engagement."

Lara shifted gears, now that she had demonstrated to the general at least an overall concurrence with the Israeli situation. "But getting back to the religious situation; that is between the Sunnis and Shi'a, do you really think Iran's ayatollahs would join forces with the Sunnis?"

"Normally, no," he replied. "But if they really think they could wipe Israel off the map, as they threaten to all the time, there is a chance. And the Mufti could be the key. We believe he holds considerable sway with the Iranians. If he can convince them that, together with the Egyptians and Syrians, they can obliterate Israel, I believe their hatred of us would overcome their ancient internecine quarrel."

"... And the fact that they have ships headed toward the Gulf ...," she began.

"Gives us plenty to worry about," he replied.

Lara realized she had drifted off-topic. Her main objective was to find out the plans for the southern front. She'd already gotten a little hint from their earlier conversation, but now she wanted to see if the general would be willing to give her more detail. "Let me get back to the point of your troop deployment here near Ashkelon," she said bluntly. "Can you tell me what the plan is once they come across your border?"

The general shifted in his chair once again and sighed. He had told her this much, and the world would see the action for itself in a matter of hours. "I'm not certain exactly why the Egyptians didn't attack simultaneously with the Syrians. It may be due to a matter of trust." He smiled. "You know, the Arabs trust each other about as much as *we* trust them. It may well be that the Egyptians, along with their new fanatical colleagues, the Hamas and Takfir, would not agree to any military action until they saw the Syrians make the first move." Actually, he knew this to be a fact based on the sat phone intercepts; he reasonably assumed she would figure that out.

"In any event, our strategy here is basically the same as it is up in the Galilee. Let them make the first moves. We have a pretty good idea where they will cross the border. As you already suspected, they would love to get their hands on our ports at Ashkelon and Ashdod. But we have no intention of allowing them to get that far. Nor will we allow them into the Negev. We have the strong line of defense protecting our port at Eilat, and points well north. As soon as they make their moves; that is, the Arabs, they're going to find themselves in what you Americans call 'a heap of trouble.'"

Lara smiled at this colloquialism, figured she had enough for one sitting, and needed to get some sleep as well.

It was at dawn the next day that Lara got the full report of the Israelis' stunning victory in the Galilee, with the capture of tens of thousands of Syrian and Hezbollah troops. The Israeli Air Force, helped by the American F-35's, had also pummeled the Syrians, After a quick breakfast, she went to see General Sharon and get the latest news on the Southern front.

"It turns out," he said, "the Egyptians had second thoughts after they saw what happened up North. Besides that, they appear to be having some internal struggles— various factions they had counted on to work together, are falling apart. This is according to our sources in Cairo."

"Does that mean they won't attack at all?" Lara asked.

"Unfortunately, no. The main force of the Muslim Brotherhood is attacking along the Sinai border. We are allowing them to move in a few miles before we strike them from two sides. You see, we have two brigades of armor hidden in the Negev, just waiting to hit them from the rear."

"So you will surround them the same way you did up North."

"Precisely. And if their Air Force makes the same bad decision the Syrians did, they will face the same result."

Chapter 30

Uri grabbed a few hours sleep on a cot and poured some hot coffee down his throat. Just after daylight the following day, he made his way back to General Zamir's tent, and was about to ask him the status of the battle when Zamir's field phone rang. The general grabbed it, put it to his ear, and moved just far enough away so that Uri could not hear the conversation. After about five minutes of extremely active exchange, the general put the phone down and looked at Uri with a mix of apprehension and delight.

"It looks like we're not waiting for the Americans," he said. "The guys at the top feel we have let them drive far enough South. The pincer move is about to begin."

Uri did not fully comprehend the implication of Zamir's remarks. "You mean the reinforcements have arrived!"

"That's right," Zamir confirmed, nodding his head vigorously. "More than a full brigade of our amphibious reserves landed at Beirut during the early evening and, as I understand it, after Naval shelling, Hezbollah offered only token resistance. Another airborne brigade came in by parachutes and gliders behind the Hezbollah lines. They were taken totally by surprise."

"Then our troops took control of the west end of the Beirut airport, where they encountered only a few dozen Hezbollah troops, who gave up without a fight. It sounds to me like they were glad to have the chance to throw down their arms and go home."

Uri was so astonished he had nothing to say; he just shook his head in amazement.

"That allowed us to land our C-130's with the rest of our airborne troops, tanks and other equipment," Zamir continued. "The whole operation ended in less than four hours."

Uri held up his hands, trying to get a word in.

"Wait a minute," Zamir concluded excitedly, cutting him off, "an additional 5,000 or so of our reservists are moving in from the East, down through the Beqaa Valley. All the Hezbollah 'fighters' were gone; they had moved south to protect the rear of their advance attack."

"So the Syrians thought just as I did," Uri said. "that we were going to let their initial attack party move as far south into Israel as they liked, until we got American support."

"What a surprise they're about to get!" The general laughed and smacked his hands together in anticipation.

"Excuse me now, my friend, I've got to get my battalion commanders together and finalize our strategy. The barrage is about to begin from two directions. The Arabs won't know which way to run." He ushered Uri from his tent and got busy on his field phone.

The Syrian 130 mm mobile artillery could be heard all along the line directly in front of them. The heavier sounds of the Israeli 150 mm guns, a mile in the distance, pounded away at the Syrians' exposed northern flank.

Uri met with the chief of liaison, Colonel Izzy Gefen, after hitching a short Jeep ride back to communications headquarters. Uri had known Izzy for years; as soon as Gefen had a break between phone calls, Uri asked him his take on the situation.

"Ah, Uri, my friend, you are about to see one of the all-time routs of our generation. We had a Marine landing at Beirut and an airborne assault all through the region to the east recently occupied by Hezbollah ..." Uri interrupted him to say that he had already been briefed by Zamir.

"Then you probably know the Arabs' reinforcement joined forces with the original Muslim Brotherhood assault. They had been prepared for an unopposed drive south. Our naval and air assaults last night were practically unimpeded. And the Syrians never expected to see our tanks come rolling down through the Beqaa this morning. All the reports I'm getting are showing our forces moving forward at will."

All this confirmed what Uri had just heard from Zamir.

"That means we should be seeing a flood of enemy troops moving in our direction within the hour!" Uri exclaimed.

Holding an earpiece to his head, Izzy nodded as he listened to the report coming in from the northern-most outfits. "Yes," he said, excitedly. "You can hear their guns. But there's total confusion: our aerial reconnaissance shows their southern lines trying to avoid those Israeli 150's you hear. In the next hour or so, our F-16's are going to be strafing their entire field."

"Let me get this straight then," Uri said, glancing at a field map the Colonel had on an easel. "You mean to say the initial attack garrisons of the Hezbollah and Syrians felt, at first, that they were at a tremendous advantage. Then when they got beat up they called in for their entire occupying force?"

"Well," Gefen added, "we know they took their lumps from our F-16's at the end of the day yesterday. So they probably felt they needed to bring their whole force into the action to protect their gains. They must feel we've already used everything we've got."

"I wish I could see all this from the air!" Uri exclaimed. "It should be quite a sight."

Gefen received a text message, complete with an updated map of the battlefield on a large electronic display. He laid it on the table, allowing the two of them to examine it in close detail, "This just came in from general headquarters," the General said. "It's been relayed to all the commanders in the field. If you look at this satellite photo, you'll see our brigades 22, 60, and 115 just to the north of us." He pointed to vague, clearly man-made objects on the second page of the transmission, with the help of a magnifying glass. "Those are our tanks and field artillery."

He moved the magnifying glass to the north and showed Uri similar images, but these were in complete disarray. "Here's the original Syrian attack force; notice, if you can, how their tanks are pointed in all different directions."

Gefen then directed Uri's attention a thousand or so yards north of the original attack force. "Now here you can see the reinforcing Syrian and Hezbollah tanks and troops. We lured them into a line about 5 miles long across the southern Galilee. Finally," he said, moving the magnifying glass further to the north, "you can see our invasion troops coming down at full speed from the Lebanese border. These are brigades 51, 82, and

122. You see these black images here—all our Sabra M-60 tanks. These smaller images are the 120 mm guns equipped with tank-destroying ammunition. Everything is equipped with rounds that will knock out the old T-54 and T-55 Syrian deathtraps."

"In other words," Uri said, "the entire Syrian force is trapped between our two top infantry divisions!"

While Uri had been examining satellite photos, Gefen had been receiving updated information, both verbal and pictorial. He listened carefully as he examined the new photographic images, nodding silently as he marked on them with a light blue pencil.

"Look at these," he said to Uri, excitedly. "These are photographs taken within the last 30 minutes from our reconnaissance aircraft. The aerial battle has begun over the battlefield!"

Colonel Idan Shachar led his squadron of the new American-made F-35's up from the military airfield north of Tel Aviv. As they made their way east at 35,000 feet, Shachar was pleased to see the morning fog diluting the sun rising behind the Judean Hills. Below him, stretched out in a line several miles long from east to west, lay the two combined enemy armored divisions. He reported back to base on the secure satellite link, *Enemy ground forces in sight. Circling up to the north to view rest of field.*

Schachar led his squadron in a broad left turn, until he could see the Israeli infantry division that had driven down from the north. These would be the crack troops that had swept down through Lebanon, pinning the Hezbollah into the Israeli vise.

The Israeli air squadron then continued east toward the Sea of Galilee so that they could report the position of the eastern flank of the enemy troops stretching almost as far as the town of Tiberius. He radioed this information back as well. Completing the circle, he could see that only 2000 yards or so remained between the original Syrian force and the defending Israeli division.

Firing from the tanks and guns from both sides of the combat area was only barely visible from his altitude, but he could see that the Syrian troops were in somewhat of a disarray. He would have liked to bring his squadron of F-35's into the land battle, but he had more important matters to deal with. Coming through his headphones, just then, was the information he had been waiting for. An unknown number of Syrian MiGs were reported headed toward the northern Israeli armored division at an altitude of about 15,000 feet. Their intent was clear: they were going to bomb and strafe the Israelis until the Hezbollah/Syrian division could at least make their way back to the Lebanese border.

Shachar's job was to attack and destroy the Syrian air brigade, and give Israel entire control of the air above the battlefield. If all had gone as planned, the "stealth" F-35's should be invisible to Syrian radar, both on the ground and on board the MiGs.

Shachar radioed his squadron, who had already spotted the old Soviet MiGs. The Israeli air squadron swept down upon the unsuspecting Syrians, cannons blazing. As a few Syrian planes tried to turn up and enter the fight, they were quickly brought down by the American-made air-to-air missiles the F-35's all carried, known as AIM–120–AMRAAM's. Shachar counted about 25 "splashes" as his squadron quickly dispatched the MiGs. A few white canopies dotted the sky, as some lucky Syrian pilots managed to eject. These pilots would be taken into captivity, since they conveniently floated over the northern Israeli troop division.

None of Shachar's F-35's was damaged. He radioed the news back to base, and awaited further instructions. It was soon in coming. Now that the Syrians were aware of the F-35's, they had dispatched a larger squadron of MiG 29's. Nearly sixty of these enemy aircraft were headed in Schachar's direction, at about 30,000 feet, according to Israeli ground radar,

Shachar knew his planes were running low on fuel; they had no choice but to engage the Syrians. He was outnumbered about 5 to 1, but the Syrians could not see his planes, except by visual contact. On the other hand, his pilots could view and track each of the MiGs, locking in with their onboard radar.

He ordered his men to spread out, east to west, catching the approaching enemy by surprise. He told them to make one pass through the enemy formation, taking whatever shots they could. As the closing speed was going to be around 1000 miles an hour, they would each get one or two shots at the oncoming MiGs.

After that initial pass, they were to re-group and come at the enemy again, as best they could. The Syrians should hopefully, by that time, be confused and scattered. Those MiGs that weren't heading back for base would be taken down in the second exchange.

The first encounter began in less than two minutes. Sure enough, the Syrians flew south in a ragged east-west line. The Israelis came at them, invisible to the Syrian radar, firing their cannons and one each of their remaining AIM–120–AMRAAM's. The Israeli planes passed through the MiG 29 formation in less than two seconds. Each Israeli F-35 knocked down two Syrian jets, without a shot being fired by the enemy.

Now that the Syrians knew was happening, they were at least ready for the second pass; however, the Israeli planes still did not show up on their radars. It was, as Shachar expected, a much more confused encounter. Of the thirty or so remaining MiGs, he could see about half cutting in their afterburners, gaining altitude and heading back toward their base near Damascus, probably scared out of their wits by the invisible enemy.

The odds now were close to even, at least numerically. The well-trained Israeli pilots each selected the closest MiG and used a burst of cannon fire to bring it down. They knew it was too dangerous to use their air-to-air missiles. In the confused skirmishes they might accidentally strike one of their own. Shachar himself picked out a Syrian jet traveling in the same direction that he was, about 500 yards off his starboard wing. The Syrian pilot must have made visual contact, because he abruptly made a sharp turn upwards and to starboard. A rookie mistake, Shachar thought to himself, as he turned underneath the MiG and released a short burst of cannon fire at the slower plane. He was immediately rewarded with a burst of orange flame as the MiG disintegrated.

In the next two or three minutes, similar encounters occurred across the now ragged field of battle. His men had brought down at least eight, perhaps more, of the remaining MiGs. He saw a few white canopies; some lucky Syrian pilots would survive. As they were now above the Israeli lines, they would be picked up and held captive.

The remaining few Syrian planes kicked in their afterburners and made for the Syrian border, just minutes away. Shachar got on the intercom and told his men not to pursue; they were running low on fuel and had given the enemy a vivid and memorable lesson.

Just then, he got a message he had been dreading. One of his F-35's had been hit, most likely by errant friendly fire. However, the pilot had managed to eject, and his canopy was seen headed toward the Israeli position on the ground. Relieved, he repeated the order to return to base.

The aerial battle had been visible to all on the ground. The Israeli troops cheered each time a Syrian MiG burst into flame. Their canopies, clearly spotted against the blue sky, quickly brought a host of infantry troops to capture the pilots. The Syrians offered no resistance whatsoever; they seemed pleased to be safely away from the one-sided conflict.

The one unlucky Israeli pilot was rescued unscathed. He received a hero's welcome from the scores of troops who escorted him to a waiting hospital van. He was chagrined, but delighted, to learn that he was the only casualty of the short air "war."

The Syrian/Hezbollah forces on the ground had now merged into a single unit, the reinforcements having been pushed southward into the original strike force. The Syrian T 54 and T 55 tanks had suffered significant damage from the Israeli field guns, M60 tanks, and M36 "tank destroyers." Unlike the Israeli tanks, the Russian T 54 and T 55's had unprotected ammunition compartments. On each direct hit, the Syrian tanks were completely destroyed, with large loss of life.

The Syrians on the ground, like the Israelis, had watched the decisive, one-sided air battle. They had seen the bulk of their air force destroyed or sent into flight back home. The canopies, signaling the pilots who had escaped death, drifted into an unknown fate at the hands of the Israelis. The commander of the ground forces radioed General Nizar el-Kuzbari, back in Lebanon, with the bad news. But it was no news to the Syrian command. The returning pilots had already been debriefed.

"Hold onto your position at all costs!" ordered el-Kuzbari. "Reinforcements are on the way!"

However, that was not to be the case. Now that the air space above the "Battlefield of the Galilee," as it was to be called, had been cleared of Syrian aircraft, it left a completely undefended enemy on the ground, pinned down on both sides by Israeli tanks and troops.

This was the moment Israeli Defense Minister Eitan had been waiting for. He instructed the Air Force to unleash two squadrons of F-16's to pound the already disheartened enemy into total submission.

The unopposed Israeli planes strafed the beleaguered enemy, tearing up what little armor they had left. The squadron commanders finally ordered cessation of hostilities, as tens of thousands of terrified Arabs ran from their tanks, and threw down their arms. Visual photographs taken from surveillance planes showed the defeated troops running in helpless confusion, waving white flags, or sitting on the ground, their hands in the air.

The Israelis now had only to round up the remaining enemy ground force and march them into a hastily-constructed POW camp.

The reconnaissance photos and video were sent to the American secretary of defense, Frank McHenry. He checked with President Seymour and Secretary of State Wright, who decided that they should be released to the press. It was felt that showing the devastation could only lead to a quicker cessation of hostilities. After all, it was clear that the aggressor force was made up of Syrian and Hezbollah attackers, and that they had been captured well within Israeli territory. Even the UN would have a difficult time decrying this defensive action.

While CNN and the other free press aired the astonishing, conclusive videos, the Arab press did nothing of the sort. They simply reported that hostilities between the invading Israelis and the near defenseless Hezbollah were continuing, and that all detailed information was considered a militarily secret. Their leading news media, however, did go so far as to say that Western news sources had been airing old footage from the 1967 and 1973 conflicts, claiming they were current.

Back at the White House, President Seymour, Secretary Wright and Secretary McHenry read the reports with undisguised exhilaration. There were handshakes all around. This was looking like a great beginning to what might be a defining battle in the Middle East conflict. Now they had to confront the looming Iranian threat.

Chapter 31

Flight Lieutenant Reuven Moraine steered his Lightning over the barren Sinai. His squadron of ten of the new F-35 Lightnings had been sent into battle shortly after the Egyptians crossed into Israeli territory. All the young pilots had been anticipating this first action with the enemy.

Reuven was barely 19 years old, having immigrated with his parents from Russia when he was 16. A tall, gangly redhead who just barely passed the maximum height requirement, he was nevertheless very athletic and coordinated. Against his parents' wishes, he joined the IDF a year ago, and went right into the Air Force. Reuven had over fifty hours training in the older model F-16s and had shown himself eminently capable. His innate skills put him at the top of the list of pilots but, being new to the squadron, he had never seen real combat.

The U.S. had agreed to deliver twenty-five of the new F-35 Lightnings two years ahead of schedule, without any disclosure made to the rest of the world. Despite his lack of experience in combat, the skill he had shown in the F-16 caused Moraine to be chosen as one of the first pilots to fly an F-35.

Reuven and a few of his cohorts needed to receive accelerated training from the American F-35 instructors. He, like the others in his squadron, found the plane easy to adapt to after their experience with the F-16. The F-35 handled remarkably easily, and the radar-guided weapons proved amazingly accurate. He and his buddies were eager to try it in combat.

He had heard, along with the rest of the air squadrons, of the rout his buddies stationed in the Galilee, had made of the attacking Syrians the day before. He was determined that his squadron would do the same to the attacking Egyptians.

Their chance came that afternoon. Egyptian tanks and infantry had been spotted crossing over from the Sinai into Israeli territory. They were aware of the planned Egyptian attack from intercepted satellite phone conversations, and so were ready with their counteroffensive. The Israeli strategy was relatively simple: They flew southwest from their bases hidden in the Negev, circled around, and came at the enemy out of the Western sun.

Reuven took a position between his two wingmen. Then, at a predetermined location, he dove to within 100 feet of the ground and headed east over the barren dunes toward the phalanx of Egyptian tanks moving into the Negev. The F-35's, with their "stealth" technology, were virtually invisible to the Egyptian ground radar.

The first group of Egyptian tanks, about thirty American-made "Abrams," tanks, were well into Israeli territory, moving at about twenty miles an hour, kicking up huge plumes of sand.

Reuven started strafing with his 25 mm machine guns as he made his first pass over the startled Egyptians. Large chunks of tank treads flew into the air, as the tanks fled in different directions. They had no warning from either their commander or their radar systems; the stealth fighter that wasn't supposed to be there hit them with total surprise. Excited, confused screaming in Arabic came from the Egyptians' unprotected communications systems. Reuven turned back to make another pass, this time aiming two of his "Brimstone" air-to-ground missiles at the tanks that flew "officer colors." Once he locked on and released the missiles, there was no doubt of their deadly impact. Passing over the disordered formation, he blasted a few more 25 mm rounds into some of the other tanks. The two hit by the Brimstones had vanished in plumes of red and black smoke.

That was enough for that group of the Egyptian 1st tank corps. Reuven heard a few more curses and screams from their radios, and saw the terrified soldiers streaming out of their tanks, waving anything white they could muster.

Just minutes later, Lieutenant Uzi ben-Even, one of Reuven's wingmen, spotted another group of Egyptian tanks further east. Uzi was a Sabra, born to Israeli parents 22 years ago. The jokester of the squadron, he was short, at 5'7" and built like a bull. Dark complexioned like his father, with green eyes like his mother, Uzi always had a bevy of girls after him.

Uzi had dreamed of being a pilot since he was a small child. He had read of the exploits of the Israeli Air Force during the 1967 and 1973 wars. Their heroic acts while overwhelmed by the numerically superior Arab air forces far outweighed the nonsense shown on American TV and movies. The exploits of the pretty-boy movie stars always drew laughs from the Israeli audiences.

Uzi was about to deploy a couple of his air-to-ground missiles, when he spotted a group of four enemy fighters on his radar. They had to be Egyptian F-16's, because the stealthy Israeli fighters would not be visible. The radar image of the F-35 was about the size of a marble. The fact that the Egyptian planes were headed for him meant that some visual sighting had occurred. One of the other Egyptian fighters must have already seen action and reported back to Cairo. At any rate, he was in for a dogfight.

He knew the top speed of the F-16 was equal to his. But he also knew that he could turn tighter and unleash more deadly air-to-air missiles. His plane was equipped with four of the new American MBDA "Meteor" air-to-air missiles. He also had electronic missile-evasion capabilities unknown to the Egyptians. It was based on the Northrup Grumman AN/AAQ-37 distributed-aperture system.

The Egyptians were closing in on Uzi fast, from about 10,000 feet. Suddenly his warning light flashed, indicating an approaching missile. His plane automatically maneuvered out of the way, easily avoiding the oncoming threat. He pulled his stick back, picked out one of the F-16's now almost directly above him, targeted it, and fired. Uzi then immediately banked to the right, dropping below the second Egyptian. From the corner of his eye he briefly saw the flash of another enemy missile as it passed harmlessly by.

Uzi remembered his dogfight training, and the Egyptians were playing right into his hand, attacking with old-school techniques. He fired a second missile at the unsuspecting F-16 just as he saw the first enemy fighter burst into flames. As he had done in training, he now banked sharply left as he passed above the two remaining Egyptian planes. But before he had a chance to attack, he saw both turn tail and head full speed toward the airbase at Abu Suwayr. No point in chasing them, he figured. Instead, he went back to his original target, the cluster of Abrams tanks.

They must have seen the air action, he thought, but there was little they could do to protect themselves from his Brimstone missiles. He fired one at the lead tank, then strafed the one just behind it with his cannons. As Uzi passed over the group and turned back, he saw a ball of flames from the lead tank, and a shower of metal from the second. As he was getting in position to fire a second air-to-ground missile, he saw white flags emerging from the turrets of the remaining two tanks. He waggled his wings at the Egyptians, indicating it was safe for them to emerge.

As he was turning, he saw the terrified Arabs piling out of the tanks, prostrating themselves in the sand. Uzi headed for home. He knew, as did the other pilots, that the IDF ground forces would be coming soon in tanks and other armored vehicles to round up the frightened and disoriented Arabs. They would be placed in a makeshift POW camp somewhere in the Negev.

Lara, sitting in the command tent, watched and listened as reports of the fight in the southern campaign headed to an early close. The senior officers seated there applauded as each account came through.

In the hours after the initial, rapid advance of the Egyptian tank and infantry brigades past the border, they were met by two brigades of Israeli tanks. Lara, along with the Israeli command, watched as the Egyptian Air Force, flying American F-16's, flew overhead as protection. But they were soon scattered and destroyed by the Israeli F-35's.

Without any air protection, the surprised Egyptians were quickly forced to surrender by the hidden brigades of Israeli tanks to their south. With most of their tanks knocked out of action by the Israeli planes, the Egyptians tried to find a way to flee. But when faced with the prospect of even more devastation, they threw down their arms and surrendered en masse.

Surveillance planes gave a clear account of the quick end to the battle.

Special infantry units had been set up by the Israelis to quickly gather up the defeated Egyptians. As in the Galilee, where the Syrians and Hezbollah were herded into temporary prison camps, the same was done with the Egyptians in the Negev. The important thing in both locations was that the enemy had been captured inside Israeli territory.

"Well, Lara," Gen. Sharon said to her, smiling. "I think we've seen the end of the Egyptian campaign. Now it's up to the politicians to see what we can do about the Iranians."

Chapter 32

Moshe Chayat, the Israeli prime minister, held the meeting with the U.S. secretary of state, in his office early in the morning. The group was small. In addition to Secretary of State Laney Wright were Lara and Uri, and Chayat's defense minister, Micah Eitan, a longtime friend and colleague.

Ms. Wright, shook hands warmly with both Lara and Uri. The residents of her home state, California, while not always agreeing with her, seemed to recognize truth over political posturing. Firm in her conviction that the defense of the United States ranked first and foremost, relegating politics to a backseat, she saw Israel as America's only true ally in the Middle East.

While initially reluctant to provide Israel with any more military capability, she had come to agree with President Seymour's decision. She saw the immense threat to world peace posed by the combined Arab-Iranian attack. Israelis viewed her as a partner in the war against terror.

"We appreciate all you've done for our country," Wright said, "Believe me, you have the gratitude of our entire nation, both of you, for the way you took down that Hezbollah gang when they tried to blackmail our country."

"We should have learned our lesson a little better," she said, "after the bombing of our Boston Marathon in 2013 turned out to be a team of ersatz international students from that hotbed of Muslim extremists, Chechnya. I would have hoped that we would have been able to spot Muslim terrorists, whether from the Middle East or the Caucasus."

Uri started to say something apologetic, but the Secretary held up her hand as if to say—the fault lies with us, and we know it. Lara said nothing; after all, it was her agency, the JTTF, that took the brunt of the blame.

"At any rate," Secretary Wright continued, "that's water under the bridge, as they say, and we have urgent business to deal with now. Let's hope we can do a better job of it." By "we" she clearly referred to the role the U.S. might play in the current crisis. "I've already gotten a brief rundown of the situation. Now tell me what we can do to help."

The prime minister looked at his minister of defense to see if he had something to offer. "Well," Eitan said, "certainly the F-35's that you sent us have played an enormous role in our victories in the field. That is, as of now. And believe me, we are extremely grateful. Who knows what kind of terrible situation we would be in if it weren't for those amazing planes of yours."

"Yes," Wright agreed. "President Seymour was adamant that you receive that aid at the very least. It was quite clear, no matter what the Arab governments have stated publicly, that Syria and Egypt, along with help from Hezbollah and Hamas, initiated this conflict."

Clearly in agreement, the Israelis nodded in approval and gratitude.

"Before we go any further," Wright continued, "I must know with certainty, how it is you identified the gang that attacked that Christian church in Haifa."

The group looked to Uri and Lara for confirmation. "We had been tailing these guys ever since they started the process of learning their trade here in your country," Uri began, "... that is, the pretense of being religious Jews—right through to their 'schooling' in your country, where they carried on their charade. Eventually, they were instrumental in attempting the complete destruction of the Zionist Christian enclave."

"And you know this for a fact?" The secretary demanded.

"Absolutely," Lara stated. "We were with them the whole way."

"What happened; how did their attack get stopped without more killing, more destruction ...?" Wright asked. "And how did the two of you manage to escape?"

"That's something of a long story," Lara answered. "The important thing is, those of the gang who survived have all been captured, and hopefully will be exposed in a U.S. court."

"Believe me," Secretary Wright responded, "we're doing everything possible to get that bunch extradited and put on trial where everyone in the world can see their perfidy."

The prime minister nodded in agreement. "Our government is proceeding in all haste to achieve those ends."

"Along the way, as you may have heard by now," Lara added, "their leader has been ... terminated ..."

"Yes!" Wright interrupted excitedly. "'The Ghost', Saleh Halibi. We've been after him for decades now. The number of innocent civilians that he ..." Laney Wright paused, clearly moved by the situation.

"Believe me, Madam Secretary," the prime minister interjected in a solemn, but congenial tone, "We know exactly how you feel. After all, your losses are our losses."

"Yes, of course," she added, regaining her composure. "You have suffered thousands of times what we have. As I say, whatever we can do..." She paused once more.

"We do have a major problem on our hands, Madam Secretary," Eitan said solemnly. "Correct me if I'm wrong," he continued, nodding at the prime minister, "but I believe we have contained the enemy forces at our north and south ... thanks of course to your F-35's," he added, smiling at Secretary Wright.

"By the way," Chayat interrupted, "those captured enemy soldiers, both in the Galilee and in the Negev, will be repatriated as soon as possible. There are nearly 100,000 of them."

"How do you plan on doing that?" Wright asked.

"Well, we're certainly not going to make the mistake we made in 1982, when we had the PLO bottled up in Beirut. We were forced, by the United Nations, to let them take their arms with them, so they appeared to leave like conquering heroes, singing and firing their guns into the air. That display, as you know, ended up killing many innocent Arabs in Beirut; shots that go up have to come down."

"And so?" Wright asked. "This time?"

"This time they will march back home; to Lebanon, Syria or Egypt, stripped of their weapons, armor and vehicles. Let the world see them as they truly are: defeated aggressors."

"I see your point," Wright replied, "they can hardly be viewed as conquering heroes."

"Precisely. We do, however, have another enemy at our doorstep—the Iranians."

Laney Wright nodded grimly but said nothing.

"As I'm sure you've seen from the satellite photos," Chayat added, "they have a convoy of ships headed up into the Gulf of Aqaba, masquerading as merchant vessels, but there is every reason to believe they carry a large number of their Fateh 110 missiles. They are short range, but very accurate."

Secretary Wright nodded again, but remained silent.

"And, of course," Chayat continued, "their missile complexes at Tabriz and Khorramabad are fitted with their long range Shahab 6 rockets. As you know, they have some of these on mobile launchers; but additionally they have hardened silos at both locations."

Secretary Wright finally replied: "Yes, we've been keeping in close contact with your ambassador. Our defense analysts agree with your assessment of the situation with the Syrians and Egyptians. Of course, we are delighted that you were able to use the F-35's to stabilize the state of affairs. Please understand that we are ready to supply you with at least fifty more on short notice."

At this point, she paused and shifted in her chair. "The situation with Iran is much more delicate. Believe me, we would be delighted to see all of their missiles destroyed before any can be launched. We're fortunate that none have nuclear warheads—at least to the best of our knowledge." She paused again and took a sip of water. "But," she said firmly, "there is no overt action that the United States can take without a declaration of war. And I can guarantee you that our Congress is not about to do that without a strike against us directly."

Prime Minister Chayat, always ready to seize upon a subtle use of words, saw an opportunity. "Do I gather, Madame Secretary, that the resolve of your Congress and President Seymour does not extend to the use of, let us say, 'covert action'?"

Wright smiled and replied, "What precisely did you have in mind?"

This was the window he had been hoping for. "What I'm asking is, is there any chance we might be supplied with the weaponry to destroy their clearly aggressive armaments before they get a chance to launch them?"

"You mean, I take it," she replied, "that defensive missiles flying the Star of David would be used in a preemptive strike against an absolutely certain attempt by the Iranians to annihilate millions of people?"

A feeling of exhilaration filled the room. Her intent was clear: the U.S. would supply the necessary "Cruise" missiles, but the launchings must be carried out from Israeli delivery systems.

The prime minister, feeling his basic purpose had been fulfilled, pushed just a bit further. "Precisely," he said. "But we must be certain to be able to hit their underground silos as well, if our combined intelligence suggests they are targeting Tel Aviv."

"You mean by that, can we supply you with our Massive Ordnance Penetrators, also known as 'Bunker Busters'?" Wright asked. Without waiting for an answer, she continued, "The president and I considered the situation before I left. We have, of course, consulted with Secretary of Defense McHenry and the Chairman of our Senate Armed Services Committee, Lawrence Jefferson. We all agree that, should the situation warrant, we would supply you with the armaments to do just that."

"You say, 'should the situation warrant'," the prime minister said, "I presume that means that in the instance you detect those long-range missiles being aimed …"

"… in the direction of Tel Aviv. That is correct." she continued. "And if any of those Shahab 6 critters gets aimed at a NATO country, you can bet the US will take care of the condition ourselves."

The general consensus among the government officials at the table indicated that a reasonable plan of action had been agreed upon. The secretary of state had certainly more than lived up to her reputation. Prime Minister Chayat, at this point, felt that the presence of Lara and Uri was no longer necessary. In fact, in the heat of the moment, he may have allowed them to stay even longer than was called for. He stood and thanked them again for their service in a manner that suggested they should now take their leave.

However, as they rose heading for the door, Secretary Wright, said abruptly, "Just a moment; there's one more thing I believe you two can do to bring this whole dirty business to a successful conclusion." She motioned for them to be seated again.

The two agents looked at each other, somewhat confused. They had no idea to what she was referring.

"Let me explain," she said, receiving the attention of everyone in the room. "As I understand the events that occurred at Haifa, the Arab gang attempting to demolish the structure and kill the American visitors, had been in training in the U.S., at Waco. That is, after their initial schooling, they pretended to be Neturei Karta at that facility you destroyed north of the Galilee." The agents nodded, not wanting to break her train of thought. "So you were quite familiar with their plan and tactics. Presumably, they accepted the fact that you were acting under the directive of the minister of that Waco church ... A Mr. Leonard Depew, correct?" she asked while checking her notes.

Lara and Uri nodded again, impressed by her knowledge of the background of the affair. They wondered where this was leading. They didn't have to wait long.

"So your true identity as government agents wasn't discovered until you aborted, or at least nearly so, the 'Destruction of the Temple.'" Her somewhat tongue-in-cheek analogy with the destruction of the First and Second Temples of Jerusalem was not lost on any in the chamber. But no one laughed. "Excuse me," she said quickly, "I meant no disrespect." Everyone smiled politely at her genuine apology.

Secretary Wright got immediately back on track. "Now this means, as I understand it, that the surviving members of the Arab gang realized at that point, that you were in fact, working for the other side; *our* side. And before their capture by our forces; that is, ours and the Israelis, these Hezbollah gangsters were witness to the fact that Saleh Halibi and his men had taken the two of you, in chains, to a nearby warehouse."

Her meaning, and her objective, were now becoming clear to everyone in the room. "As far as they know, 'The Ghost' and his men took you away to be tortured and killed, in a manner typical for that monster." At this point she looked around the room to see if anyone had anything to add to this analysis.

"These Hezbollah 'gangsters' as you so fittingly refer to them, have been kept in the dark, both literally and figuratively, since their apprehension," added the prime minister, thus agreeing with her analysis of the situation. "As far as they know, Halibi and his lieutenants survived, and the two of you," he said, indicating Lara and Uri, "have both been eradicated."

"Perfect!" exclaimed Secretary Wright. "This means when you show up in that courtroom in New York, their pretense as Orthodox Jews is going to suffer a sudden and dramatic setback."

Lara and Uri looked at each other as they caught on to her plan.

"But do you suppose that will be enough to expose their scheme?" Lara asked, implicitly accepting the roles Wright had set out for Uri and herself.

"Perhaps not. They have asked for a Jewish defense attorney, and an Orthodox one at that. We have kindly supplied them with someone who fills the bill, Mr. Steven Horowitz, a very well known New York defense lawyer, and staunch member of the Orthodox community."

"So they plan to continue their charade on into your courts," Uri added.

"Exactly," Wright agreed. "And that is going to make their denouement that much more devastating."

"I trust you have more up your sleeve than just our two agents," Chayat inquired hopefully.

"Oh yes, indeed. The arraignment hearings should be most interesting, if our plans come to fruition. I wish I could tell you more, but we're holding our trump card in total confidence until the last minute." Wright smiled and sat back in her chair. Even her Israeli allies were not going to be privy to this strategy.

"In any case," Wright added, "we are hoping your government can allow you," she said, indicating Uri, "to spend a few days in New York. I have already requested from Mr. Parkinson, the presence of agent Edmond." She looked at Lara, who nodded in approval. The stage was set for a very interesting time in New York.

Chapter 33

Uri and Lara received an urgent message from the Israeli military headquarters:

You are needed in Washington tomorrow. Report to the military airfield north of Tel Aviv by 1800 hours this evening. A military jet will fly you to Andrews Air Force Base, ETA 2100 Washington time tonight. You will be assigned VIP lodging at the base hotel. A limousine will pick you up at 0800 tomorrow morning, and you will be escorted by the Secret Service to your destination.

Uri asked the Israeli colonel who passed along this message, the reason for this urgent trip. He replied only that they would receive further instructions once on board the aircraft. They had no time to speculate, although they imagined it had to do with the ongoing hostilities.

It was Lara who first realized the purpose of this trip: the captured terrorists had already been extradited from Israel to the U.S., and their trial was about to begin. She and Uri were needed at the prosecution table, in the role Secretary Wright had outlined for them. Uri thought about it for only a second, agreeing this must be the case. The defendants might just be frightened into exposing themselves. Uri and Lara tried to speculate on who or what else Wright had in mind. They could come up with nothing.

It took them less than an hour to pack up their necessities, including presentable clothing. They were almost certainly headed to the district court in New York.

The Israeli colonel warned them not to carry or pack firearms of any kind. Uri would have to leave his beloved Desert Eagle behind. The colonel assured them that all personal property left at the base would be held for them under lock and key.

A Jeep took the two agents to the military airfield and drove them directly to a waiting Gulfstream G-550 aircraft, an impressive plane with a large, blue-and-white Star of David painted on each wing. An even larger emblem was emblazoned on each side of the fuselage.

Israeli airmen hoisted their bags into the rear of the passenger compartment, and led them into the front, where huge, comfortable, leather seating awaited them. They settled into adjacent seats until a male flight attendant, an Air Force Lieutenant, instructed them to buckle up in preparation for immediate departure.

The Gulfstream was configured to hold fifteen passengers and crew. It boasted 4 distinct seating areas, a full gallery, modern office and communications center, and two lounges complete with restrooms and shower. The entire aircraft gave the impression of comfort and security at the highest lever. *And this is all for us,* Lara thought. *Being treated like a VIP has its advantages.*

As they moved up the aisle, they had noticed several 'suits,' U.S. Secret Service types, already seated behind them. Lara and Uri hoped that shortly they would be told of what lay in store in Washington.

The pilot informed them they were ready for takeoff, and the flying time would be about fifteen hours, depositing them at Andrews at about 2100 local time that same evening. Lara and Uri both contemplated a leisurely time during which they could discuss the tumultuous events they had just been witness to. But that was not to be the case.

Two of the suits came forward as soon as the Gulfstream reached cruising altitude, exhibited their credentials, and politely asked the two weary agents to rotate their seats around so they were facing the rear. Uri and Lara did as instructed, and found themselves eyeball to eyeball with the Secret Service men, a small pop-up table between them. *This is going to be a long trip,* each thought. As consolation they would be treated to a full night's sleep on arrival.

The two Secret Service men, who asked to be called Russ and Todd, were efficient, courteous, and not given to small talk. Russ, a young man, perhaps in his late 20s, with red hair cut very short, had bright blue eyes that were so piercing that they never seemed to blink. Dressed in the generic blue serge suit, with white shirt and black tie, his shoes, what they could see of them, were standard government-issue black oxfords.

Todd, clearly the man in charge, was about 35 years of age, with close cropped black hair and brown unsmiling eyes. His dress was almost identical with Russ's.

As they settled in, the flight attendant asked if they would care for some snacks or drinks, non-alcoholic. They would be served dinner in about three hours. Lara and Uri asked for some peanuts and ginger ale; chips and 7UP would do in a pinch. The Secret Service men appeared to be impervious to hunger or thirst.

After the attendant deposited their food and drink on the table in front of them, they devoured it all, both being ravenous. Then the anticipated inquisition began. The Secret Service men placed identical voice recorders on the table; they had backup for everything. Todd started the questioning: "Could you please, just for the record, state your names and nationalities?"

The agents, becoming wearier by the moment, recited the information clearly into the voice recorders. "And can you tell us, Ms. Edmond first, exactly the reason for your presence in Israel?"

"We were here on assignment, or perhaps I should say there, to act as liaison between the United States Joint Terrorism Task Force and the Israeli government. My chief is Mr. Hadley Parkinson, whose office is in New York City. I was responsible for transmitting any information permitted, concerning the conflict, to Mr. Parkinson."

Todd and Russ wordlessly turned their eyes to Uri. "Well," Uri began, "I am an Israeli citizen, member of the Mossad, and given highest level clearance by the U.S. government. My assignment was to act as liaison in the other direction; to transmit whatever information permitted, to my superiors in Tel Aviv. I am not permitted to disclose their names. This was agreed upon between our two governments." The Secret Service men looked at each other without saying a word, and each wrote something on a small pad.

"If you don't mind," said Todd, glancing at Russ, "we'd like to speak with you now individually." He rose, nodded his head towards the rear seating area and indicated that Uri should follow him. Lara and Uri glanced at each other; this truly was going to be a long flight.

Todd and Uri arrived at a similar seating arrangement in the aft section of the plane. They sat across from each other, a small table between them. "Now," continued Todd, "when did you first arrive in-country?" Uri detailed their adventures since arriving in Israel, beginning with the raid on the training camp, the ensuing firefight, and the arrest of the Arab masqueraders. He went back through their experiences with the church in Waco, then moved to Haifa and the ensuing exhausting battle with the Ghost. By this time nearly three hours had gone by and it was time for a break.

Lara, meanwhile gave her version of the story to Russ in the same excruciating detail. She told him about being sent to the southern front, meeting General Sharon and following the details of the battle along the Sinai border.

Neither Secret Service agent was willing to share any information from their side. When asked, they simply said, "This is strictly for the record."

And so it went all through the long flight. They were given three breaks, during which time they could eat, drink and relax.

Uri and Lara had a chance to compare notes. Uri had decided that the U.S. government was taking every precaution to ensure the two passengers were the bona fide agents they claimed to be. Lara, on the other hand, came to a more reasonable explanation: they truly wanted a recorded timeline of events from each of them.

Finally the Gulfstream landed at Andrews Air Force Base, at about 2130 local time. They disembarked on the tarmac, were given a quick check by an Air Force sergeant and driven in an SUV to the VIP hotel on the base.

The desk sergeant, an attractive young, red-haired woman, inquired if they would be needing separate rooms. Uri quickly responded, "Yes, that would be great. Would you happen to have any adjoining?" The young sergeant, whose name tag read simply, "O'Brien," smiled discreetly, and said, "Yes, second floor, rooms 204 and 206." She gestured to two airmen who had magically appeared with their baggage, and the exhausted warriors were whisked up in the elevator to their rooms. The airmen deftly put the bags in the separate rooms and disappeared without waiting for a tip.

Lara and Uri used their separate keys to enter their rooms; each immediately noticed the interconnecting door. Without any conversation, they each, individually, enjoyed a long, hot, relaxing shower. On the beds, they found light blue, unisex pajamas complete with Air Force logo, white bathrobes similarly adorned, and dark blue slippers.

Uri waited what seemed like forever, but was probably only fifteen minutes, before gently knocking on the interconnecting door. "Who is it?" came the laughing reply. "It's the maid," he said in a falsetto, "May I turn down your bed, ma'am?"

He didn't wait for her to stop giggling before entering her room. They gathered each other up in their arms and fell onto her bed. He kissed her hungrily, saying, "You know how long I've been waiting for this?"

"If I didn't, I could certainly tell now," she replied happily from beneath him. It took only seconds for the robes and pajamas, complete with logos, to join the slippers on the floor. They made love quickly, as though trying to make up for lost time. Then they lay quietly in each other's arms for some time, until Lara suggested that they get under the covers.

"You always were the practical one," Uri replied as they dove under the covers, greedily exploring each other with a passion born from the long, tense adventure they had experienced.

They fell into a deep, coma-like sleep, cradled together, as if to protect each other from the outside world. It was only the phone ringing at 0700 that brought them back to reality. They looked at each other, quizzically, trying to figure out who should answer. After about three rings, Lara realized they were in her room, so she should answer. Only later did they realize his phone had never rung.

Chapter 34

Staunton Richardson had been sitting in his sumptuous new office in their new house in the suburbs, the one Sally had been so excited about, the one paid for by Simmons. He had been watching the developments unfolding ever since the announcement of the Mount Zion bombing.

At first, things seemed to be going as planned: destruction of the facility had not been as extensive as expected, but still a slap in the face of American Christians. Two Americans had been killed; that was unfortunate; but worse, all of the attackers had not. The plan for the attackers to be identified as Neturei Karta suicide bombers, resolute in ending American Zionist Christian influence in Israel, was now in jeopardy.

Some of the saboteurs had been captured; this was a serious complication. Things had gotten worse when the Israeli courts quickly acceded to United States' demands that the perpetrators be extradited for trial in the U.S. Even more disturbing, the trials would be held in civil court, rather than military tribunals. The U.S. government had come under fire recently, for trying suspects involved in "9/11" and other terrorist incidents, in secret military courts. The press demanded access.

As Stan watched the scenes unfold, switching back and forth from CNN to Al Jazeera, the doorbell rang. Sally, who really didn't understand Stan's obsession with the whole affair, answered the door expecting a FedEx package or kids soliciting for one thing or another. She was surprised, therefore, to see two impressive men in dark blue suits standing there quietly.

"How can I help you?" Sally said sweetly, full of southern charm.

"Is this the residence of Mr. Staunton Richardson?" the larger of the two asked. He was a sturdy man, with close-cropped, dark hair, about 35 years old, carrying a small briefcase. His compatriot, slightly smaller, and a few years younger, had lighter-colored hair, cropped similarly short, and also carried a leather briefcase.

"Why, yes it is," Sally said charmingly. "May I tell him who's calling?" innocently giving away his presence.

Stan, in his office with the door closed, was unaware that he was about to receive visitors. Sally knocked lightly on his door. "Honey," she said, opening the door, "there's two men from the government here to see you. They wouldn't say exactly what it's about, but they do seem to have proper Federal government credentials."

Luckily, Stan hadn't eaten in the last few hours; otherwise, there would have been a mess all over the floor. "Stan, are you all right, can I let them in?" Sally said, seeing the loss of color in his face.

It took just a second for Stan to recover, "Sure, honey, bring 'em on in." In the second or two that he had before the men came in, Stan stood, took a couple of deep breaths, and used the time to draw two chairs over to his desk. He put his jacket on and stood there, trying to appear the calm businessman about to receive clients.

"Mark Davis," said the first man holding out his badge and shield for Stan to look at. "Timothy Shelton," said the other, holding out his credentials. As Stan made a cursory attempt to verify their identity, he realized the TV was still on, with coverage of the breaking news. *Fortunately*, he thought, as he reached over to his desk, grabbed the remote, and clicked it off, *it's tuned to CNN, and not ... the other.*

"Sir," said Davis in a somber tone, "are you Mr. Staunton Richardson?"

"Yes, I am ... that's me," replied Stan, trying to pull himself together. He noticed both men flipping closed their creds and replacing them in their breast pockets. As they did so, Stan caught just a glimpse of what appeared to be a leather holster under Davis' jacket. "What's this all about, may I ask?" Stan queried Davis.

"Sir, all I can tell you is that we serve in the United States Department of Justice. We are here to ask if you would oblige us by accompanying us to our downtown office."

"Where exactly is that, and how long will you need me?" Stan's mind was whirling out of control; he didn't know quite what to say.

"Sir, the office is at 800 Franklin Avenue in Waco. You shouldn't be gone long. But, if need be, you can call your wife." Davis said conclusively.

Richardson wildly tried to put things together, figure out what to do. "What's this about?" Stan asked again, trying to buy some time.

"As I said, sir, we are merely asking you to come downtown to answer a few questions. That's all I can say."

"Am I under arrest; can I call a lawyer?" Stan asked, his voice rising an octave.

"Sir, you always have the right to a lawyer. But before you make use of that right, you should know that we are asking you only for a voluntary appearance --- at this time."

"So, I'm not under arrest?" Stan added weakly.

"No, sir, you are not. Not if you choose to come with us voluntarily."

"… and if I choose not to …?" Stan now knew what an animal felt like in a trap.

"Then, sir, we would be obliged to get a court order and place you under arrest."

That about did it. Stan's knees started to collapse, and the second man, Shelton, immediately grabbed him to keep him from falling. "Are you all right, sir?" Shelton asked. "Would you like some water?"

Stan took a couple of big gulps of air. "No, I'll be all right," he said, trying to appear calm and under control. After his near collapse, the effort no doubt looked ridiculous. "Do I need to … uh … bring anything?"

"No, sir, just your ID, driver's license, passport, whatever," Davis replied brusquely.

"All right, then," Stan said hoarsely, "I guess I'm ready to go." He felt like a character in a cartoon.

As the three exited Stan's office—Davis leading the way, then Stan, followed by Shelton—Stan saw Sally standing at the front door, clearly terrified. "You're not going to, uh ... 'cuff' me or anything are you?" Stan asked abruptly. He had visions of the neighbors staring out of their windows as Staunton Richardson, churchman, solid Christian businessman, was led out of his own house, handcuffed like a murderer, or embezzler. He was glad his boys weren't home to see this.

"No, sir," Davis replied. "As I said, sir, you are not under arrest. You are merely complying with a voluntary request for your appearance."

Stan looked at Sally, who did not appear mollified by the agent's remarks. In her eyes, he might as well have been headed to the electric chair.

It was a short ride downtown to the Federal building. Stan had been there a couple of times for matters of routine licensing, and so on. As far as he could recall, there was no FBI office in the building. That was a relief.

Shelton parked the car outside the building in the space marked, "Official Vehicles Only," and they headed up the granite steps, into the building, passing quickly by the front desk. The agents were clearly known here. Stan, however, was required to pass through a double set of detectors. As they stood in front of the elevator, Stan was still desperately trying to think: *Why am I here? If this is about Mount Zion, what can they possibly know?* The elevator appeared, and they headed up to the third floor, where they passed some offices without names on the door. Davis opened one, and gestured for the others to follow. Shelton then closed the door. They were in a plain room; no windows, a simple wooden desk with four chairs around it. A fluorescent light centered above the table gave the room a sterile, blue quality. The only adornment on the walls, Stan noticed quickly, was a mirror on one; the wall Stan was facing as they sat him down.

Stan had already engorged himself with a series of questions while they were in the car; he figured now was a good time to let them spill out. "Can I call my lawyer now?" his voice trembled as he asked. He had no doubt in his mind that this meeting was being recorded, both picture and sound. He wanted to make sure they had on record that he had asked for legal advice. He'd seen enough cop shows to know that.

"As I said, sir, you may always ask for legal representation," Davis immediately replied. "However, before you 'lawyer up,' you might want to consider your alternatives. If you do get an attorney in here, we will have to read you your rights, and then you will be, at least technically, under arrest." Davis knew he wasn't dealing with a common criminal here, and the man had probably never been put in a position like this before. He would probably, Davis figured, like to get this over as quickly as possible.

Stan thought about this for a second, then said, "All right, let's say I don't 'lawyer up' right now. What exactly is all this about, what can I do for you ... that is, without needing a lawyer?"

"All right," Davis said, sitting down directly across from Stan. "Here's the deal. We caught some of the gang that tried to blow up the Christian Center, Haifa. I'm sure you know what I'm talking about." He held up his hand to indicate Richardson need not offer anything yet. "The point is, Mr. Richardson, every one of them, names you as their contact man here in the States. We know you didn't train them; but we also know that you were the one who set them up here in Waco, got them into school, got them into the church ..." Richardson just sat there, listening.

"We also know about the financial arrangements."

Stan looked up quizzically. "Don't give me that look," Davis shot at him. "We have all the bank drafts. The one to the church for 30 mil, the ones to your account at the Cattlemen's Bank in Waco ... do I need to go on?"

"What about them," Stan asked, his throat drying rapidly.

"Listen, Mr. Richardson," Shelton said softly, "the quicker you play ball with us, the easier it's going to be on you, understand?"

Stan just sat there, trying to digest everything. He needed to think.

"Don't tell me you never saw these!" Davis stood, drew a couple of papers from a manila folder and shot them across to Stan. Stan looked at them, saw the amounts, then looked more closely at the name of the bank from which they had been drawn: "The Royal Bank of Dubai" was written in English just below some ornate Arabic lettering. Stan looked for a glass of water, anything.

"There's more," Davis added. "The real brains of the outfit, the guy that set the whole thing up, Saleh Halibi—you probably know him as 'The Ghost'—he's dead. Had his balls cut off, stuffed down his throat." Richardson blanched, and reached up involuntarily, touching his neck. "Point is, Richardson, you're the best thing we've got in terms of the next link up the chain. At least right now. Follow me so far?"

Richardson sat there, thinking for a moment. He hadn't been arrested, hadn't been read his rights, so he was pretty sure they weren't planning to put him on trial. He didn't know that with certainty but he was willing to go one step further. "I understand what you're saying. At least I think I do. You're not planning to charge me with anything, any crime I mean, is that right?" he asked.

Davis glanced at Shelton; to Richardson it seemed the men felt they'd gotten their point across, and were ready to move on.

"What we want from you, Mr. Richardson," Davis said, sitting again and leaning forward, speaking more quietly, "is simply to appear in that courtroom when these scum are arraigned in New York. That's all, just appear at the prosecution table where they can see you."

Stan noticed that Davis had not answered his question, about his culpability, their intention to charge him with a crime. These guys didn't want that on the tape. *Alright*, he thought, *I haven't been arrested ... I haven't been charged ... I'm not getting thrown in jail, even though they have all the criminal terrorists involved in a murder, naming me as an accessory. If I call in a lawyer, I get formally charged, I go on trial, I make headlines ... I'm gonna take the risk,* he decided.

"Can you tell me," Stan asked, "have they been assigned a lawyer, I mean here in the U.S.?"

The two federal agents huddled for a moment, then Davis said, "We can tell you that; it's already been made public. Name is Steven Horowitz. His services offered by the New York branch of the B'nai B'rith."

That told Stan a lot: the criminals were still pretending to be Jews. But what could he do for the prosecution? They must have assumed that he knew their real identity. It was clear they knew he had met, or at least knew of, The Ghost. He knew the terrorists to be Arabs parading as religious Jews. Stan had nothing to do with that deception, and the feds knew that. So what ...

"So what's your answer, Stan? Do we have a deal? The arraignment is set for Monday in New York Federal court. You go there, you show up at the prosecution table, and your part is done."

Stan noticed that Davis had addressed him first as "Richardson," then as, "Mr. Richardson," and now, finally, as just "Stan." He frankly didn't see what he had to lose. He hadn't admitted a thing, wasn't being charged, wasn't being jailed. He would talk to his lawyer as soon as he had a chance, but for now he was playing their game.

What about Simmons? Stan suddenly thought. *They've got me involved in all this, they must have something on him.* Then he remembered how Dale had gotten him to handle all the transactions, financial and otherwise, with the Arabs. *Maybe they didn't have any evidence on Simmons. Wouldn't that be the clincher?* He laughed bitterly to himself.

"All right," Stan said, rising and extending his hand. "When do we leave?"

The agents both smiled, clearly relieved, and shook hands with Stan. "Our plane leaves tonight," Davis said simply. "We'll get you some clothes, toiletries, that sort of stuff. You can call your wife, but just tell her the basics, and, remember, we'll be listening. Just say you have to be in court in New York, that you have to leave tonight, but that you're not being charged with anything. Tell her also to keep this to herself, at least until after Monday. That's it—no details, got it?" Davis knew this last warning couldn't be enforced, but the woman might worry for her husband's safety. Chances are, she'd keep quiet.

Stan nodded. This was going to be some weekend.

Chapter 35

Lara and Uri got word as soon as they reported to the State Department the next morning. They would indeed be flying to New York almost immediately. After a quick meeting with one of Secretary Wright's deputies, they were on their way by limousine to Air Force Base, and from there to JFK.

The pair were flown by military jet to a small terminal, located at the far eastern end of JFK and used by government VIPs. A black, unmarked limousine waited to take them to the US District Court in Brooklyn.

On the way, they made a quick stop at the Israeli consulate in Manhattan. David Peretz greeted them warmly, expressing Israel's gratitude for their heroic efforts. David used the short time they had before the arraignment at 1400 hours this afternoon to set up the situation for them as best he could.

David explained that despite all the pleading by legislators from New York, New Jersey, Illinois, and Florida, the President had sent word through the Embassy that the United States was not able to do anything more in Israel's defense. Congressional delegations from Southern states, vigorous supporters of Israel in the past, now deferred. Influential senators from Texas, Georgia, Alabama, and Mississippi voiced their disappointment in the actions of Orthodox Jewish Israelis against evangelical Christians.

Word had been withheld from the public about the true culprits in the bombing of the Brooklyn synagogue. The JTTF did not want to alert the terrorists to their knowledge of the true situation.

Public opinion at first held that it was an act of Islamic terrorists; however, in the weeks since the blast, the official word became: an ongoing investigation.

But when the evidence was made public, the facts seemed incontrovertible. Orthodox Jewish immigrants had blown up one of their own American synagogues. Then when word came of the bombing of the Evangelical Christian Center in Haifa by the same group and widespread animosity against the state of Israel rose.

Senator Jasper Willoughby of Alabama, ranking Republican member of the Senate Armed Forces committee, and devout evangelical Christian, put it most succinctly:

"We who have been strong supporters of the Jewish State are sadly disappointed in the actions of a large organized group of its citizens. This group, with the implicit support of the Israeli government, has carried out acts of terror against citizens of the United States, both here and abroad. It is especially disturbing that this group has targeted an American Christian organization that has aided the state of Israel with substantial political and financial assistance. While we do not wish for physical harm for the people of Israel, especially from known enemies of the United States, we cannot and will not authorize military assistance in light of the loss of American life and property due to the acts of these Israeli citizens."

More shocked than Uri at this statement, Lara asked, "So you mean these people really think the government of Israel is sponsoring terrorist acts against the Zionist Christians? Why would the Israelis do that? The prime minister and his cabinet have repeatedly said how much they appreciate the efforts of the evangelicals. They have poured hundreds of millions of dollars into Israel. The Christian tourists come away with a wonderful impression of the ..."

Uri stopped her with a gentle hand on her shoulder. "I understand how the more rural areas of your country might react. Folks in the southern states might never run into a Jew in their whole lives. They also tend to be opposed to foreign aid in the first place. So when kind-hearted evangelical Christians are killed while trying to do good ..."

Lara interrupted him: "... but what about states like California? Highly educated people, lots with Jewish ancestry. Why don't they step forward?"

David shook his head. "I'm afraid there are a lot of what we call 'self-hating Jews' in the more liberal areas. Some supposedly charitable organizations have planted the notion that Israel is the aggressor in the region, not the Islamists. A tremendous amount of money is being quietly spent behind the scenes, by these and other sorts of organizations to reinforce this notion. Because of them, some studies show a substantial number of Americans think Israel was behind 9/11."

"What about those terrorists we captured at Haifa?" Lara asked.

"As Secretary Wright explained," Uri said, "when they are exposed in court as Islamists masquerading as Jews, there will be a tremendous impact."

Peretz agreed. "The United States government has ruled that foreign terrorists who target American civilians must be tried, in public, in a U.S. civilian court. In this case, it would be the District Court for the Eastern District of New York. Which happens to be at 225 Cadman Plaza in Brooklyn, only two miles from the scene of the synagogue bombing!"

"How come that family who blew themselves up, the Barlevs, have never been exposed in the press?" Lara asked.

"It's our fault really, I mean the consulate's," David replied. "We pressed the District Attorney here to hold off until we had concrete proof. We were afraid it could look like we were charging Arabs for something Israeli Jews had done. Remember, we didn't have any witnesses. Now that the whole cell you guys busted in Lebanon is in custody ..." David managed to say before Uri leaped in.

"Have both sets of Arabs been extradited, the ones captured in the training camp and the ones from Haifa?" Uri asked.

"Both sets are in that New York courtroom right now," David replied.

The Brooklyn courtroom was absolutely still. Those who had stood in the rain overnight and managed to get seats were warned to remain silent during the proceedings. Television monitors and speakers lined the sidewalk around the block. This, for people who weren't able to get into the courtroom. Some commentators said the worldwide audience might exceed even the O.J. Simpson trial.

The defendants, from both the raid on the camp in the Galilee, and the bombing of the Christian visitor center outside Haifa, sat at a long table in the center of the courtroom. They numbered sixteen, all dressed in Orthodox Jewish clothing. All were men. The eight women, captured at the training camp in southern Lebanon, asked for, and received permission on religious grounds to be absent from the proceedings.

U.S. District Court Judge Nathan Siegel, highly respected for his impartiality, especially in high-profile cases, presided over the proceedings from his dais high above the tense scene. Stephen Horowitz, the well-known Orthodox Jewish attorney, was lead counsel for the defense. His team of mainly Jewish lawyers, all well-known, sat to the judge's right, next to the defendants.

Howard Rosen, U.S. assistant District Attorney, led the prosecution. He and his team sat at a table to the judge's left.

All the main players were Hebrew. For those who did not recognize that on their own, the point was made clear by the television commentators.

In the end, it had not been difficult to get Israel to abide by the U.S. court orders. The U.S. Attorney General ruled almost immediately that both crimes, in Brooklyn and in Haifa, had been committed against U.S. citizens. It was ordered that the jurisdiction lay within the United States; trial would be held in civilian court.

The Israeli prime minister, aware of all of the circumstances; agreed that the facts in the case be withheld until formally produced in court. There were to be no cries of partiality.

Questions, of course, abounded. Why was Israel so easily persuaded to allow its citizens to be tried in an American court? Why would Israeli Jews choose to murder Zionists, even if they happened to be Christian? And most puzzling, why kill their own countrymen and co-religionists?

Worldwide, Muslim extremists were overjoyed. That, of course, included the American Muslim associations, who populated every Sunday TV news show

Al Jazeera, the Arab news agency which had quietly gathered quite an American audience, toned down their rhetoric. The facts were there for everyone to see. Al Jazeera was now the voice of moderation

As Judge Siegel gaveled proceedings to order, a pair of witnesses quietly made their way from the back of the courtroom to the prosecution table. To most of the observers, nothing out of order seemed to be occurring. To some, however, the man with the black patch over his left eye brought a murmur of recognition. His partner, an attractive blonde woman, was not quite so recognizable, at least to most in the courtroom.

At the defendants' table however, the reaction was swift and obvious. These were their two "associates," all the way from Waco to Haifa, the pair who then interfered with the destruction of the Christian Center. How could this man and woman have possibly known the defendants' true nationality or mission? And how could they possibly have escaped the massacre at Haifa? Lara and Uri's appearance here was totally unexpected, throwing the defendants into near panic. They began muttering in clear discomfort. They asked their lawyer, Horowitz, to get them some time.

Horowitz approached the judge and asked for a 10 minute discretionary recess.

The defendants gathered in the judge's chambers, without his presence. They were assured they would not be spied upon. Once alone, all their confidence vanished.

The one who called himself Michael, silenced the others immediately. "Do you recognize him now?" he asked tensely, but in a hushed tone. "The eye patch? He's Mossad. The famous one, from the Hezbollah bomb scare in the U.S. a few years ago!"

The group became quiet. Their mission had been sabotaged by the Zionists from the first. But these two impostors at the prosecution table were supposed to have been terminated at Haifa. The Ghost had assured them. When last seen, they were being hauled away to their death by Halibi's executioners.

In any case, there was no way the pair could have known the defendants to be anything other than ultra-religious Israeli exchange students. How then could they know about the plan to destroy the Christian Center? Their appearance in the courtroom was astonishing to say the least, and might indicate more surprises to follow.

Equally disturbing to the defendants was the fact that they were to be charged, somehow, in the bombing of the Brooklyn synagogue some months ago. How was that connection to be made?

The only American who had known their true identity was Staunton Richardson, who had been their compatriot all through their time in Waco, and since. He had paid them, harbored them, and seen to their every need. If it became necessary, they were certain he would come to their defense; if for no other reason, than to save himself. Even their Jewish court-appointed attorney knew them only as ultra-religious Israeli Jews. He had even spoken in Hebrew with them.

Michael, the most well-spoken of the bunch, assumed the role of leader. He tried to assuage the fear that gripped them. "Do not worry, my compatriots." he said loudly in English, just in case the chambers were, in fact, being monitored. "Our friends will not let us down." To anyone listening in, nothing in his statement of reassurance could be used as evidence against them.

The gang of disguised murderers took comfort in Michael's confidence. They regained their composure and knocked on the door, indicating they were ready to return to their place in the courtroom.

They had just been re-seated and order restored, when one of the policemen guarding the door at the rear of the courtroom, opened it, looked at some paperwork, and allowed a group of three men to enter.

The main attraction had just appeared. Mr. Staunton Richardson entered, escorted by a pair of heavily-armed policemen. Richardson was known to many who had been following the case, as one of the leaders of the Zionist Christian Center in Haifa. His presence at the proceedings did not seem at all unusual. After all, it was his center that had been desecrated by the Orthodox Israeli terrorists.

The reaction of the defendants was tangible; a sense of relief came over them. Michael had been right; they had no need to worry. Richardson was here to get them released.

Their relief however was short-lived. To their astonishment, he and his guards walked directly to the *prosecution* table. At first the defendants just stared at him in disbelief. Their friend, their sponsor, the man who had led them through this entire journey was now to testify against them?

It was Michael himself who first leapt to his feet in rage. The only reason for Richardson, if that was in fact his name, to be seated with the prosecution was to aid in their execution. He was the only one who could have saved them, and now, he had turned on them, to make certain they were convicted.

They had been lied to from the first. Why, they had no idea, but they certainly weren't going to sit there pretending to be Jews any longer.

After a few seconds consultation with Michael, the Arab masqueraders rose, almost as a single entity, ripped off their Orthodox Jewish costumes, and hurled them in the direction of Richardson.

Papers, folders, and other objects from the defense table, along with false earlocks, flew across the room as shouts of Arabic invective filled the air. The two dozen uniformed New York police assigned to the courtroom moved swiftly into action as the defendants rushed towards the object of their hate: Staunton Richardson. They tackled the incensed Arabs, securing their hands with plastic cuffs. The two Secret Service agents who had brought Richardson lifted him completely off the floor and rushed him into the judge's chambers, locking the door.

Judge Siegel, after about 10 seconds of useless pounding of his gavel, hid terrified under his elevated desk.

The astonished defense team of Orthodox Jewish lawyers, including Horowitz, stood transfixed at the unbelievable scene unfolding before their eyes. Their presumed Hasidic defendants were now seen for what they truly were: rabid Islamic imposters.

250

A mixture of reactions spread across the spectators in the courtroom ... some wide-eyed, shocked at this turn of events; others, eyes smiling and corners of lips turned up in suppressed amusement.

With the police totally occupied securing the defendants and protecting the lawyers, the way was open for the journalists and photographers. They hurtled over simple barriers and sent live images of the chaotic scene to all corners of the world. One young newsman from NBC described it to his viewers as "something like a Marx Brothers movie, perhaps titled: 'A Day in the Courtroom,'" in a reference to their famous "A Night at the Opera."

Instead of the martyrdom the perpetrators had been promised—the glory for them and their families—they would be exposed as the cowardly assassins they were, hiding like women in the clothes of their very enemy! Instead of the fatal blow to Zionism, they had dealt a devastating blow to their own cause. They would be cursed forever, here and in the hereafter.

Only a very few in the courtroom had any idea what had occurred, as it were, backstage. Richardson, when presented with the facts, really had no choice: Be the final and damning witness for the prosecution, or face the rest of his life in jail and the ignominy requisite to the betrayal of his church and country. This way, by appearing as the obvious threat that he was, he had the promise of a lifetime of anonymity under the federal witness protection program. Hopefully, he would be safe, or at least reasonably safe, from Arab assassins. Whether his family would receive equal protection was yet to be decided. He could only hope.

The television commentators pieced together the events as best they could. It was clear now that the defendants were not Israelis, not even Jews. They were in fact, Islamic terrorists masquerading as Hasidim as they committed acts of extreme violence against American citizens, both at home and abroad.

The unmasked defendants were hustled out of the courtroom and order restored. News was quickly forthcoming.

251

The defendants instantly demanded that their Jewish defense attorney, Stephen Horowitz, be removed from the case. The American Muslim Society, secretly funded by Iran, immediately offered their assistance in the person of Mr. Ibrahim Haleef of Detroit, Michigan, well known for successfully defending Egyptian and Jordanian immigrants accused of defacing American synagogues and cemeteries.

Haleef, already present in the courtroom, quickly accepted the responsibility. After an hour's recess, he assumed control of the defense.

Mr. Haleef, an immaculately dressed, clean shaven, olive-skinned man who exuded the confidence of a successful businessman, immediately asked for change of venue, on the basis that these unfortunate and wrongly accused Arabs could certainly not get a fair trial in this location. The implication being that the location was in a highly Jewish neighborhood.

The defendants, remanded to federal custody until the matter could be resolved, insisted on their right to publicly defame Israel, or as they called it, "the Zionist entity," and to demand the restoration of all "Arab lands."

Over 100 NYPD uniforms maintained the swell of the crowd. Uri and Lara left the court by a side door in their effort to avoid the main horde of reporters and photographers The pair circled around back behind the building where police and other official vehicles were parked. Even here, they encountered a mad rush of all sorts of people looking for identifiable personages.

In the parking area, they were met by two police officers who came up on either side of them. One politely said, "You two are quite well-known; we've arranged an escort for you back to the Federal building in Manhattan." A seemingly welcome idea, until the policemen grabbed their arms in painfully tight grips. Taking a closer look at them, Lara noticed the man holding her arm had a Middle Eastern look about him, and in fact, looked somewhat familiar.

Uri had the same impression. As they were being hustled along toward a black minivan, Uri said loudly, "Quite nice sneakers you fellas have there! Thought you guys all wore cop shoes." Uri and Lara both could see the telltale markings of uniforms purchased in a costume shop. The badges and patches had no relation to the NYPD.

"Hey," Uri said, didn't we meet you guys in Waco, a couple months ago?" Uri really didn't remember them, but it was a signal to Lara to be ready to make a move. She quickly stepped down with her left foot onto her captor's unprotected instep, causing him to lean forward in pain. She simultaneously struck upwards into his throat with her doubled-up fists. Then, as he bent over in agony, she punched him on the back of the neck, perfectly hitting a nerve center. As he crumpled, she concurrently brought her right knee up into his nose, breaking it, and driving the bone partially into his brain. He fell in a shower of blood, unconscious but not dead, a result of the "Crav Maga," technique she had learned called "bursting." A multiplicity of concurrent moves especially effective against a larger or more heavily-armed opponent.

While Lara put down her attacker, Uri twisted the pinky finger of his captor upward, breaking it instantly. He simultaneously spun him around, putting a knee into his crotch and a claw of fingers into his eyes. The Arab masquerader went down screaming, temporarily blinded, and obviously in terrible pain.

Mr. Haleef, the Muslim attorney from Detroit, met with the defendants twice that same day. They demanded, as citizens of Lebanon, that they be allowed to return home. No American court could have jurisdiction over them, they argued. Haleef tried to explain to them that was not possible; they had attacked and killed American citizens. Their only recourse, he told them, was to throw themselves upon the mercy of the court. They scoffed at that and demanded their story appear in the court of public opinion. Haleef, realizing he could do nothing to help them, asked for, and received, removal from the case.

The press quickly pieced together the defendants' astonishing and horrific story of treachery and murder. The public reaction, both in the United States and elsewhere in the

West, was swift and one-sided. The evidence was clear: the defendants had convicted themselves.

The story, downplayed in countries with large Muslim populations, was said to have been merely the actions of just a few misguided individuals. In the Arab countries, it was treated as a lie manufactured by the U.S. press, controlled largely by Jews.

In the end, the court ruled that the defendants were to be treated as enemy combatants and tried as such in a military tribunal. Judgment would be swift and harsh, that was certain.

Congress and the White House overwhelmingly backed immediate support of Israel's defense. Legislators from those districts who supported the Zionist Christian movement and the concept of "Revelation," moved back to their original position, in defense of Israel.

Now that Israel's enemies to the immediate north and south, namely: Syria, Lebanon and Egypt, had been subdued, there remained only Iran to deal with.

Secretary of Defense Frank McHenry, proposed that Israel be given sufficient Cruise-type missiles to knock out any of the Iranian ships in the Gulf that did not immediately reverse course and return to their ports of embarkation.

Additionally, Laney Wright, the secretary of state who had initially opposed any such action, now advised that the long-range Shahab 6 missiles aimed at Tel Aviv, be struck with munitions capable of destroying the hardened bunkers.

McHenry agreed, but suggested Iran be given 72 hours to disarm rockets at their western launch sites, and turn back the ships entering the Gulf of Aqaba. Furthermore, he said, it would be wise to blanket western Iran with printed warnings, written in Farsi, advising civilians and military alike to vacate the launch regions at once. The U.S., the warnings would clearly state, was not waging war against the Islamic Republic of Iran; merely protecting its, and its allies', lives and property.

Near unanimous agreement came from the Senate Armed Services Committee, the lone holdout a senator from California, with a strong electoral base in the Bay Area.

In Washington, a surprise announcement stating that the secretary of energy, Mr. Roy Blankenship, of Texas, had abruptly resigned, no reasons given. Hints suggested an investigation into his financial dealings, especially with the oil-producing countries.

The state of Texas, however, was justly proud of its secretary of defense, Mr. Frank McHenry, for showing the resolve of the United States when confronted by Islamic terrorists.

Chapter 36

Iran's spiritual leader sat glumly, gazing at his president, dressed up in his "Himmler suit." The president, strutting around with his swagger stick, nervously awaited comment from the ayatollah. When none was forthcoming, he repeated his query, "So, Your Eminence, when shall I give the order to commence our attack against the Zionists?"

The ayatollah shook his head, paused, and shouted just one word directly to his second-in-command: "*Bisho'ur*!!"

The little president's ever-present smile disappeared for just a second and he reacted as though slapped in the face. Never in his 62 years had he been called an *idiot*, and certainly not by Islam's top religious leader. His body reeled as he absorbed the shock. "What have I done, what is wrong, your Holiness?"

"What is wrong, you say! Have you not just seen what happened to the stupid Sunni Arabs? Have you somehow missed the spectacle of two entire nations being defeated, humiliated by the Zionists? Where have you been this past week, while our so-called secret allies have been sent home like beaten dogs?"

The military leader, in his custom-made, black, Nazi-like uniform, staggered under the barrage of blows. Somehow he must regain his stature. "But, Eminence," he implored, "surely the military strength of the enemy must be exhausted after having to defend itself against two giant armies. Now is the time to pounce, whilst they lick their wounds."

"Lick their wounds, indeed!" shouted the aged tyrant. "Can't you see the Jew has had the unseen support of the great Satan? Are you somehow blind to the fact that the United States has taken this opportunity to test its most powerful, secret, new weapons on those people they consider the scourge of the earth, the Arabs? I might point out to you that, before our secret alliance with them, we had the same opinion. Now it is once again justified!"

The tiny president staggered under the relentless attack on his sensibilities. "But surely, your Reverence, when we strike the Jew with our long range rockets, and pounce on them with our missile-laden ships, they will have no way to protect themselves, let alone retaliate!"

"Are you deaf, as well as blind, you fool?" The white-bearded potentate struggled to keep his temper. "Do you not realize the Americans have a full fleet of ships in the Persian Gulf, and another in the Mediterranean? All of NATO would support an attack on us now. The Americans would merely have to supply the Zionists with the weapons they need to avenge our puny assault."

Overwhelmed, the president had no retort.

The ayatollah continued his attack: "You realize, don't you, that even our most dependable sponsor, Russia, will not come to our aid. They have told us in so many words—we are on our own."

"But our oil reserves ... surely our oil remains our greatest weapon ..."

The ayatollah concluded his lecture. "Do you not remember how the other oil producers easily filled the needs of the world without us? They merely raise the price, and suddenly new sources appear, seemingly from nowhere. Our best option, our *only* option, is to now divorce ourselves from the Arabs once and for all. Our time will come. For now we must be patient and allow Allah to provide us the proper opportunity. The Shi'a will triumph!"

And so the Iranian military made a show, for all the Western drones and satellites to see, of disarming the missiles along its western frontier. Its "merchant" ships reversed course and headed back to their home ports, their weapons never fired. The battle, at least for now, was over before it began.

"Our time will come ... it must ..." muttered the defeated little man in his black costume. Over and over he repeated it, until finally he believed it himself.

Back in New York, at Lara's office in the federal building Uri received a message from David Peretz. He was ordered to call Shimon in Tel Aviv immediately. He and Lara raced over to the Israeli consulate building, so that he could use the secure line. Lara waited outside for what seemed like 30 minutes, but was actually only about five.

He came out, a grim look on his face. He couldn't look directly at Lara. "Bad news?" she asked, fearing the worst.

"I've been called back. Some sort of emergency. Now that I've proven myself in the field again, they can't wait to put me back in action, one eye or not." He finally looked up at her, and she could see the ambivalence in his face. They looked around the room, and seeing no one, grabbed each other in a fierce embrace. "You better go back to the hotel and get your stuff," she said, holding back her tears.

"Won't you come with me to the airport?" he pleaded.

"No, it's better this way," she said with finality.

"We'll be together, and soon," he said.

"That's what you said last time." She turned and walked away without looking back.

A black Citroen sedan made its way slowly along the road from Ramallah to the Jordan River crossing at the Allenby Bridge. The Arabs like to call it the "King Hussein" bridge.

The eastbound traffic on the road was light, as usual, early in the morning. The sedan made its perfunctory stop at the Israeli border gate. A sleepy-looking Israeli sergeant motioned for the driver to roll down his window. The driver complied, handing over three sets of documents. The sergeant looked into the car and saw two Arabs in the backseat: one an overweight, middle-aged woman, cloaked in typical Arab dress; the other, a young man, wearing typical street attire.

The Israeli border patrolman glanced casually through the papers given to him. Vehicles leaving Israel for Jordan got little scrutiny. The only "targets of interest" were known terrorists. These three did not fit the characteristics of any currently sought. The Citroen was allowed to pass on to the Jordanian side of the checkpoint.

Two Jordanian border guards looked in the car, saw the occupants, then looked at their paperwork. Inside the passports they saw two American hundred dollar bills. They swiftly snatched the money, glanced again at the occupants, and waved them through onto the highway to Amman.

After traveling about two miles along the short, divided highway into Jordan, the driver was told to pull over to the side of the road. The "middle-aged woman" savagely pulled off her head and face covering, throwing it aside. With the help of the young man, "she" wiped off the thick coating of cover-up makeup, with a sigh of relief. The young man giggled as he cozied up to the Grand Mufti.

"I like you much better like this," he said adoringly. The Mufti gave the order for the driver to continue. *This is just a small setback,* he told himself. *There will be another time. Another time.*

Epilogue

In the end, it was Gaza and Hamas that suffered the worst political and economic damage, even among the Arab world. Their leaders were humiliated, as the Israelis had been careful to warn the civilian population of the danger of any aggressive military moves against the state. The Arabs living in Gaza under the rule of Hamas, by that time were pretty much fed up with their lack of adequate living conditions, jobs and respect. The large majority of their population felt their despair was due strictly to the intransigence of their leaders.

The populace recognized that their children had been used as human shields in largely ineffective military operations against the Israelis. They were ready to join hands with the Palestinian Authority, who at least were ready to recognize Israel, and proceed with negotiations.

However, the Palestinian Authority, which supported the Mufti and his treacherous acts against non-Jewish civilians, did not fare much better in the worldview. Nations around the globe that had become uniform in their resistance to Israel's needs were now taking a second look at establishing economic and military ties.

In the east, Russia, who had once been great friends with Israel, but lately had developed a more adversarial stance, now saw the advantages of a more open trade policy, allowing them access to Israel's remarkable advances in communications technology, medicine, and agriculture, just for starters.

China also saw Israel's emergence as the clear victor in this latest failed Arab offensive. With their growing sophisticated population, China could make good use of open trade with the small, but highly advanced Israeli high-tech industry. This trade, as it has been for several years now, was not publicized; the products were advertised to the local population as being developed by the Chinese themselves. This was fine with Israel, as the income generated was significant—in the multibillion dollars per year.

The United States, of course, was ecstatic with the development of the Jewish-Christian coalition. Congress was now heavily in favor of continued alliance, both military and economic, with the Jewish state. The one-sided military victories were seen in the U.S. as largely due to the American assistance. This also was fine with the Israelis. Only in the far left liberal community was there any dissent. These people got their news mainly from left-leaning periodicals and Al Jazeera.

Iran, fortunately, suffered very little from the whole affair. Their wise decision not to enter into the fray had kept the country and their leaders largely unaffected. However, they were now keenly aware of the danger of a military exchange with Israel.

Europe, on the other hand, was a different matter. The huge influx of radical Muslims had a marked effect on European politics. Especially in the southern European countries, notably Portugal, Italy, Greece, and Spain, the influx of poor, largely uneducated and unskilled immigrants caused tremendous economic difficulties and even threatened the continued existence of the European Union.

But a greater threat to these countries' stability was seen as coming from jihadist attacks, both from their immigrants and outside organizations like Al Qaeda. Furthermore, the weak leaders of these countries feared a cut-off in their oil imports would result in losses at election time. To them, their careers were more important than the stability of the region.

The continent of Africa continued to be a complex situation for Israel. Up until the Yom Kippur war of 1973, Israel had markedly good relations with most of the African nations, the exceptions being the North African states dominated by radical Islamists.

After the Arabs were humiliated in that war, more than forty years ago, the oil-producing States, most notably Saudi Arabia, blackmailed the African nations, almost to a one, with the threat of loss of oil imports. This, despite the fact that the hostilities were initiated by Arab surprise attacks on all sides of Israel. Central and southern African countries fell like dominoes. Almost none would have anything to do with Israel, diplomatic or economic. The situation slowly improved over the years, as many of the countries in these regions recognized the aid Israel could give them, both in terms of agriculture and medicine.

Most notably, in East Central Africa, Israel was responsible for improving irrigation systems to the point where these countries were self-sustaining. Sudan had been war-torn for many years, with violent attacks by the Islamist radicals in the north, on the largely unarmed Christian villagers in the south. When South Sudan became independent in 2011, they became good friends with the Israelis, who helped develop their agriculture. Friendly relations continued across Central Africa for the Israelis at a slow, but steady pace.

However, after the Islamist attack on the Christian settlement in Israel, countries in Africa with large Christian populations recognized that radical Islam was not their friend. They once again established formal relations with Israel and as a result, saw some improvement in medicine, agriculture, and perhaps more importantly, tourism. The dramatic drop in tourism in the countries that had been swept over by the Muslim Brotherhood had not gone unnoticed.

As often happens in armed conflict, the victors gain substantially in stature. It is, after all, how the United States gained world dominance after World War II. Though some might argue against it, this dominance has allowed the United States to give untold billions of dollars in aid to the distressed countries of the world.

Perhaps the same picture will unfold in the Middle East.

Jack Winnick

A Middle East scholar for over 40 years, Jack Winnick has been interviewed on a number of TV and radio stations, and has had editorials in major newspapers and magazines across the country, including a front-page piece in the prestigious Washington-based newspaper, *The Hill*.

Winnick has spent most of his career as an academic, having taught at such universities as Georgia Tech. He has remained deeply involved in foreign affairs, centered mainly in the Middle East. He participated as project leader of a U.S. led team of technical experts who have established liaison with counterparts in the Arab world. The goal has been to bring about enhanced quality of life in the region through utilization of scientific and engineering expertise.

Winnick has called upon this wide knowledge base in writing *The Devil Among Us*. His first novel, *East Wind*, has received excellent reviews.

Made in the USA
Lexington, KY
14 December 2016